ALSO BY TYLER McMAHON

How the Mistakes Were Made

KILOMETER 99

Tyler McMahon

 ST. MARTIN'S GRIFFIN ⚏ NEW YORK

KILOMETER 99. Copyright © 2014 by Tyler McMahon. All rights reserved. Printed in the United States of America. For information, address St. Martin's Press, 175 Fifth Avenue, New York, N.Y. 10010.

www.stmartins.com

Designed by Anna Gorovoy

The Library of Congress Cataloging-in-Publication Data is available upon request.

ISBN 978-1-250-04708-3 (trade paperback)
ISBN 978-1-4668-4745-3 (e-book)

St. Martin's Griffin books may be purchased for educational, business, or promotional use. For information on bulk purchases, please contact Macmillan Corporate and Premium Sales Department at 1-800-221-7945, extension 5442, or write specialmarkets@macmillan.com.

First Edition: June 2014

10 9 8 7 6 5 4 3 2 1

For Skip and Susan

KILOMETER 99

1

On shore, the mariachis struck up with a flourish of horns. The first wave of a new set rolled toward us. Ben and I paddled hard for the outside. Atop the still-unbroken swell, a would-be lip feathered white against the wind.

"We're too shallow," I said.

"I think we'll make it," Ben shouted back.

I paddled up the face. Ben turned to commit. The wave jacked along the point, then stalled. I duck-dived my way through before it broke, board twitching in my grip. From the backside, I caught a glimpse of Ben's red hair rising once against the curl, then disappearing down the line.

The next wave looked even bigger. As I was the deepest surfer out, it belonged to me. I turned around and rose with the crest.

One of the rich kids from Santa Tecla took a couple tentative strokes, incredulous that a girl might catch the best set wave so far today. I shouted "*¡Voy!*" and fixed a stink eye on him. He stopped paddling and floated over the shoulder.

The mariachis played a minor chord and I made the drop. The face opened, broke top to bottom. It was big: double overhead at least. I took a high line and kept a lookout for the Mother Rock.

Through the first section, I pumped cautiously and built speed. The wave fattened up farther down the line. I unloaded a turn at the top of the lip, sending a fan of spray at one of the local guys. "Chinita!" he hooted. The wave re-formed for another speed section.

Some mix of instinct and guesswork took over. I pulled into the upper part of the face and crouched lower to my board. The lip turned sharp and silver. A land breeze blew mist backward off the wave. I stuck my front arm into the water, up to the elbow. A loud rumbling drowned out the mariachis. My feet shuffled forward on the deck, almost off the wax. I crouched lower, my free hand nearly pressed to the board's nose.

With eyes turned upward, I watched as the lip reached over like a rainbow, covered me up, and touched down by my opposite rail. Surrounded by water on three of four sides, I felt a moment of woozy vertigo. The board wanted badly to creep up the wave and spin out inside the barrel. Only my body weight kept it down. I stood higher, hoping to pump up some speed. The top of my head hit water and I returned to a crouch.

I've had lots of in-and-out barrels before, quick cover-ups in hollow beach breaks. If asked, I'd have said, Yes, *I've been tubed.*

But never like this: setting it up, stalling with a hand in the face, stepping forward as if in a surf film. This was no fluke. Barrels didn't get any more legitimate than this one.

Afraid of going too deep, I took my arm out of the water. Through the almond-shaped eye of the wave, I saw more ocean, the pier, and—to my surprise—Ben paddling back out. He pumped a fist in the air and cheered at the sight of me. I smiled so hard, my ears popped.

I wished I could always see the world that way: from out of the inside of a wave, through a telescope of salt water, a swirling set of blinders that block out all the second guesses.

And then, a fraction of a self-satisfied second later, the whole thing came undone. My head was struck sidelong by a blast of aerated seawater. The wave closed out, with me inside, and soon I was spinning about underwater, connected to the board by nothing more than a rubber cord.

Back at the surface, Ben grinned a few yards away. El Salvador's swell season was only beginning. The mariachis came together in a festive waltz.

Side by side, Ben and I paddled back out toward the lineup.

"Wave of the day," he said.

I smiled and nodded.

"You were in that tube forever." He laughed.

"Ben, I love you." It was the first time I'd ever said that to him. Maybe it wasn't the best moment. But something about the ecstasy and the power of that wave made clear the fact that I'd never have had the chance to ride it if not for him. I couldn't hold the words in a second longer.

He smirked and said, "I love you, too, Malia."

Another set loomed on the horizon. We stopped talking and sprinted for the outside.

We didn't know then about all the troubles that were only a

few months into our future. Back then, I didn't know how hard I'd try to regain that view from inside the tube. Not just the quality waves—though I certainly would want to get those back—but also the perspective. I'd want my life to look the way it had for that too-brief instant before the barrel collapsed: fast, obvious, moving forward in one direction, with Ben at the center. In some ways, it's what I'd always looked for in El Salvador: a small, safe space where I fit in, between layers of violence and gallons of water.

2

They call him Chuck Norris. I'm known only as Chinita. Maybe you've heard about La Libertad. El Salvador's coast faces straight south. Punta Roca reaches half a mile into the sea. It's a perfect point break—long, hollow, without sections. Only local beach kids, a few wealthy sons from the capital, and a handful of adventurous travelers surf here. It's the sort of thing Ben and I grew up dreaming of.

Libertad is a Spanish word that means "freedom." Puerto La Libertad is the largest coastal city in the country, and not far from the capital. Poor campesinos buy fish off the pier, while rich San Salvadorans eat seafood in the oceanfront restaurants.

In the mid-nineties, a local drug syndicate set up shop in a house a few blocks from the point and began to refine cocaine into crack rock. It took the locals by storm, especially the young men. La Lib cornered the market on three commodities: fish, crack cocaine, and perfect waves.

Ben's handle is based on his beard and hair. Chuck Norris is a fairly common name for pets in this country. The aging action hero seems to be more famous here than in the States. Mine is even less creative. "Chinita" says only that I'm small, Asian, and female—qualities that are, I suppose, rare among La Lib's visitors.

Our nicknames were given to us by a local crackhead named Peseta. Peseta's own moniker refers to the Salvadoran twenty-five-cent piece. At one time, he'd been the best surfer in La Lib. Now, he begs quarters from tourists in exchange for nicknames.

A cemetery occupies the last piece of land on the point, before it becomes a pile of rocks. A sewage canal runs through town and empties on one side of the graveyard. It carries La Lib's runoff and gray waters like a sick river and expels them onto the town's greatest resource. They dump their shit and bury their dead on the one thing that rich Californians would sell their souls for.

La Posada is a horseshoe of a hotel wrapped around a dirt courtyard. One wing holds expensive rooms with air conditioning and private baths. We sleep in the cheaper wing, with ceiling fans and shared toilets. The third wing consists of the kitchen, office, and dining room. A wonderful Salvadoran woman named Kristy looks after our boards and runs the place whenever the owners aren't around.

Ben and I spend most weekends and holidays here—and

any other time the surf is up. It's our second home, in a sense; we both have our own project sites, our own actual houses in two different inland villages. But in another sense, La Lib has always been the primary residence for us together, for our relationship. While Ben and Malia may live in distant villages in the campo, Chuck Norris and La Chinita live here, together, in La Libertad, full-time.

3

The children ask if I know karate. With index fingers, the little girl pulls at the sides of her own eyes and speaks an invented language of *ching-chong* sounds. The little boy kicks and chops at the air. Their mother cuts fruit and does her best to ignore them.

I buy green mangoes. The vendor's stand is set up in front of her house, off the main street. She drops the slices into a plastic bag and asks which condiments I want: salt? Hot sauce? Ground-up pumpkin seeds?

"Everything," I say.

Her smile shines with a gold-framed front tooth.

The date, January 13, 2001, will later prove ripe with meaning for amateur numerologists. This new century isn't yet two weeks old, and already it looks like it might turn out to be even crueler than the last for this little country.

From inside the house, a ranchera plays over a crackling radio: a guitar's single bass note, then the jangling of other strings, some vibrato vocals riffing over the top. Tired of speaking their fake Chinese, the children head inside.

I wear the denim skirt that Niña Tere made for me from an old pair of blue jeans. From the change pocket, I fish out a couple of coins and lay them flat upon the rough plank of a counter. The vendor nods her gratitude.

She takes the full mango bag by two corners and spins it end over end. Soon she has a twisted thread of plastic in each hand. As she goes to tie them in a knot, the earth moves below us.

At first I'm unfazed, and guess that a bus is passing. But the sensation intensifies. The street we stand upon bounces like a thin surfboard through chop.

Mangoes roll off the splintery counter. High-pitched screams sound from all sides. People emerge from other houses along the street. The shaking grows stronger still. My mind takes a second to recognize the Spanish word for earthquake.

Something hits me in the calf and my knee almost buckles. Another object flies past my ear and smashes against the ground. Red roofing tiles are falling from the buildings on either side. The walls sway and dance.

The vendor's two children materialize at each of my hips and hug my thin legs as though they are trees. Their snot and tears moisten the skin above my waistband. I put my hands up over their heads to protect them from the flying tiles. The three of us crouch together in the center of the road. They cry out for their mother. I try to hush them. There comes a series of breaking sounds: the splintering of beams, the grinding together of clay shards, the heavy thuds of ancient mud and straw blocks against each other. One tile catches me in the shoulder; another bounces off the forearm I hold across these two little skulls. Eyes closed, I picture a ravine opening up out of this very street and swallowing us. Another desperate second passes, and I'm ready to surrender: to throw my hands in the air, or lie flat in the path of the falling walls, tell these two kids to find somebody stronger to protect them. And at that moment, the shaking stops.

I look up. In the space where the children's house stood a moment before, there is now a brownish dust cloud.

The sound of wails and cries gives way to shouted prayers— desperate pleas to the Virgin and the Señor. The fruit vendor demands divine explanation: "Why, Lord? Why us? What have we done to deserve this?" Her face points upward, her mouth tweaked in a scowl, fists tightened together against her chin. The kids abandon me and gather around her—stroking her hair, hugging her waist—as she asks, "Haven't we suffered enough?" I cough out loud and cover my mouth. The remains of this family's home are stuck in my throat.

On the main street, every second or third house has turned to dust. They float in place like wispy architectural ghosts. Buildings I presumed to be brick or poured concrete turn out to be made of bamboo and earth—covered over with a thin cement finish.

I stand upon the rutted asphalt of the main road. My house is in a smaller village outside of town, a twenty-minute walk south. The aqueduct I've been working on for the past year is an hour-long hike to the north. My lover lives a hundred miles to the west, without a telephone, inside a tiny adobe hut. My father is five thousand miles away.

The Peace Corps issued me a mostly worthless pager, which now buzzes and vibrates in the pocket of my jeans skirt. I take it out and see the word STANDFAST spelled out in pixels — whatever that means.

People scream out names. Some of the calls are answered. Others grow more distressed. I stand in the center of the road, wondering which way to go—wondering, even now, if this is a beginning or an end.

Rubber flip-flops on my feet, I start south, downhill, toward Cara Sucia.

Twenty minutes later, I'm in front of Niña Tere's still-erect home. The house beside hers has partly collapsed and leans over, cockeyed, like a kneeling giant. Everyone stands outside. Shirtless men hold babies and inspect walls. A group of evangelicals gather by Don Israel's to sing hymns. In a courtyard across the street, a grandmother uses a blanket to cover the body of a teenage boy, his chest and neck discolored by blood and dust. I knew him; he was called Felix, and his grandmother used to scream at him for being lazy and watching too much television. The whole village could hear them argue.

"I'm all right!" Niña Tere emerges from the entrance to her house, her dog oddly silent at her side. "They say El Terrero suffered the worst. Every house down."

El Terrero is a smaller village farther south, tucked into the valley alongside of us.

"The pueblo is bad, too," I say.

"That slab of bedrock,"—she stomps her foot on the ground—"the one that prevents us from finding any groundwater, it did us some good this time."

"And Nora?" My voice quivers as I ask after her daughter.

"In bed." She points back to the house with her thumb. "She stayed home sick today, thank God."

I nod. Outside, the evangelicals beg forgiveness in song.

"And the aqueduct?" Niña Tere asks, as if it's my own child.

"I'm heading there now."

"Be careful."

In my own little house, a favorite coffee mug has fallen off my desk and shattered upon the floor. A crack creeps its way between the seams of cinder blocks on the inside wall.

I put on long pants and hiking boots, throw a water bottle and a sweater into a backpack that's still half-full, and set out on foot to check the damages. I have to turn my head as I pass Felix and his grandmother's house, but I can hear her crying and saying what a good boy he was, how much she loved him.

Back in town, people begin to grind away against the tragedy. Cars are commandeered to take the injured to the capital. Bodies are placed under bedsheets. The literal dust had settled, but that now seems a cruel insult to the metaphor.

I walk toward the ANTEL public telephone office and see a crowd spill out its doors. Hysterical parents shout numbers for their sons and daughters in the States. Phones ring and ring. The clerk tries his best to calm everybody down. There's little chance of getting a line to the Peace Corps office, to my father's house, or to whatever phone is closest to Ben; it will be a long while.

I walk uphill and to the north, up the network of tiny roads and trails that I've come to know well over the past year. Fields of corn and corn stubble give way to coffee forests. The landscape turns from brown to green and grows more vertical. Here the homes—modest one-story affairs made from wood and corrugated metal—have survived intact.

In an hour, I reach the house that served as our bodega. We paid the owners to look after our pipes and cement back when we worked in this area. One of their outbuildings—a kitchen, perhaps—has collapsed. No bodies lie in their courtyard. Nobody cries or prays. I don't stop to say hello.

I start down the trail toward the river. The rush of water and the calls of birds fill my ears. Soon, a silver line of galvanized pipe shines from afar. Another, similar line appears from out of the dark foliage. Its angle is, as I'd feared, off-kilter from the first.

At the trail's next switchback, I see the brown scars on the hillsides where earth and rocks have rolled free. To descend farther is clearly dangerous. But I don't feel scared. In a way that soon after will strike me as silly, disrespectful, and self-absorbed, I feel I have nothing more to lose.

The pipeline is totaled. Boulders—a big round variety familiar to me only from Roadrunner and Coyote cartoons— have knocked the galvanized stretch all over the valley and into the river. The mouths of disconnected pipes gape at me as if begging for mercy.

I walk upstream. The spring box has come undone at the seams. I think back to my college courses on concrete. It makes sense: The weakest bond would be to the surrounding rock.

Water rushes out from the cracks at the sides. I open the top hatch. It's nearly empty.

I close that worthless spring box, like it's a chapter of my life, and walk back toward town, now very worried about Ben.

In the ANTEL office, all lines are still tied up as far-flung families try to reach one another. Salvadorans in the States call for news of their loved ones. Local families send word of their suffering and survival to relatives.

After several tries, I get through to the Peace Corps office and tell Astrid I'm okay. I ask about Ben; he's not yet checked in. I give Astrid my ANTEL number and beg her to relay it to Ben if he calls.

In the meantime, I ask the clerk to place a collect call to my father's house in Honolulu. It takes a while to get a line out, but once we do, my father manages to accept the charges despite the language barrier.

Straight away, he asks if I'm okay, where I am, how the quake felt. I didn't expect him even to know about it. Apparently, El Salvador has become international news. This makes me even more fearful for Ben, but my father has other concerns.

"Is the aqueduct okay?" he asks. "Have you heard anything?"

"It's ruined." I exhale so hard that my breath sounds through the earpiece. "Crushed by landslides and boulders."

"Oh my," he says. "At least it happened while nobody was working up there, right?"

"True." That was a stroke of luck. Had the quake hit a few short weeks ago, workers would've died. I might've been among them.

"I'm so glad you're all right, Malia. That's all that matters. The aqueduct is *manini*. You'll fix it, by and by."

"Honestly, Dad, what worries me now is Ben. I haven't heard if he's okay or not."

"Ben?"

"You remember. You met him. My boyfriend." An adolescent note rings in the final word. My father and I have never really figured out how to talk about my love life.

"Oh yeah," he says. "The redhead."

"Right. He lives in a little mud hut." As I describe it, my mind's eye pictures those blurry house-size clouds from a few hours earlier.

My father goes silent.

"It's good to hear your voice, Dad. I should free up this line."

"Okay, Malia. Thanks for calling. And don't worry about the aqueduct. Take care of yourself."

I spend the next few minutes on the steps of the telephone office, waiting to hear from Ben, fearing the worst, all our good times replaying through my mind like a highlight reel. In those hours, it becomes clear that I'm witnessing the end of what might be the best year of my life: working on this aqueduct, surfing with Ben in La Libertad. It's been a golden age of sorts. I wait to hear just how over it is.

A sheet of corrugated-metal roofing rings out against the street. I turn to see the house it came from, a few doors down the hill. Next comes a shriek so high-pitched that I wonder if it's human, not the cry of some giant bird or jungle cat. More shrieks. Two men pry a crying woman up off the ground, but she slips their grip. Standing on my toes, I watch her throw herself atop somebody else, a body. The two men get a better grip and finally force her out to the curb.

As I watch that woman sit there sobbing, her face buried in her hands, one thing becomes abundantly clear: I can't just sit here by the phone and wait for news.

Back inside the ANTEL office, I ask the clerk to dial the pager service. He passes me to the operator; I give her the message I need sent to Ben: "Don't move. I'm coming to find you."

4

Outside, I stand on the street and stick out my thumb. A pickup stops within seconds. In the back, a man with a bandaged face lies upon an old mattress.

Another man shouts, "Niña Malia! Going to El Centro? *¡Vamos!*"

It's Don Antonio, the khaki-clad municipal health promoter whom I once worked with to gather data on water usage. He kneels inside the pickup bed, tending to the injured man.

I nod and climb in the back with both of them. The driver guns it toward the city.

The patient is wrapped up like a Halloween mummy; blood

and facial hair poke out between the bandages. He's conscious, breathing hard, and steeling himself against pain. After several minutes, Don Antonio leans away from him and whispers into my ear, "And the aqueduct?"

I shake my head.

He seems to understand.

At the turnoff for Panchimalco, more injured gather, hoping for rides. Our truck doesn't stop. I wonder about the old cathedral in their town, the one that's weathered so many tremors and other disasters. Has it survived this quake as well?

Once we approach Los Planes, Don Antonio points toward the Puerto del Diablo, as if spotting some damage to the iconic rock face. It looks the same to me. We zoom past Nora's school. Beyond the gate, its roof has sunken inward; it sags below the walls like a saddle. The wealthy houses in Los Planes proper appear intact, but armed guards stand in all the entrances, shotguns and tin badges at the ready.

Nothing prepares me for the situation in El Centro, San Salvador's downtown. The street signs and traffic signals are ignored. Pedestrians, buses, taxis, and private cars all crowd against one another helter-skelter. The traffic spills out of the roads and onto the sidewalks. In the market district, a gigantic lot—normally filled by a labyrinth of vendor stalls—has been taken over by slow-moving vehicles. Right-of-way seems determined only by the size of the car and the recklessness of the driver.

We inch our way through the automotive mosh pit, driving up curbs and over poles and tarps that have been abandoned by the vendors. Mangoes and bananas squash beneath our wheels.

Along the hillsides above the city, the ravines run brown with mud and the detritus of humble squats. I strain my eyes to make out a few antlike figures clinging to shrubs and rock.

We start toward a faster-moving avenue in the distance, then the truck brakes hard. Two men jog past the front: tattooed Salvatrucha gangsters, arms full of electronics and fake designer clothes. One wags an index finger at us and offers a sinister grin. They keep running and then disappear between the cars.

The bandaged man groans at each start and stop. Don Antonio takes a syringe from his bag but can't seem to fill it, what with all the bumping and braking. We make progress toward our avenue but are bottlenecked by a bus heading in the same direction. Inside it, the passengers all point and stare at something on the other side. Don Antonio and I turn to look.

A knobby-kneed elephant and two underfed giraffes—ribs and pelvic bones poking out of their hides—come around the bus and gallop past the back of our truck. They continue on through the traffic, the giraffes' long necks still visible above the smoggy din. I slap myself on the face, sure I'm dreaming or hallucinating. Don Antonio puts a hand on my shoulder.

"The zoo." He points back to a damaged wall in the direction from which we've come.

I nod, hoping that the lions and tigers went a different way.

We follow in the bus's wake and finally make it to the *avenida*. The driver gets the truck up to a dangerous speed, and that somehow seems to soothe the bandaged man.

In another few miles, we obey our first stoplight and pull up next to an empty flatbed truck, wooden slats along its sides.

It's covered in black soot, as are the two workers standing in the back. The whole rig still reeks from the syrupy char of sugarcane.

I whistle at them and ask, "Santa Ana?" It's a good guess. Most of the cane comes from the west, near Ben.

"*Sí.*" One worker nods. "*Vamos.*"

I hop from the pickup bed onto the wooden side of the cane truck. "Good-bye," I shout to Don Antonio.

"May you go with God," he says. Most likely, he thinks that I'm heading off to some sort of water-related emergency, and not just hoping to find out if my lover is alive or dead.

The light changes and we speed off, with me still clinging to the outside of the cane truck. I manage to scale the wooden slats and drop onto the bouncing floor of the flatbed. The two workers and I all spread our stances and try to maintain balance—one hand on the side—surfing our way over the bumps and turns.

Soon, we pass a still-standing hospital in the process of evacuation. Nurses carry out the sick by the corners of their bedsheets, then line them up along the sidewalk. Doctors kneel over bodies, taking pulses and hoisting bags of fluid. The building must have been judged structurally unsound. I wonder where they plan to put everybody. Is this the final destination of Don Antonio and my first ride? Will the bandaged man get any attention at all?

Somewhere near Santa Tecla, one of the workers points to the north. A giant white *colonia*—a subdivision of identical attached houses—is painted down the middle by a mile-wide stripe of muddy brown. The men in the truck curse, then cross themselves. It's the biggest landslide I've ever seen—in real life or in pictures. A huge section of the hillside has collapsed into the houses. Dozens of homes are invisible beneath the mud. So many people buried alive. I think again about Ben and his adobe shack. Is the epicenter even closer to him than I'd anticipated?

The engineer in me can see what a bad idea that *colonia* was—built in such a place, without retaining walls along the hillside. But who am I to judge, after what happened to my water system? Though I'm not at all religious, and have never been to Mass, I find myself making the sign of the cross along with these workers.

Once on the Pan-American, we make time. The traffic's all going the opposite way—more pickups with mattresses and injured people hoping to find a working hospital in the capital. On either side of the road are endless fields of sugarcane, the stalks invisible behind the thick green foliage. It was in fields like these that my grandparents first met.

Our truck must be up to eighty miles per hour. The two workers giggle and point up ahead. I climb the first rung of the wooden slats to see. At the spot where the road meets the horizon, a bank of dense black smoke rises into the air.

"Get ready." One of the workers laughs out loud. "It's about to get hot."

I have another look. The fields on both sides of the road have been set on fire. I know they do this before harvest, to get rid of the leaves. But I've never seen it up close.

As we approach, the Pan-American fades into a tunnel of fire. A bus blasts out of it, coming in the other direction. I expect our driver to pull off or slow down, but instead he seems to be gunning the throttle and gaining as much speed as he can.

"*Mamasita.*" The other worker puts a gentle hand on my shoulder. "Down!"

I do as I'm told. The three of us crouch with our backs to the cab. The men hoot and holler. The sun and the sky disappear. I'm instantly coughing and covered in sweat. My eyes burn, but I can't help but look around at the fiery landscape: black lines of cane stalk surrounded by orange flames, and farther on surrounded by blacker smoke. It so resembles the cartoon versions of hell that I half-expect to see a cloven-hooved red devil standing around, pitchfork in hand.

We emerge from the fire just as abruptly as we entered. Even the humid, exhaust-drenched highway air feels fresh and cool by comparison. The two workers curse and cheer. I find myself smiling along with them for half a second, as if this whole day has been some sort of scary carnival ride. But it doesn't take long to recall that pile of pipes in the jungle, the bodies under blankets, and, most of all, Ben. My stomach sags inside me. Soon, the three of us wipe at tears, and I'm not sure if they're due to guilt over that fleeting celebratory moment, or simply from all the smoke and fire.

We reach the outskirts of Santa Ana, El Salvador's second city. I see the same unfair pattern of fallen houses as I had in my own town, the same bamboo-and-earth construction exposed. This city has several old colonial buildings in its center—a municipal palace, a theater, and a tall Gothic cathedral. I wonder if they've survived intact. Mercifully, this truck has no business downtown.

At a stoplight, the driver hollers back to ask where I'm heading. I shout the name of Ben's nearest town, and the driver seems to understand. Minutes later, they drop me off at a crossroads. I thank the driver, say good-bye to the workers, and wait by the road.

A pickup truck with a rebar cage welded to its sides finally shows up, a dozen people standing up in the back. For a few coins, I'm allowed to climb aboard with the others. We head down the dirt road toward El Porvenir, knees bending with every bump in the dirt road.

I still have no idea where the epicenter is, whether I'm getting closer to or farther away from the heart of the destruction. I try to apply some makeshift science to it—after all, I've traveled nearly halfway across this country today—but nothing adds up. The levels of damage seem to have more to do with the style of architecture than with anything else.

The pueblo of El Porvenir, at any rate, does little to raise my hopes. I've been here only a couple of times before, but I always considered it a charming town, full of friendly *pupuserías* and pastel-colored stores. Now, the very hue of the place has dulled. So many buildings are down, it's hard to tell where the blocks begin and end. Even the police station and the mayor's office have suffered damage; black tarps are set up in their courtyards as they try to mitigate the disaster.

The pickup comes to a short stop and we all climb out. Ben's tiny village, El Cedro, is up a steep hill, and I know there's little chance of getting a ride the rest of the way. I set off on my own, the sun now low in the western sky, this long day finally drawing to a close.

No one passes me on the rutted path, and no houses line the way up. A pair of indifferent cows stands by themselves in a field. They stop chewing and stare at me, against a pink-and-blue background of fading light.

The first house I come to in El Cedro is simply a pile of brown adobe and red tile, with a door and door frame still proudly erect in the center. A mother and four small children sit in a circle off to one side. She prepares a meal for them on a clay *comal* placed atop a small open fire. Chickens pace around the remains of the house, pecking out a supper of bugs and worms. The children turn to see me, but we don't exchange words.

The next two houses are much bigger, but they have also fallen to the ground. I make a conscious effort not to study them too closely, and quicken my pace. My nerves come unraveled. Through the heart of El Cedro, I hold my hands up against the sides of my face, making literal blinders against the ruin. I have yet to see one house still standing here. Out of the corner of my eye, I catch a glimpse of the tiny wooden store where Ben bought beer and snacks. Yellow-and-red Diana brand packages are strewn about the ground. The shack itself seems to be held up only by the refrigerator within.

Once the road ends, I head up the path toward Ben's. It's nearly night once I finally catch a glimpse of his house. It's just as leveled as any other home in El Cedro, a pile of broken adobe blocks, some splintered beams, and the red crumbs of a roof. Not even the door frame stands.

I take two more steps, then stop and collapse there upon the path. Tears fall hard from my eyes. Sobs buck and kick their way out of my chest. On my hands and knees, I know that I can't go any farther. I can't be the one to find it, to unearth my boyfriend's body from the ruins. I'm simply not that strong, and won't pretend to be even for one second longer. How has it come to this? How did we let it happen?

You only get to be in love so many times—if ever. Why didn't we take better care of it? Why didn't we stay together, in a little hotel room in La Libertad or someplace similar, for as long as we could or until the Peace Corps kicked us out? Why was I always saying good-bye to him? So I could go play engineer on

some stupid water system that's now worthless anyway? None
of it makes any sense. But I'm sure I did it all wrong.

Night has now fallen, and brought along a cold wind. I lie in
a fetal position upon the packed dirt of the path. Can I sleep
here tonight, I wonder, then find somebody who might help me
deal with Ben's body in the morning? Can I simply run away at
first light, pretend I never went farther than San Salvador, and
then act surprised once the embassy releases the news about
Ben? Anything but this: to face him now, here, all alone.

"Malia? Is that you?" It's the first English I've heard since
the phone call with my father.

"Ben?"

"I'm over here. My leg's hurt and I can't move too well. Are
you okay?"

"I'm just fine." I stand up. The very last bit of daylight fades
along the horizon.

"Over here."

I follow the voice.

On the other side of his downed house, Ben has himself
propped up on a couple of rocks, one foot elevated.

"Sorry." An emotional crackle sounds in his voice. "It's hard
to get up." He begins to shift his weight to his arms and raise
himself.

"No," I say. "Stay there."

I fall to the ground and we embrace so tightly, it's as if we're
protecting each other from falling debris. He rubs a hand all
over my back and neck, checking my spine to see that it's fully
intact.

Into the whiskers of his cheek, I whisper, "I was so scared."

"I was scared, too. Thank God you had the wherewithal to
send me that page. I couldn't do much but wait anyways."

I sit down on the dirt beside him; we lock hands. I'd never noticed it before, but at this angle there's a view down to the lights of Santa Ana. We sit and watch the lit-up city. From this distance, it might be any night at all.

"Did something fall on your leg?" I ask.

"No." Ben sighs. "I was working in a steep cornfield and turned my ankle. It's an old injury. A couple of guys helped me limp my way home just in time to watch my house collapse." He takes a big breath. "If the quake had hit two minutes later, I'd be at the bottom of all that." He gestures to the pile of adobe blocks behind him, but I don't turn my head.

"Jesus," I say. "Did a lot of people die up here?"

Ben shrugs. "I've heard of only two so far. Both older folks. It was such a hot morning; most of us were outdoors. Had it happened at night, everybody in El Cedro would be dead."

It's the first time that I've even considered how things might've been worse.

"How's your neck of the woods?" Ben asks.

"Cara Sucia fared better than here. Supposedly, the bedrock slab that blocks the groundwater kept it stable. Our pueblo is bad, though, and the capital is the worst."

Ben squeezes my hand a little harder. "You must've seen some shit today."

I do my best to paraphrase it for him: the vanquished shantytowns, the freed zoo animals, the looting gangsters, and the awful Santa Tecla *colonia* swallowed up by the earth. Finally, once all those more tragic facts have been related, I manage to say, "The water project is totaled."

Ben turns to me in the darkness. "Your aqueduct?"

"Boulders rolled down the hillside and smashed up the pipes. The spring box broke off the rocks."

"I'm sorry, sweetheart."

I shrug. "They're just pipes, right?"

"I guess. I know it means a lot to you anyway. You worked hard."

I nod, saying the words *just pipes* over and over to myself, like the very repetition might make me believe it.

"Listen," Ben says. "I've had some time to think today. I'm not sure if I'm up for staying."

"What do you mean?"

"Look at this place." He gestures backward, toward a village that we can't see, that isn't really there anymore. "I mean, what am I supposed to do for the next three months? Sleep under a tree and try to talk to these guys about using natural pesticides? They've got bigger problems right now."

"That's true."

"I know people need help after this earthquake, but what do I know about that? And if I stay, where will I live? In some shelter that ought to go to somebody else? Somebody who needs it a lot more than I do?"

"Right." I hadn't thought about the future all day. It was as if some cosmic reset button had been pressed, like a bigger pair of hands had shaken up the ant farm that is my life.

"I know we've talked about traveling once we finish our service," Ben goes on. "But now, with your aqueduct destroyed . . ."

"What are you saying?"

"Why don't we just quit now? Together. Start our trip a few months early? The handwriting is sort of on the wall, don't you think? If there were any walls left."

I let his words settle for a second. "It's true; I don't know if I can start over. I don't know if the agencies will even want to fund a rebuild like that." And it would definitely take way longer than the few months that are left of my service.

Ben puts his arm around me and pulls me closer to him. I can see the Santa Ana cathedral below, and it looks intact.

"Those are the logical reasons, Malia. And they make sense. But more important, I can't stand to be apart all the time. Not seeing you for a week or two was hard enough already. Now, after this earthquake, it'd be impossible."

My mind's eye still sees those pipes littered through the river valley, all the hours and effort that went into them. My heart still stings with those first awful seconds of finding Ben's flattened house. Less than five months are left of my service. What does that number mean to anybody besides me?

"Count me in," I say.

Most of the time, my story feels utterly trivial: a footnote about a small measure of second- and thirdhand suffering, stuck between the pages of this nation's history—a history that flows over with far greater suffering.

But other times, my story seems to beg the most fundamental question of our age: What's a decent person supposed to do when confronted with a fallen world?

5

Ben and I spend that first night in the dirt beside the remains of his El Cedro home. In the morning, he finds a neighbor with a pickup and arranges to hire it for the day. We pull his backpack, his camping gear, hiking boots, and a few other valuables out from under the wreckage, then have the driver take us straight to La Libertad.

Once at La Posada, I help Ben hobble his way to our usual room. For the first couple of days, we hardly leave the hotel. We speak mostly of weather, food, and the lack of waves. I begin to wonder if all that talk about quitting the Peace Corps wasn't just some posttraumatic moment of weakness.

———

On the third or fourth day, I decide to paddle out—if only for the exercise. Though he's now walking on his own—albeit with a slight limp—Ben thinks it best to give his ankle more time.

La Lib wasn't hurt badly in the quake. Sitting on my board, bobbing in the midday chop, it isn't hard to forget about the disaster—which is, I suppose, exactly what we've been trying to do.

The ocean surface wears a dull, grayish look. A current pushes toward the pier; I spend most of my time trying to stay clear of its crusty concrete legs. I feel conflicted about Ben's plan, to say the least. It's true what he said: It is silly to stay. There's no time or resources for a fresh start. And I hate the idea of not being with him all the time, of once again living on opposite sides of this country.

But on the other hand, something simply feels wrong about walking away now, in the aftermath of this disaster. We'd volunteered to help this country, hadn't we? Now we would leave it in its greatest hour of need?

I finally get to my feet on a knee-slapper that has no face and doesn't last half a second. Once it's over, I tread water for a while, then decide to head for the beach. Ben and I need to talk. On the way to La Posada, my surfboard under my arm, I wonder how to best breach the topic of our next step.

"Check it out!" Ben meets me by the entrance, a massive smile across his face. He sits in the driver's seat of an older-model Jeep Cherokee. There's a crude paint job on the hood: two unfamiliar flags. The back seats have been torn out and replaced by a plywood shelf. It has Utah plates.

"Whose is this?" I find myself grinning along with him.

"It's ours, sweetheart!" Ben hasn't looked this happy in days. "I just bought it."

"You what?" I nearly drop my board onto the dirt of the courtyard.

"Did you meet that Kiwi guy who was staying at Hotel Rick? He drove this thing down from the States. Today he got a call from home, sick mother or something. Had to leave right away. I got it for a song."

"So, that's the New Zealand flag." I point to the blue one with the Union Jack. "What's this?"

"Switzerland. He started the trip with a Swiss girl, but they broke up somewhere in Mexico. Met at a ski resort, I think."

I nod, trying my best to process the whole thing.

"Get in!" Ben says. "Let's take it for a spin."

Still in my bathing suit, I stash my board in our room and then climb into the passenger seat. We drive east—out of town, to a section of the Litoral that follows the coast and winds around a series of hills and cliffs. We hoot and giggle, as if having a good surf session. It is, by far, the best I've felt since the earthquake. My faith in our plan is instantly restored. The road, the coast, this car, and Ben—this will be my home for the foreseeable future, maybe for a full year. I can't imagine anything better. The sound of the wind rushing past my ears drowns out all the second thoughts. It's not unlike that barrel I had half a year ago.

"When we get back," Ben shouts, "we should call the Peace Corps office. We need to do the paperwork and get our money."

"Right."

————

The next morning, a loose itinerary materializes from our hotel bed. We'll surf our way south through the rest of Central America, then continue on to the South American continent—find wet suits somewhere in Peru, surf the Pacific coast, see the Amazon, the Andes, Patagonia. The hardest part will be crossing Panama's Darién Gap. There's a rumor that the ferry service no longer travels around it. Ben's confident that we'll figure something out.

He talks about this for hours while I lie beside him, nodding. Sunlight seeps in through the jalousies in broad horizontal stripes. Above us, an oscillating table fan is bolted to the ceiling—upside down—and points at our bed; it moves from side to side with a series of jerks and clicks.

Ben props himself up on one elbow. His other hand runs back and forth along my thigh.

"Are you stoked?" His fingers pause at the bony rise of my hip.

I smile. "Stoked. I can't believe we're doing it." The doubt that I felt in the water yesterday has become a distant memory.

Ben turns toward the window. "Once we get to the bottom of that big old continent"—his slight Southern drawl emerges while talking about our trip—"down to the Tierra del Fuego, I want to throw one stone out into the water." His arm makes a mock throwing motion.

"I never thought I'd see something like that," I say. "Make it that far from home."

"Why don't we go to the office tomorrow morning, get things settled. After that, we can pay off our tab, get on the road. If we don't make it all the way to San Juan del Sur on the first day, we can stay the night in Managua."

"Okay." I nod.

Ben lies back down at my side, wraps his arms around me. I turn closer into him.

A car pulls into La Posada's dirt courtyard—*norteño* music blaring on its stereo—and quells our conversation. The oompah bass line shakes the doors and windows, an accordion riff maxing out the little speakers. The dust cloud drifts all the way to our room with the onshore breeze. Ben and I sit up and have a look.

It's a taxicab. To its roof is strapped a large surfboard case: the wheeled, hard-shelled, expensive kind called a "coffin"—not the sort of equipment carried by the low-budget surfers we're used to meeting here.

The taxi parks by the air-conditioned wing. The driver kills the engine and the music. Kristy stops sweeping and greets the new guest.

"Shit." Ben rolls his eyes. "I guess the earthquake didn't scare all the rich cocksuckers off."

"It's just a cab ride and a decent board case," I say, lying back on the bed. "Don't jump to conclusions."

Ben shrugs, then follows me down to the mattress.

I can tell the new arrival is a gringo from his Spanglish. Poorly pronounced words like *amigo*, *dinero*, and *gracias* carry in as he dismisses the driver. The taxi's engine turns over and the music resumes. A lesser dust cloud follows its exit.

Ben moves his hand back to my thigh, tracing the small ridge and valley made by waist and hips, lingering at the hard crest of my pelvis.

"It'll be cool to see all those places." He speaks right against my ear. "But this is what I want the most: to get some waves during the day, and to wake up next to you every morning."

I smile. It all sounds too good to be true.

6

Jim, the Peace Corps country director, says, "It's not your fault," and for a second I wonder if he means "fault" like responsibility or "fault" like the lines that cause earthquakes.

"Don't blame yourselves." Behind him, ribbons tied to his air-conditioner grille flap and flutter in the artificial breeze. Framed degrees and commemorative plaques hang upon the back wall, dividing it up into squares of dark wood and shining glass.

"We don't blame ourselves." Ben kneads his beard between his fingers. "It's not like that. We want to be together. Our villages, our projects—they just didn't work out."

Jim furrows his brow, then nods. "All right, then."

He places two official documents in front of each of us. We sign and date them without reading a word. I reach over and lay my hand—palm upward—upon Ben's knee, so that he'll hold it.

"I feel terrible about this, truly." Jim struggles to look us in the eye. His gaze settles on our two interlocked hands.

"You shouldn't feel bad," Ben tells him. "It's not meant to be right now; that's all. We're just rolling with it."

Jim sighs. "You can use my phone, to call your families."

"No thanks," Ben says instantly. Both of them turn in my direction.

The thought of calling my father brings me close to tears. All he'll understand is that I've quit, given up work on the aqueduct. I want badly to hear his voice, to beg for his understanding. But I can't imagine doing that here, in this office, while Jim and Ben watch. My eyes linger on the shining plaques behind Jim's head, all those communities, all that thanks.

"It's too early," I say, "in Hawai'i."

"That's it, then," Jim says. "Go see Astrid about your plane tickets." He stands and gives us each a firm handshake. "I am sorry that things turned out this way."

Ben says, "Don't be sorry."

I manage a nod.

In a smaller, less impressive office, Astrid calculates the cash equivalent of our airfares home. My San Salvador–Honolulu ticket turns out to be more than double what Ben gets for a flight to North Carolina. She hands us each a white envelope of American currency.

"There you go." Astrid is businesslike, and casts no judgment.

"Your readjustment allowance should show up in your bank accounts by the end of the week. Good luck."

The second we step outside the office, Ben and I share a reassuring kiss in the carport. I half-open the envelope full of money and run my thumb across it.

"Hey, guys." The greeting comes from over Ben's shoulder.

The two of us turn and see a lanky gringo walking up the driveway. He's dressed for something official—pleated pants and collared white shirt. His sleeves are long, in spite of the heat. A red speck below his chin shows where he's nicked himself shaving. The skin of his face is sunburned. One pronounced blood vessel squiggles its way down the side of his forehead.

"Alex," I say.

Ben offers him a handshake that morphs into a one-armed hug.

I kiss Alex on the cheek. "What are you doing here?"

"I'll bring the car around." Ben speaks in a gentle voice. He points his thumb in the direction of the gate, then starts toward it, his limp barely noticeable. "It's good to see you, Alex."

Ben suffers from a mile-wide jealous streak; I'm pleasantly surprised by his willingness to leave me alone for a few minutes to say good-bye to an ex-boyfriend.

"You have a car?" Alex tips up his sunglasses. He takes two lone cigarettes from his shirt pocket and holds one toward me. "I heard you guys might early terminate?"

I wave away the offered cigarette. "Yes, and yes. We just signed the paperwork and cashed in our airfare. Ben bought the car yesterday."

"That's cool." Alex lights up and looks puzzled. "So what's the plan?"

"Surfing." I nod and hug my own elbows. "We're heading south, soon."

He lets out a mouthful of smoke.

I feel smaller and somehow younger than he is—though I know us both to be the exact same age. A gust of his second-hand smoke tingles in my throat and almost makes me cough.

"Going back to Cara Sucia?" Alex squints against the sun.

I shrug. "Maybe. How about you? How are things in El Vado?"

"I'm not so much there anymore."

"What do you mean?"

"I'm with the Red Cross now. I was here in the capital for the quake, you know. And my bus wasn't running, so I went down to the refugee camp at La Feria."

"I heard about that." It's all a bit ironic: Alex was a notoriously unproductive volunteer before the earthquake. It wasn't laziness, exactly. He was constantly sick, and spent much of his time traveling back and forth between doctors' offices.

"After the first couple days, they put me in charge. I've been living in the city ever since. Jim worked it out so I'm technically still a volunteer. He's looking the other way on my salary. I signed a year's contract with the Red Cross."

"Wow." I haven't seen Alex this happy and together in a long time.

"That's the reason I'm here, actually. I wanted to see what you were up to. We're thinking more about reconstruction now. I'm sure we could use somebody like you—an engineer, with the language and experience in the campo. But I guess . . ."

Outside the gate, a car horn plays a sloppy version of "Shave and a Haircut."

"I have to go," I say. In truth, to hear myself talked about this way—an expert of sorts, qualified for things, needed—unnerves me so much, I can hardly speak.

"Right." He reaches into his back pocket.

"It's good to see you."

"Take this." He hands me a business card with his name and the Red Cross logo on it. "I've got a place not far from Metrocentro, if you're in the city again, before you go."

We share another cheek kiss, and I run over to meet Ben.

"How'd that go?" Ben hands me a beer as I climb into the passenger seat, a barb of suspicion in his voice. He must've bought the six-pack at the supermarket where we parked.

"Not bad." I pop the top off the can. "Earthquakes seem to bring out the best in him."

"Some people love tragedy."

I take a long pull from the beer. Alex and I came here in the same group. We were a couple in training and then during our first few months as volunteers. We had an ugly breakup. A few months later, there was an incident: Alex cut his wrists. They sent him to D.C. for counseling. After six weeks, he returned to El Salvador.

I was with Ben by then, and it became an all-around awkward situation. Part of me was disgusted that the Peace Corps would send Alex back so quickly. Another part could tell that he'd be worse off if they forced him to stay home.

I hold the beer can between my legs and open my purse. I tuck the envelope of cash and Alex's business card inside my purple Guatemalan wallet, alongside my passport.

"So, we did it," Ben says. "How's it feel?"

"Weird," I say, "scary." I take another gulp of beer. The giddy excitement over our money and our freedom has faded as fast as it arrived. All those second thoughts I'd felt in the water yesterday roll back up like incoming tide.

Ben turns onto the La Libertad highway. The traffic untangles and the car gets up to speed.

"I've always been the girl who did what she was supposed to, you know. This is new territory for me." It's true. My tendency was to avoid hard decisions. I never cared about engineering; that was what my father wanted. Studying on the mainland was fine by me, but it wasn't my idea. Applying to the Peace Corps might be the most decisive thing I ever did, before quitting today.

Eyes still on the road, Ben leans across and gives my knee a reassuring squeeze. "It's all right. This is a big change; it should be scary." He pats the top of my leg a couple times. "We're in it together, you know. We can lean on each other when we need to."

I nod. "Thanks."

Ben turns to look at me, his eyes fixed on mine through the tint of his sunglasses. "I love you."

"I love you, too." I smile.

"Hey." Ben points out the window toward my side of the road. "Looks like snow."

I turn and see the brown mounds of dirt, covered at the top by white powder, like a miniature version of a mountainous landscape—from a place like Utah, perhaps.

"That's lime," I say. "It's a mass grave."

7

First thing in the morning, we ask Kristy for the bill. I check the math on the stack of stapled-together guest checks. Ben goes back to the room for our cash.

"What heat," I say to Kristy.

"Tremendous," she agrees.

I've always been curious about Kristy's age. If forced to guess, I'd place her in her early thirties—within ten years of my own age. She wears too much eye makeup, and a couple of her teeth are framed in metal, but she is quite beautiful. Based on her dark skin and fine hair, I'd guess she has a lot of Mayan blood. She's shorter than I am, her build a bit thicker than mine—bigger breasts and hips. I wonder if she has any children, but I can't bring myself to ask.

"You're good with numbers," Kristy says, watching as I whisper myself through the arithmetic.

"I'm an engineer," I admit. "Or studied to be one, at least."

She nods. "So intelligent."

"Here we go." Ben returns with the white envelope of currency he was given at the Peace Corps office. Kristy makes our change with a mix of dollars and colones. It might be handy to have a little of both on the drive. We'll do our final exchanges at the Nicaraguan border.

"We'll finish packing in another hour or so," Ben tells her. "We can check out then."

"So soon?" Kristy asks.

Ben shrugs. "Can't stay here forever."

"Don't leave without saying good-bye." When she says that, I can't help but think of Cara Sucia, Niña Tere and Nora and the others to whom I never said a proper farewell.

We walk out of the dining area. A door on the air-conditioned wing swings open as we pass. A cloud of pot smoke drifts out, along with the new gringo we saw arriving yesterday.

"What's up?" he says with a scratchy rasp.

"Morning," Ben says.

"Hey, Chuck Norris! Remember me?" He's excited to see Ben.

"Have we met?" Ben asks.

"It's Pelochucho." He points his thumb back at his own chest. "I was here last year."

Ben doesn't seem to recognize him, but he plays along. The word *pelochucho* roughly translates to "hair like a dog," and must refer to the guy's curly mop. It does sound like a name that Peseta would give out.

This Pelochucho is older than we are, but in good shape. His upper body is health-club fit, covered in the hard, round muscles that come from lifting weights and taking supplements. He wears designer board shorts and sandals, bug-eyed sunglasses. The orange hue of his skin betrays time on the tanning bed. His floppy head of hair shines with product.

"Hi." I reach out my hand. "I'm Malia."

"Chinita." He kisses me on the cheek. "You don't remember me? We totally surfed together. You're from Honolulu, right?"

"That's right." I have no recollection of him.

He doesn't seem to care. "Fucking sit down," Pelochucho says. "Let's hang out."

He takes the big seat by the entrance to his room—an easy chair made from thin strands of colored rubber strung across a rebar frame. Ben and I pull up two plastic patio chairs. Pelochucho leaves his door open, so that the chill of the conditioned air seeps out.

"Got something for you." Pelochucho runs back inside his room and returns with a plastic bag of marijuana and a pack of rolling papers. He throws them into Ben's lap. From the blue-green hue of the buds, it's obvious that they were not bought locally.

"Roll a fatty for us, Norris," Pelochucho orders.

"Where are you from?" I ask.

"All over the place, really. Nowadays, I split my time between Orange County and Vancouver Island."

"Vancouver Island?" I had him pegged as a Southern Californian, but I didn't expect Canada. "How's the surf there?"

"Good." He smiles hard and reveals a mouth packed full of brilliant white teeth. "Cold, though. And full of bears."

"What do you do there?" I'm not sure where all these questions come from. He seems a person in need of explanation.

"What do I do? You mean for work?"

Ben holds his head down, balancing the papers and the pot upon his knees.

"I own a company that buys other companies." Pelochucho crosses one leg over the other. His flip-flopped foot bounces in the air. "It's kind of complicated. But not really. We buy businesses that we think Microsoft will buy, then jack up the price before they get them."

"I see." None of this makes any sense to me.

"But I don't work that much, to be honest." He puts both feet on the ground. "I flew down here just for this swell."

"What swell?" I ask. "It's a lake out there right now." It's not even the season for groundswells here.

"Trust me." He smiles again, his teeth looking even bigger and closer together. "I've been online, watching the buoys."

"I've been watching the ocean." I say it with more sarcasm than intended.

Pelochucho stares at me and closes his lips.

"I hope you're right," Ben says, diplomatically.

He passes the joint off to Pelochucho, who fishes a lighter from his board shorts and sparks it up.

Ben turns to me. "Maybe we'll score it down in San Juan del Sur."

"San Juan del Sur?" Pelochucho coughs out the words along with the first exhalation of smoke. "Nica-fucking-ragua? Are you joking? This is a real swell. You want to score it *here*." He uses the lighter to gesture backward over his shoulder.

"We paid our bill. We bought a car." Ben shrugs and tilts his head toward the Jeep. "Time to get on the road."

"That's your car?" Pelochucho passes Ben the joint. "Then you guys have to stick around. Listen." He speaks only to Ben now. "I'll pay for your hotel, your food, your gas, whatever, if you hang out for a few more days."

"You don't have to do that," I say.

"I want to." Pelochucho turns to me and pushes his sunglasses up to his forehead. "Look, I might be doing this land deal out at K Ninety-nine. I could use some help getting around."

Kilometer 99 is a semisecret surf spot up the coast, slightly shorter and less perfect than Punta Roca, but far from any sizable town. Ben and I sometimes hitchhiked to it for waves. There's nothing there, only a mile marker and a cove with world-class surf.

"You can rent a pickup and a driver," I say. "Just ask Kristy."

Ben sips smoke from the joint. I can tell this offer appeals to him.

"So, this is embarrassing, but I'm not great with the language," Pelochucho says. "This could work out for all of us. I want you guys to have an epic trip. Forget the food and hotel and shit. I'll give you a hundred bucks a day if you stay here and help me out, drive me around a little, translate the odd conversation. A hundred bucks each."

"That's awfully generous." A red-eyed Ben pushes the joint toward me.

"No thanks." I hold up a vertical palm. He passes it back to Pelochucho.

"It'll be fun." Pelochucho lowers his sunglasses. "We'll score some sick waves. You'll make some cash. Take a minute. Think about it." He looks back and forth between the two of us. "Talk it over."

———

"Flat," Ben says.

On the concrete and stone stairs that lead down to the beach, we take a seat. The sun sags low at the horizon. Not a breath of wind. Were there any waves at all, conditions would be perfect.

"It could help out a lot." Ben stares seaward, his Southern drawl returning. "Costa Rica, Chile, those places will be pricey. We're only spending like twenty bucks a day now—between the two of us. If we stick around here for a week, it could add another month or so to our trip."

Two stray dogs dig a hole farther up the beach. Sand flies out from between their hind legs. One of the restaurants must've buried bones or fish guts in that spot.

"I know." There's no point arguing with the math. "Our hotel bill was more than I thought. We could use the money. But that guy, he gives me the creeps. What's this business about a swell? There's nothing."

"Chuck Norris!" The call comes from behind. "Chinita!" We turn and see Peseta approaching in that urgent, rhythmic gait of his.

Considering his lifestyle, Peseta has a beautiful head of hair. His shining curls bounce as he hurries over to us. We nod and say hello. Ben bumps his knuckles.

"¿Qué ondas?" Peseta asks. "There're no waves."

"No waves," Ben agrees.

"Have you got mota?" Peseta asks Ben.

"Sí." Ben stifles a laugh, still recovering from Pelochucho's pot. "Plenty."

Peseta is La Libertad's jack-of-all-trades. If a strange tourist shows up in town, he helps them with their luggage and leads them to a hotel, where he'll ask for a tip from both the client and the hotel manager. His mother is a local weed dealer; Peseta earns most of his income from trips between her house and the rooms where the surfers stay. He's more than happy to run to the crack house for something stronger.

Peseta nods. "Listen, both of you. Some guys, they've been waiting by the cemetery to rob surfers. Be careful, eh."

Peseta also fancies himself a sort of ambassador between the surfers and the city's criminal element. He issues warnings like these as though they're weather hazards, and expects money in return.

In this instance, the information isn't too useful. The cemetery stickup is a fairly common thing.

"Hey, Chuck Norris." Peseta puts on a pouty face. "Have you got a coin for me? You know, a little gift."

I roll my eyes.

"Oh, right." Ben taps the pocket of his board shorts and pulls out one colón. "Here." He holds it out.

"*Gracias,* Norris." Peseta smiles, his thin mustache edging up at either side of his mouth. "You let me know when you need more *mota.*"

"Peseta?" I say.

He turns to me.

"Do you know this guy Pelochucho? Have you met him before? Did you give him that nickname?"

"Pelochucho? Of course. He's returned, no?" Peseta raises a mischievous eyebrow. "He's a lot of fun. *Mucha plata.*" He rubs together two fingers in the international sign for money, then walks away.

"See?" Ben says to me. "The guy likes to throw his cash

around. It could be a while before we have another chance to earn any money at all. Let alone easy money."

The ball is in my court. I get bad vibes from Pelochucho. But another side of me likes the idea of sticking around here a little longer, getting some kind of closure. Everything has happened so fast since the earthquake, I could use some time to catch my breath.

"Fuck it," I say. "Might as well take this guy's money for a day or two."

Ben smiles and puts an arm around my shoulder.

I look out at the ocean. "I mean, how bad could it be?"

8

It wasn't long after I'd broken up with Alex, a few short months into my service, a year and a half before the earthquake. Some girlfriends from my training group talked me into a weekend at the beach. Four of us rented two rooms in La Posada's cheap wing—which was the first time I ever saw the place. Once our backpacks were shoved inside, we all went to a shorefront restaurant for midday drinks.

I'd not surfed in years, and never outside of Hawai'i. It hadn't occurred to me that there might be waves in El Salvador. Straight away, I could tell a swell was running. The rocky point—which began at the restaurant—stretched far out to sea. It was as long as any wave I'd seen on Oahu and had no closed-out sections. I studied it while the other girls smoked and chatted.

Soon, I saw a bearded gringo, prone on his surfboard, riding white water into shore.

I leaned over toward Courtney, my closest friend in the group, and pointed. "Do you know that guy?"

"Him?" She squinted. "That's Ben. He's Agro-Forestry, from the group before us. They say he comes here a lot. You never see him in the capital. I think he's from North Carolina."

He climbed out from the frothing ocean and undid the leash around his ankle. He was shorter and thicker than Alex; his body was fit except for a small paunch at his belly. The water made clumps out of his reddish beard and matted together the hair on his chest and shoulders. He tucked the board under his arm.

"He's kind of cute," Courtney said over my shoulder. "In a dirty, hippie, surfer sort of way."

He walked up the beach toward us. Afraid to be caught staring, I faced the girls. Seconds later, Ben leaned his board against the concrete platform of the restaurant. I turned back to him. He pushed wet hair out of his eyes, then set his elbows up on the platform.

"Spare a sip?" He pointed at the liter of Regia I'd been working on.

I picked up the amber bottle and passed it down to him.

"Cheers." He took a big swallow.

"Good waves." I meant it as a statement, but it came out of my mouth sounding more like a question.

"Really good." He took another sip. "I'm about to grab my bigger board and head back out. Just snapped the leash." He held up the length of broken plastic, as if I didn't know what a leash was.

Courtney and the others giggled behind me.

"Are you the girl from Hawai'i?" Ben asked. A Xeroxed face book of new volunteers was circulated among the veterans. Maybe he'd seen my picture in it.

"Malia." I nodded. My feet were at his eye level. I stole a glance at my toes to check for filth and dead skin.

"I'm Ben." He reached up his hand.

I crouched and shook it.

"You come from Hawai'i but you can't surf?"

"Who says I can't surf?" Still crouched, I took back my beer bottle and had a drink.

"You should get out there," he said. "We haven't had a swell like this in months."

I shrugged and handed him the beer again. "You say you got another board?"

"Yeah." In an instant, he went from flirtation to logistics. "Two boards but only one working leash. Let me think. . . . Maybe Napo would loan me one."

"I don't need a leash," I said.

He cocked his head like a confused dog. "You sure?"

"Those things are for haoles." I smiled and lifted his board by the nose. It was full of dings, but a good size for me. "I'll take this out. Grab your other one and meet me back here. I've got a bikini on under this." I pinched a bit of cloth from my T-shirt.

Ben grinned. "Suit yourself." He sprinted off toward La Posada.

I turned to the girls. "Would you guys take my stuff back to the room? There's money in the pocket—for my beers." I pulled my T-shirt off over my head, wiggled out of my shorts. "I'm going surfing with him."

By the looks on their faces, you'd have thought I said I was going to eat broken glass with him.

"Out there?" Courtney stood up. She pointed to the ocean, mouth agape. Her height and her short tufty hair gave Courtney a certain ostrichlike quality: legs too long and thin for her body, center of gravity a bit too high. Her shape—with its thick, pillowy torso—had an endearing maternal aspect when she was in a good mood. But when frustrated, she turned squawky and comical.

"At the point, I suppose." I craned my neck to see the take-off, then turned windmills with my arms.

"What about, like, sharks?" asked Kathy, a blond girl from my training group, whose fair skin already looked to be burning under the sun.

"More people are killed by vending machines than by sharks." What did worry me was my strength. I remembered how to surf, but I hadn't paddled in years.

"Malia!" Ben called from below, a second beater surfboard under his arm.

"See you guys back at the hotel," I said. "We'll probably stay out for the sunset."

I followed Ben along the point. We picked our way across the big black stones. Every minute or so, he glanced over his shoulder to check on me. I hadn't expected such a hike. Perhaps the wave was even longer than it looked from shore.

Finally, we came to a spot where two rusted-out pipes headed straight into the water. I shuddered to think what they carried. Ben put in. With his board at knee level, he leaned on the deck, pushed off a couple of rocks, and started paddling. I did the same.

A handful of local surfers were out, but not many, considering. The swell was bigger than I'd anticipated, the wave even better shaped.

Ben led me to a tight inside position. From here, we'd be able to pick off smaller waves, but also scramble outside for the big ones.

"Watch out for the Mother Rock." He pointed toward a huge boulder half-exposed in the lineup. "Other than that, it's pretty user-friendly."

We didn't wait long for a set. One of the local guys took off way deep on the first wave. Ben and I paddled for the outside. A bodyboarder had position on the second one but wasn't going to make it. Ben turned. A couple of strokes and he was atop a long drop wall.

I wasn't sure how many waves might be in this set, so I cut toward the point for the next one. It looked smaller and like it might back off. I paddled for it anyway. My wave pitched more than Ben's; the takeoff was hasty. As I made the drop, that round Mother Rock rose below me like a whale coming up for breath. I was so shocked, I nearly wiped out then and there.

Once on my feet, I set the rail and gave two hard pumps. The borrowed board felt nice. The volume offered extra glide; the weight from all the dings gave it more drive down the face. Once past the takeoff section, I was home free.

This wave was unbelievable; it kept opening up. After a couple big carves, I spotted Ben paddling down the line. He flashed me a *shaka* and hollered some inaudible word over the roar of the sea. I crouched, rode high and tight against the curl. The wave's power built up under my feet. The next section went vertical and I unloaded. With a stomp, I shifted all my weight to my front foot, shot down the face, did a bottom turn, and hit the lip.

It didn't work out as well as I'd hoped. I scrubbed too much speed at the bottom and miscalculated the distance to Ben. Still, I managed to get him with a small arc of spray, on my first wave in years. I'd leaned so hard into the top carve that I fell off in the shoulder.

Underwater, I remembered that I was unleashed. I surfaced and swam for my loose board, but Ben got to it first. He grinned wide.

"Damn right you can surf." He pushed the board back my way.

"This wave is amazing!"

"Nice, huh?"

We paddled back to the lineup. As the next set came in, a band of mariachis started up from one of the seaside restaurants. It felt as if we were heroes, their cinematic horn lines our theme music. The sunset glowed pink and orange on the horizon.

But how can I truly describe that first session at the point, with a boy whom I began at that moment to fall in love with? Surfing is something I grew up around, that I did as a kid. In high school, surfers were a sort of caste—like the jocks or nerds from mainland movies. Once we hit puberty, older sisters warned that our boobs would turn flat from too much paddling, that sharks would attack when we had our periods. Early in my high school years, I started playing volleyball and put waves on the back burner. For teenagers and twentysomethings in Hawai'i, surfing tends to get competitive and serious. It's not playful the way it is for little kids or adults. I'd forsaken the sport for so long now. I'd always enjoyed it but never wanted it to be my identity.

Here there was no slang, no fashion, no accoutrements; there was only the ride.

So surfing that first wave—a nearly perfect wave, which I'd surfed well—was like a celebration of my past. And knowing that this break was this good, this empty, and this close to where I lived—that was a glimpse at the greatest possible future.

A celebration of my life so far, plus the promise of better days to come—it was, I suppose, a bit like falling in love itself.

We went back to La Posada cold, hungry, and grinning. Courtney and the others had set up at one of the tables in the dining room: beer, cigarettes, and the remains of dinner. The three of them shouted and slammed playing cards upon the table in some unfamiliar game. They whispered to one another as we came in. I couldn't have cared less.

Ben put the boards away. I showered, dressed, and joined the girls. Ben talked Kristy into making us a late dinner— something she seemed accustomed to. We all sat around drinking and chatting for a while. Ben went to bed first. He told me that I could join him for the morning glass. I said good night to the girls, and I was so exhausted, I didn't hear Courtney stumble in beside me later on. In fact, I barely woke up once the screaming started.

I thought it was a bad dream at first. But it kept up, and changed from incoherent shrieks to English. "In my room, he's in my room . . ."

"That's Kathy," Courtney said.

We threw clothes on and went to the door. In the court-yard, I saw Kathy's blond hair. Her pale limbs were tangled up with those of another figure; four arms contorted in all directions, as if attached at the wrists. Kathy kept shrieking, "My room!" along with less coherent words. Courtney and I stood in our doorway, frozen by a mix of fear and confusion.

Less than a second passed before Ben materialized and pulled the two bodies apart. He put a sort of wrestling hold on the intruder, grabbed both his arms at the shoulder. Ben's hands were laced together behind the stranger's head. Lights clicked on in the kitchen. A fat Salvadoran man in tighty whities—who, I'd later learn, was the owner of La Posada— came to the door.

"Don Adán," Ben hollered. "This *mañoso culero* was in one of the rooms!"

"Tie him up," Don Adán yelled back.

Kathy was in tears. My heartbeats felt like punches against the inside of my chest. Finally, we could see the thief. He was small, wearing only a tattered pair of cutoff jeans. His four limbs flailed in Ben's grip like the legs of an upside-down crab.

More lights came on, and I noticed the broken surf leash upon a chair outside Ben's room. As he wrestled the guy to the ground, I went and grabbed it.

Leash in hand, I hesitated to close the distance between myself and the two of them. I flinched from a few feet away, as if afraid the robber might somehow sting me with one of those thrashing limbs.

"It's all right," Ben said, reading my mind. "They never have knives or weapons. These guys trade anything of value for rocks." He put his knee in the middle of the thief's back, then took the leash from me and began to tie his hands together.

"This happens . . . often?" I asked.

Ben pulled tightly on the cord. A wince came from his

prisoner. "The town's got a bit of a crack problem. You shouldn't leave doors unlocked."

"How do they get in?" I looked up at the ten-foot-tall wrought-iron gate that enclosed the courtyard, studied the spikes along its top.

"Tree over there." Ben pointed to the roof above the hotel's expensive wing. "I sometimes use that route to dawn patrol, if they haven't unlocked the gate yet."

He went through the thief's pockets. First, he found a slim glass pipe, snapped off at one end, along with a lighter and a folded square of tinfoil.

"No rocks," Ben said. "Big surprise there."

From the next pocket, he pulled out a compact pair of binoculars and a leather billfold. "Are these hers?"

I carried them over to Kathy, whose teary face was pressed to Courtney's chest. The two of them still stood by the room at the far end of the courtyard.

"Guess we need to keep our doors locked." I handed over the items.

I went back to Ben. With now-dilated eyes, I could see that the crackhead was tiny, hardly a man at all, possibly still a teenager. Lying still in those ragged shorts, with no fight left, he reminded me of a deflated Incredible Hulk.

The hotel owner put on pants and took control of the thief.

Ben trembled from the residual adrenaline. "Well, Malia. You've already gotten the full La Lib experience: the upside and the downside."

"In less than twenty-four hours."

He laughed and nodded, walked over to his room, and put on a shirt. "C'mon," he said.

I followed him up a set of stairs to the roof of the hotel's expensive wing. Strands of rusted-out rebar sprouted like saplings from the concrete. A forgotten stack of red bricks lay by a pair of patio chairs and some makeshift ashtrays. We sat down. From his shirt pocket, Ben pulled out a hand-rolled cigarette and the lighter he'd taken off the crackhead.

"My hands are shaking so bad, I can hardly light this thing."

I'd have offered to help, but my nerves were in no better shape.

From below, we heard the big gate rattle, a string of Spanish curse words, then another clang of metal.

"Is he letting the guy go?"

Ben nodded and drew smoke. "It's for the best," he said without taking a breath.

By then, I could tell he wasn't smoking a cigarette.

"*Pakalolo*?" I asked as he handed it to me, forgetting where I was.

"They call it *mota* here."

I took a small and cautious drag.

"Sun's coming up." Ben looked over his shoulder.

"This is the grossest pot I've ever had in my life." I coughed and handed it back to him.

He laughed. "You're not in Hawai'i anymore."

"You got that right." I put a hand to my chest.

"Is it true that *haole* means 'white devil'?" he asked.

I stopped coughing long enough to laugh. "Not a devil; more like a ghost. Definitely a foreigner. But, yes, it's what we call white people."

Ben nodded and drew more smoke.

"It's no big deal, like saying *gringo* here. They call me *hapa*—which means 'half'—for being part Hawaiian and part Japanese."

For several minutes, we sat in silence and stared at a square of ocean visible between the buildings. The corners of the sky began to brighten with the impending sunrise.

"Fuck it," Ben said. "We might as well paddle out."

We changed, got the boards, and returned to the roof.

Ben climbed down the tree first. I handed him each of the boards, then went down myself. For nearly an hour, we were the only people in the water. The tide was higher than yesterday, and I was exhausted, but it was a fun session all the same—more playful than the day before.

Afterward, I was surprised to find my girlfriends all packed up at the hotel. I figured they'd have slept in. Still rattled by the robbery, they wanted to be rid of this town as soon as possible.

"We're all waiting on you," Courtney said.

I gathered my towel and a change of clothes. "Already? It'll probably be a while, with showering and breakfast and stuff. I'm starving."

Courtney looked at her watch. She seemed upset with me, as though I'd not treated the crackhead incident with the proper gravitas. Or perhaps it was all the surfing: I'd failed to play my assigned role in this girls' weekend at the beach.

"Why don't you go without me?"

"Fine," she said. "We have the room until noon."

We said our good-byes before I even got to shower. After breakfast, I took a sweaty nap, the same modified fan turning back and forth above like an automated dummy from an old wax museum.

An hour later, I woke up, needing to pee. I emerged from the room bleary-eyed, in a tank top and sarong, and went straight for the toilets.

On my way back, still confused and half-asleep, I saw Ben in the hammock outside his room. A Salvadoran newspaper lay across his lap.

"What time is it?" I held a hand above my eyes like a visor.

"Almost noon," he said.

"I have to check out."

"They're pretty flexible here." He turned one of the pages. "Or you could stay another night."

Maybe it was the dreamy half-awake state of my brain. Maybe I knew it could be weeks or even months before our paths crossed again. Maybe, after all the great waves and the robbery, the tedious rituals of flirtation and courtship were drained of their normal weight. Whatever the reason, this is what I said to Ben one day after first meeting him: "Could I stay in your room?"

He dropped the newspaper flat to his lap. "I'd like that."

Courtney had already made a pile of my things atop my backpack. I used my arms like alligator jaws to clamp it all and carry it over to Ben's room. I offered him a half smile as I passed. He kept the newspaper down at his waist, and I wondered if he was hiding an erection.

A smaller room, it had a thin single bed but a proper ceiling fan. I starfished across the mattress and felt the air blow down. It took only a minute to realize that I'd not be falling asleep. A wave of self-consciousness washed over me, woke me up, and forced me to feel silly for the self-invitation.

As if reading my mind, Ben appeared in the doorway. He stood there for a second. I propped myself up on my elbows. We exchanged a volley of loaded eye contact. And though it was only Ben who stood on a literal threshold, we were both about to enter a whole new chapter.

He closed the door and locked it. I sat up on the edge of the bed, my body language doing its best to confirm his assumptions. He took the couple of steps toward me, then went down to one knee. The bed was so low that our heads were almost even with each other.

I'd never kissed a man with a beard before, and so I flinched when he first leaned his head in toward mine—thinking of the prickly stubble Alex used to get after days without a shave. But Ben's beard was soft and fine. In a way, it felt gentler against me than regular skin.

I put my hands upon each of his round shoulders. All his paddling had formed a loose, flat layer of muscle. It felt like a manta ray affixed to his upper back. He grabbed the bottom edge of my tank top. I barely had a chance to raise my arms up before he pulled it off and over my head.

I sat up a little straighter as he went to kiss my nipples. To me, this was always the most tedious part of foreplay. I never minded my tiny breasts; what I hated was the way that boys felt the need to reassure me by paying so much attention to them.

But Ben's beard tickled my chest in a pleasant way. It gave me chicken skin in spite of the heat. I'd always considered myself deficient in whatever nerve endings make this area so sensitive to most women. Now, I wondered if I'd simply never been touched in the right way.

My fingers traced the shape of his shoulder blades. I spread my knees wide. The sarong around my waist melted into the bed. I lay down and closed my eyes. The hiss of Velcro ripping undone and the crisp brush of synthetic fabric sounded as Ben removed his board shorts.

I felt the tickling bristle of his beard against the inside of my thigh. My whole body shuddered at the first touch of it.

One leg kicked as if hit by a doctor's mallet. Scared he might take that as a sign of protest, I said, "Don't stop."

And he didn't stop. I clenched my knees around the edge of the mattress to keep from further squirming. The bearded face between my legs sent electricity all throughout my limbs. It had the feel of something alive yet unfamiliar, like the rubbery muzzle of a horse.

My orgasm was a relief once it finally happened, like walking out a cramp or sending blood to a sleeping limb. I shuddered and panted and pushed his head away.

Ben climbed into the bed. He made love to me in a way that was lighthearted and generous—the opposite of Alex. In spite of the ceiling fan, both our bodies were soon covered in a slick film of sweat spiked with sand and a trace of sunblock.

Once it was over, we lay uncovered on the little bed. I put my head upon his shoulder. Staring up at the spinning fan, I once again craved reassurance, some confirmation that this was the right thing to do. How did I know then that we were getting ourselves into more than a one-off weekend?

Ben wrapped his arm around me more tightly, careful not to displace my head. His fingers settled on the slightly softer, slightly paler triangle of skin at my breast. They searched it for a second, came across a nipple sore from rubbing against surf wax, then backed off.

"Sorry," I said. "I don't have any boobs when I'm lying down."

"That's okay," he said. "I don't have a dick after I've been out in the ocean for a while. It's like an eel in a cave."

I laughed out loud. The bed shook beneath us.

"Seriously, it looks like a second belly button down there."

I turned my face into his chest and felt the hair against my cheek. Even after the laughter ended, I couldn't stop smiling.

"So you spend a lot of time here, then?" I asked him.

"Depends," he said. "Couple weekends a month. More if the surf's good."

From then on, La Libertad became a part of my life. In El Salvador, most volunteers stay sane by going to the capital or visiting friends every two or three weeks. Now, Ben and I went to La Lib exclusively.

I became La Chinita. Though it was perhaps Peseta's least inspired nickname—and though I'm not Chinese—it was nice to have the status. My surfing skills came back quickly. The point was the perfect place for a regular footer to practice.

Kristy prepared our meals and looked after the boards while we were gone. I brought her gifts from the Peace Corps medical office: lotions, tampons, ibuprofen.

Those long weekends—sometimes whole weeks—in La Libertad became the best days of my life. The locals—crackheads and surfers alike—knew who I was and flashed *shaka*s and thumbs-up signs as I walked by. We surfed the morning glass, breakfasted on beans, eggs, fresh cheese, and tortillas. We passed the sweltering daytime hours with naps, sweaty lovemaking sessions, and ice-cold Regias. During sunset surfs at the point, the low clouds turned a weird mix of pinks and blues. The water calmed and took on a reflective, oily sheen. At the far side of the sky, fires from the cane fields sent up columns of smoke that glowed purple in the evening light. Mariachi bands serenaded us. The waves were as good as waves get.

Was I afraid of the crackheads and the other dangers? To some extent. But it wasn't so different from the rest of El Salvador. There was a simple set of rules: You didn't go out at night, never left anything unlocked, never carried more money than you needed. In a sense, the crackhead thieves were more predictable than other elements of the criminal class. Also, I was always with Ben. From the first day I met him, I believed that he could handle anything. That he could keep me safe.

9

We wake early. No signs of stirring from Pelochucho's room. Ben and I walk to the beach for a morning surf check—a ritual that's become more about procrastination than actual forecasting. We take a seat on the stone staircase that leads down to the sand.

"Small." Ben yawns. He's brought along his multitool and a bit of tie wire to fix my broken flip-flop.

"This is Pelochucho's monster swell?" I hand him the bad sandal. "The one we're sticking around for?"

Ben shrugs. "Surfing's a way of life. Waiting is part of it."

I run my finger through the sand at the bottom of the steps.

How many days and hours did I spend thinking about sand in the past two years? How far the men would have to carry it and how much, whether it was fine enough to aggregate the cement. That was river sand, of course; you can't make concrete with ocean sand.

"Here we go." Ben fashions a sort of wire pin to keep the rubber plug from pulling up through the flip-flop's sole.

"I'm not going to get lockjaw from that, am I?"

"If you do, then it's time to buy a new pair." He hands the sandal back to me.

"Thanks." I slip it onto my foot, then rise and take a couple steps. My toes hardly feel the wire. "It works."

"Course it works." Ben grins. "I may not be an engineer, but I've got a few tricks up my sleeve."

Peseta wanders up to join us, a T-shirt draped over his head. "No waves," he says.

"No waves," we repeat in unison.

Peseta looks as frustrated as we are, though he hasn't entered the water in years.

"Ben," I say. "Would you mind if I take the Jeep and go to Cara Sucia? I feel like I need to say some good-byes, at least to Niña Tere." Now that we plan to stick around here a few more days, I can't justify not returning to my village one last time.

"Today?" He takes his eyes off the hapless surf. "I don't mind. Want me to go with you?"

"That's okay. I'll do it on my own."

Ben nods. "Not like you'll be missing much here."

El Salvador's coastal highway, the Litoral, is the smoothest and fastest stretch of road in the country. Eastbound, not many miles outside of La Libertad, I cross the Santa Cruz Bridge, where the women of Cara Sucia—my former neighbors—do their laundry in the dry season. I crane my neck to try and spot a familiar face, but speed makes everything a blur.

I find my turn and head inland. The engine winds hard with the quick gain in elevation. The landscape grows familiar. Coastal sugarcane and coconut plantations give way to hills full of corn and beans, a few cows and pigs, humble houses of adobe walls and red clay roofs.

Soon I pass the tiny refugee camp of El Terrero. Their community—which had been a lovely hamlet tucked deep into a valley that runs parallel to this road—was demolished in the earthquake. The residents now live along the dirt shoulder in shacks made from black plastic sheeting and corrugated metal. Over the shelters hangs a homemade banner begging help from both God and the government.

Seconds later, I'm in Cara Sucia proper. A few heads turn as I park next to Niña Tere's house and climb out.

A young man named Chago, who was a tireless worker on the aqueduct, turns and smiles, looking confused by my presence. What does he think? That I still live here? That I've returned from vacation? Who knows what rumors might've followed my exit.

Across the street, a blue-and-white cross is planted in the courtyard, covered in flowers. It's the spot where Felix died. His grandmother must've built the memorial.

"Niña Tere?" I round the corner of her house. "It's me, Malia."

Her dog, Rambo, howls. His claws click upon the packed dirt of the floor.

"Come in, child." I recognize Tere's voice. Then I hear Nora's excited squeal: "Niña Malia!"

I enter the house that is, in many ways, the beating heart of my time in El Salvador. It looks as I remember it: thick adobe walls whitewashed on the inside. Wooden beams and columns—all milled by machete—hold up a roof made of red clay tiles and bamboo crosspieces.

Upon my arrival in this village, Niña Tere took me in—long before I'd become a local celebrity with the aqueduct, back when the rest of the Cara Sucians wanted to trade me for a white male, a *real* gringo. I stayed here for several weeks while Tere helped me arrange for the house I eventually rented. I continued to eat with them almost every day.

Niña Tere's husband, Guillermo, lives in Texas and works construction. He sends down generous *remesas*—mainly for Nora's tuition at the private school in Los Planes. Niña Tere is a natural entrepreneur. In addition to his earnings, she mends clothes for extra money, sells tamales and bags of sweetened fruit drinks at all the local soccer games. She serves as secretary for the village council and is the only reason that body gets anything done. The other members are more interested in making speeches and granting titles. Without Tere, I doubt the aqueduct would have enjoyed its year of fruitless construction.

"Have a seat." She uses her hand to dust off a plastic chair. "Did you bring hunger? We're about to eat lunch."

I nod and sit down.

"Will you stay here tonight? Do you need to bathe?" She gestures toward the cistern behind her house.

"No, Niña Tere." I look down at the table, then finally raise my eyes. "I came to say good-bye. I'm leaving El Salvador."

She grimaces for a half second, then nods. "I understand. With the earthquake, it must be very difficult."

"There's no time or money to finish the aqueduct. It simply doesn't make sense."

"Indeed." Her voice chokes up a tiny bit. "*Pues,* we were lucky to have you. I'll get the soup." Niña Tere disappears into the small and smoky outbuilding that serves as the kitchen. Nora and I sit alone at the table.

"Is that your car outside?" Nora asks.

"More or less," I say. "You remember Don Benjamín? It belongs to the two of us." Ben and I never spent much time here, but I made sure to introduce him. "We're going to South America, in that car."

"That's a long way," she says.

"It's a very long way," I agree.

Niña Tere returns and places steaming bowls of soup before us: rice, potato, squash, the small dark leaves of *chipilín*—a wild herb said to be healthy. The stringy lace of egg white promises a hard yolk somewhere at the bottom. On her second trip, she brings a dish of salt, a stack of fresh tortillas, and a couple of quartered limes.

When I first arrived, I found the Salvadoran custom of hot soup in the sweltering midday hours ridiculous. Now it feels nice, familiar. How many days have I eaten this same meal here at this table, on this same red-and-white oilcloth? Surely, this time will be the last.

"How are things?" I ask. "With the village council?"

Niña Tere shrugs. "Not much interest in the water project. All you hear about is the earthquake now."

I tear a tortilla in half and touch one of the corners to the coarse salt in the dish. "What do you mean?"

"The council solicits help from different agencies: clothing, plastic, food, things like that." She speaks without enthusiasm. "That's taken up most of their time."

I'm confused: Cara Sucia's homes fared relatively well during the quake. The village is in much better shape than its surrounding communities. More homes are standing than not. Certainly, there's no lack of housing or food.

"It's foolishness," Tere admits. "Somebody brought out a load of blankets and mattresses last week, and people went crazy. They didn't have enough for everyone, so they cut them in half. Can you imagine? What do you do with half a mattress?"

"But most people here have bedding, right? They should've taken those things down to El Terrero," I say.

Niña Tere shakes her head, as if this episode exhausted her reason long before I learned of it. "People like free things," she explains.

Nora commits to her soup, a few grains of soft rice stuck to her chin. I try to remind myself that this isn't my problem anymore.

Once my soup is finished, I lean back in the chair. Niña Tere brings a soccer ball–shaped watermelon from the kitchen and sets it in the center of the oilcloth. It's so ripe that when she touches the blade to one side, the entire shell splits all the way around.

We suck down the fruit until I think I'll burst, gossiping and reminiscing. Niña Tere laughs out loud, recalling the sight of me in muddy work clothes, heading off to supervise all the village men.

"We'll never see something like that again, not in this village," Niña Tere says, nodding her head.

"Something like what?"

"You." She points at me with her lips. "A North American, from Hawai'i no less, coming down to work for this community." She laughs aloud and claps her hands together. "While the rest of us are trying to sneak into your country to find work."

We share an awkward second of silence.

"I should go," I tell her.

"So soon?"

We say our final good-byes. Each gives me a hug.

I climb in the car but drive only a few doors down the road and stop again.

My old house already looks abandoned; vines climb the walls and front fence. I find my key and walk through the yard. A half dozen bats fly out as the door swings open. The inside looks much as I left it. The same shattered coffee mug lies across the floor. The same long crack reaches up between the cinder blocks. The only difference is the fresh bat guano, spread about the walls like hasty brushstrokes.

I've been living out of the backpack I grabbed on my way out of here last time; luckily, it was still half-packed from an earlier weekend trip. Now I gather up some spare clothes and other valuables and stuff them into a larger bag. I make sure to take a sweater and raincoat for the cold legs of our South American journey. At the doorway, I pause for one last look around my old home. Then I pull the door shut and leave the place to the bats.

There are other friends in this town to whom I owe good-byes. But I'm simply not up to it. I drive back to La Lib with the windows all the way down. The air feels nice against the soup-caused sweat that covers my skin.

10

The most unexpected thing about meeting Ben and rediscovering surfing was that it corresponded with a breakthrough in my Peace Corps work. The water project—which had spun its wheels through months of bureaucratic limbo—finally took off. Materials arrived by the truckload. Cara Sucia's men gathered each morning with picks and shovels.

My first six months in that village had been spent ticking away the hot hours reading books, painting my little house, and asking questions for a useless health census. Almost overnight, I switched to twelve- or fourteen-hour days, walking through the jungles and coffee fields in jeans and boots, checking elevations, making work schedules, measuring the depth of ditches, and asking landowners for permission to lay pipe.

I became a hero in Cara Sucia. The villagers had all been suspicious of me at first. With the start of the project, I won them over. Even the old boys of the council took my opinions seriously. They called me *ingeniera*—"engineer." I was offered food and invited into homes. If I complained of any problems with my house or my cistern, a man would arrive to fix them. I had to invent excuses for not being godmother to several local children.

All the while, my surfing life was in full swing. Though I never lied about where I went on the weekends, rumors spread that I was off advising on other aqueduct projects. It didn't matter much; there was no need for me to supervise every second of the construction. What counted most were the results, and I was producing those in spades. Nobody questioned what I did with my own time.

And it wasn't only the villagers who were enthusiastic. The Peace Corps office heard great things about me. I was asked to speak to incoming trainees. Suddenly, all of those bizarre courses I'd taken in college—building concrete cubes in the lab, or tiny models of suspension bridges—finally made sense. I *was* an engineer after all.

I called home frequently and spoke of my work with pride. My father had been against my Peace Corps service in the first place. He'd seen it as an indulgence, a waste of time. But with the news of the project, everything changed. He was rapt, asking detailed questions, always wanting to know how I learned to do this or that.

My father loved to work with his hands—to build things—but he never had a chance to attend college. The landscaping business was something he inherited—and grew—but his heart wasn't fully in it. His favorite part, I believe, was tinkering with the broken lawn mowers. He's the one who pushed me to study engineering.

To my surprise, he decided to fly to El Salvador early in the second year of my service. I was shocked when I heard. In fact, I had to call off a weekend in La Lib with Ben.

The three of us had an awkward dinner in San Salvador the night my father arrived. I don't think he understood who Ben was, or why they should meet. There was no room for socializing or boyfriends in my father's vision of my life here. Ben rolled with it well enough.

The next morning, my father and I rode a rattling chicken bus out to Cara Sucia. It was a Sunday; nobody was working. I took him to see the spring boxes—the most complete part of the project. Soon into our walk, he slipped on the trail and muddied his pants and golf shirt.

At the river's edge, I showed him the two concrete boxes we'd built, and lifted the cover so he could watch the water gushing inside. He asked how we worked in the river and I explained that we made a wall out of red clay—the kind used to make cookware and roofing tiles—to divert the water's flow while we poured the first layers of concrete.

"Amazing," my father said over and over, as if I'd invented these techniques, not learned them from the locals.

It was a beautiful day along the riverbed. Butterflies clung to wet rocks. We followed the four-inch galvanized pipes downward on their way. I showed him the suspension bridge we'd constructed to span a wide and rocky ravine, told him about the Salvadoran teenagers who'd worked up there, while the pipe was supported by only a series of machete-hewn tree limbs. I pointed out the forked mango tree where we bent the galvanized pipes, with eight guys pushing on either end, whenever the aqueduct needed to turn corners.

My father listened with a brand of awe that I'd never before seen in him. On that day, I realized that raising me alone had been his life's work. This project must've meant a certain measure of secondhand achievement for him.

We had a look at the beginnings of the tanks, where the work was currently going on. Along the road, I pointed out where the distribution lines would run to the houses. A couple of families had already planted taps beside their cisterns, in anticipation of the water.

My father was less interested in getting to know the community. He didn't enjoy being studied by the Salvadoran villagers, dragged around and introduced in a language he couldn't understand. Little kids pulled at the sides of their eyes and demonstrated kung fu moves they'd seen on television. I'd ceased to notice such things long ago. But my father looked bothered by it all. Even at Niña Tere's house, he remained quiet and withdrawn. He passed a silent judgment on the village, as though it wasn't deserving of the water project that had so pleased him.

By the time we went to the airport for his departing flight, I was exhausted. Playing the tour guide had worn me out. He bought us a dinner of fried chicken at the terminal's Pollo Campero. For the last five minutes or so of his trip, with fast food and soda spread across the table, I felt like a child once again. In fact, once the boarding calls began, I had to remind myself that I was staying here. Having won my dad's approval for this project, it felt like a finish line of sorts.

Once back in Hawai'i, he continued to follow the progress

of the aqueduct. He bought the first computer he'd ever owned. Through frequent e-mails, he continued to offer me his pride, an emotion I'd not quite figured out what to do with.

We spoke on the day of the earthquake, of course, but not since. I haven't managed to tell him about quitting the Peace Corps, or about the Jeep and South America. I suppose I thought it better to wait until we're actually on the road—until there's no chance he might talk me out of it.

11

"Okay, that was not cool, but whatever. I can look the other way." Pelochucho stands beside Ben. Both wear button-down shirts with short sleeves and collars. They seem to be waiting on me.

"Come again?" I climb out of the driver's seat.

"You guys are on my clock here. You can't go disappearing." He glares down at an expensive-looking wristwatch—all shining metal and dark leather. "We need to be at Kilometer Ninety-nine like now."

"K Ninety-nine? There's no surf. And you weren't even awake." I look toward Ben, hoping for some support. "Are we supposed to wait outside your door all day?"

"No worries." Pelochucho smiles and holds up his hands. "Miscommunication. But seriously, we've got to go."

A ping sounds from the Jeep's engine. The three of us stand on the driver's side. My mouth hangs open, still eager to defend my right to take my own damn car when and where I please.

"Chuck, you drive," Pelochucho says. "I'm riding shotgun." He walks around the car and opens the passenger-side door.

That means, of course, that I'll be left lying across the plywood shelf in the back. Pelochucho's door swings shut.

"Do you want to drive?" Ben asks me halfheartedly.

"Oh, I almost forgot," Pelochucho calls from inside the car. "Your money."

A Velcro pocket rips open. Pelochucho's hand, clutching two hundred-dollar bills, is thrust in Ben's direction through the open driver's door.

Ben takes them both and is about to hand one to me.

"Chinita, here's yours." Another two bills come through the car door.

I look inside the Jeep and see a thick wad of hundreds in Pelochucho's other hand.

"I figure you guys were technically on the clock yesterday, you know." He passes Ben one more hundred. "And this is like a signing bonus or something. Let's go."

I'm about to ask why I need to go along in the first place, but at the sight of the cash, I think better of it.

"Hold on to this for me?" I pass my two hundreds back toward Ben.

He nods and puts all five bills in his pocket. He was right: That money might represent weeks, perhaps another full month, of traveling for us.

I climb onto the wooden platform in the rear and ask Ben to close me in.

The road to K 99 undulates along the rugged coastline. In the back, tossing about with every curve, I have vertigo and mild nausea. I can't decide if the pot smoke, wafting over from another of Pelochucho's pungent joints, makes things better or worse.

"You'll turn right just before the surf spot," Pelochucho says in a hoarse voice. "There, that's the one."

Ben shifts into four-wheel drive. We head uphill on a steep dirt road. My body slips backward along the shelf. After a minute or two of climbing, Pelochucho says, "Stop."

Ben kills the engine and comes around to let me out. Pelochucho calls to someone in his awkward Spanish. Once out of the car, I look around.

We're in the campo. The ruins of several small adobe houses are flanked by temporary structures. For me, it's like instant déjà vu from the scene at El Terrero hours ago: makeshift walls of corrugated metal and black plastic, smaller yellow tarps bearing the USAID logo. Women tend fires built safe distances from the remaining walls. Children and dogs poke their faces out from behind the shored-up fragments and stare at the car. One young mother carries a baby suckling at her breast. In all, there must be five or six families holding on to this hilltop community.

"Don Miguel!" Pelochucho shouts. He greets a light-skinned Salvadoran man who's stepped out from one of the shelters.

Miguel is short but long-limbed and lean, built like an Olympic wrestler. The index and middle fingers are missing from his right hand.

"*Mis amigos.*" Pelochucho points at Ben and me.

"Pleased to meet you." Ben shakes Don Miguel's three-fingered hand.

"A pleasure." I do the same.

"The papers?" Pelochucho almost manages to pronounce the word correctly in Spanish.

Don Miguel seems to understand what he wants and goes to fetch it from his house.

Pelochucho then speaks to us in English: "Who's got the better Spanish, between the two of you?"

"Ben," I say.

Don Miguel returns with a small stack of typed documents.

"Him." Pelochucho points at Ben. "Read."

Ben smiles at Don Miguel. "He's asked me to look over your documents."

"Of course." Miguel seems to like Ben.

"*La vista*," Pelochucho says, pointing seaward. Then, in English, to Ben and me: "Check this out!"

The three of us walk away from the houses and shelters toward a shoulder of land on the ocean side. We step over dry corn stubble in an out-of-season field. Ben stares up and down from the documents, all of which bear the bluish seal of a Salvadoran notary.

"Pelo," I ask, "what's going on here?"

"Me and Don Miguel are doing a little business. He wants out of the corn and beans racket. I'm looking to invest in this country, and this break."

We climb up the small ridge and catch a view of the ocean. A blast of offshore breeze lifts my hair. Straight below are the cove and the point of Kilometer 99. We watch miniature swells struggle to break.

"There it is." Pelochucho flashes his overpopulated grin.

"Put this view on a magazine ad or a Web site. Tell me it won't have the gringos flocking."

It is quite beautiful. I have to turn my head from side to side to take it all in. In the afternoon wind, whitecaps on the rough ocean shine like diamonds. Not far from the point, a lone pelican dives deep for a fish.

"This looks legit to me." Ben stares down at the paperwork. "But I'm no lawyer."

"Are you buying this cornfield?" I ask.

Pelochucho turns to me. "This field has grown its last corn. It's about to become the K Ninety-nine Surf Hotel."

That gets Ben to put down the papers.

"The outside wall will go here." Pelochucho takes a couple steps down the steep hillside and tries to walk a straight line. "I want every bedroom to get a view of the surf. The suites will have their own— What's that Hawaiian word for porch?"

"Lanai," I say.

"Exactly. We'll put the pool over there." He points back toward the farming hamlet. "But what will make it great is the service. I'm talking shuttles to the airport, all English-speaking staff, drinking water in your room, safe food, rides to the other breaks. . . ."

"You'll take the adventure out of it," Ben says.

"I'm after the surfers with money," Pelochucho says, "not the ones with guts."

"Pelo, you cannot build here." Since he said the word *hotel*, I've been studying the angle of the hill, the consistency of the soil.

"Now don't get all high-and-mighty. This will be huge for the local economy."

"It's not that; it's the land. Look at this hillside. You see those ruts over there?" I point to a deep ditch running down the far side of the field. "This place has probably been eroding a few inches a year. Corn is terrible for soil conservation. I doubt you could even pour a foundation without a massive landslide. And what if there was another quake? Every one of those adobe homes came down in this one." I point back toward the hamlet. "Imagine what would happen to a two-story hotel, built here!" I kick the ground.

"What are you?" Pelochucho asks. "Some kind of—"

"Engineer," I say. "I'm an engineer. And I'm telling you: Do not build on this spot."

"I was actually thinking more like three stories."

Ben speaks up. "She knows what she's talking about, Pelo. The thing about corn is that it doesn't like the shade, or other root systems. These double black-diamond cornfields tend to get steeper and steeper, with nothing underneath to hold them together."

Pelochucho stares down at the dirt about to be his, lets out a long sigh. "You guys make some good points. I'll have to take this into consideration."

"Are you buying the land all the way up to his house?"

"That's the deal. I want to put the pool over there."

"Move your hotel back to the far side of the ridge." I take a couple steps inland, point toward the abandoned set of walls from which Don Miguel retrieved his documents. "You'll lose the view, but it'll be worth it."

Pelo turns to see the panorama of the point one more time.

"You could make an observation deck here." Ben does his best to sound optimistic. "Get some telephoto lenses; have a guy filming the sessions. Weekend warriors love that kind of shit."

Pelochucho sighs again. "Let's go buy some land."

He walks back toward the hamlet, several strides ahead of us. Ben and I trade glances and shrugs.

Don Miguel sets up a table with plastic chairs and a pen.

Before sitting down, Pelochucho pulls that thick roll of hundreds from his board shorts and hands the whole thing over to Don Miguel. "For you," he says in Spanish. He uses the second-person familiar, which is technically an insult. Miguel doesn't seem to mind.

I can't decide whether or not to protest. I have no faith that Pelo will build responsibly. But I don't want to step on Don Miguel's plans, whatever they might be.

Don Miguel counts the money once, then twice. I try to follow with my eyes. My best guess is two or three thousand. Not a lot, but probably more than he'd get from a local buyer, especially since the quake, with so many people trying to liquidate their land. I wonder what the other families think of this. Do they know about the hotel plans?

Pelo sits down and asks Ben for the paperwork. He turns straight to the signature page and signs his name. Don Miguel does the same, a broad smile across his face. Pelo stands up again. There follows a flurry of handshakes and thanks, a few pats on the back. Pelochucho looks impatient with the whole process.

Don Miguel follows us to the car. He tells Ben and me that he's glad to have met us.

"Where will you go now?" I ask him. "What will you do?"

"The rest of my family is in Chalate," he says, suddenly somber. "We'll go there for a while, stay at my mother's house. With this money, I can afford a good coyote. I hope to find my way north, maybe in time for a harvest. My brother-in-law has agreed to receive me."

"You're going north?" I ask. "To the States?"

"That's right." He shrugs. "It's what one must do to make a living in times like these."

"Good luck to you," I say. It hardly seems a worthwhile deal for him: giving up his home, which is practically beachfront property, for a chance to pick citrus or wash dishes in Texas or California. Does he have any idea what kind of rare resource this view is? I wonder how he thinks of the ocean. A source of fish? A cause of rust? The reason his cornfield catches too much wind? Certainly, he doesn't see it as added value to this land. Do these other families have any idea about the quality of waves in their backyard?

Pelochucho is already in the passenger seat as we say our final good-byes. I climb into the back and Ben shuts the hatch.

Pelo stays silent on the return trip, then goes straight to his room once we reach La Posada. His A/C unit hums hard the second his door shuts.

We go up to the roof. Ben makes a spliff from the local brown weed and his moist Dutch tobacco. I roll myself a cigarette.

A dog-eared surf magazine—abandoned weeks ago by some other traveler—lies on the concrete at our feet. Ben picks it up and wades through the pages for anything of interest.

"Look at this." He points at one of the ads toward the back. It reads WAVE ESCAPES! EL SALVADOR ADVENTURE.

Rumors recently circulated about a company running tours to isolated surf spots in the east, several hours from here. Apparently, they drop their clients off by boat and then take them back to a nice hotel where everybody eats pasta and drinks imported beer.

"Rich fuckers won't stop until they ruin all the good spots." Ben's camped and surfed in that part of the country several times—once with me. It has a special hold on his heart.

"That was published before the earthquake," I say. "It's probably not so popular anymore."

"'The Wild East'—that's what they're calling the point breaks out by El Cuco. Ridiculous." Ben throws the magazine to the floor.

We go silent for a moment and focus on the smoking. Both of us stare out at the ocean as though hypnotized. The midday winds have ceased; the surface is flat and still.

"You ever have flat spells like this in Hawai'i?" Ben sounds stoned already.

"Sure we do."

"Where do you surf mostly?"

I let out a lungful of smoke. "Waikiki when I first started. It's consistent, but full of tourists. Once I got more into it, I'd go to Diamond Head or Ala Moana. Some other places you probably haven't heard of."

"North Shore?" he asks, as all mainland surfers tend to.

"If I could get a ride," I say. "When they hold the contests in the winter, it's a zoo up there. Hard to find an empty parking spot, let alone an empty wave."

When I say the word *wave*, the roof trembles under our feet. Both Ben and I hop up from our chairs. Some gasps and whimpers sound from the street below. Aftershock.

"Jesus." Ben sits back down. "You have a lot of this in Hawai'i?"

I shake my head. "Where I'm from, not too much. It's more

of a problem on the Big Island, with the volcano and all. You probably never felt one before last month, huh?"

"No," he says. "In North Carolina, we only worry about hurricanes. But you get a bit more warning with those." He readjusts his fingers around the spliff. "And the surf picks up at least."

"I don't think I could ever get used to them," I say. "Even if I lived my entire life on a fault line."

"Fuck it." Ben seems suspicious of sitting on the roof all of a sudden. "How about a beer at La Punta?"

We return to the place where we first met: La Punta, best of the local seaside restaurants. The owner is a salty Florida expat who came here during the seventies and pioneered the waves at the point. He weathered the entire civil war in this same location. Now he has a Salvadoran family; his son has been the national surfing champion several years running.

It's a beautiful evening. The wind is dead, the sea glassy. Still a little shaken by the aftershock, we ask to sit downstairs, at a table not underneath the second floor's concrete deck. A waiter in a white shirt takes our order. He brings back two amber beer bottles, along with two dishes of mealy ceviche, a toothpick sprouting from the center of each.

"So tell me," Ben says, "how was Cara Sucia?"

"Good." I had almost forgotten about the first trip of the day. "I'm glad I went. It was nice to say some good-byes." I swallow a mouthful of beer so big that it burns the back of my throat. "It made me feel a little better about the situation."

"Better?" Ben brings his beer bottle up to his lips but pauses before drinking. "What situation?"

"It freaks me out . . . abandoning things." I push ceviche

around the dish. "Makes me scared that I might turn into my mother."

Ben laughs out loud. "An earthquake leveled your aqueduct, Malia. That doesn't make you your mother."

A part of me wants to argue with him, to suggest that parenting might also be fraught with setbacks and obstacles, which wouldn't justify giving up. Instead, I nod.

I'm not sure how well Ben understands my issues with quitting and leaving. As an Agro-Forestry volunteer, his projects—diversifying crops and fighting erosion—were largely unpopular in his community. It's important work, but he wasn't raising anyone's expectations. Could he appreciate how many hopes and dreams—let alone thousands of hours of labor—were hung on my water system?

A part of me envies Ben's work. Every expensive piece of infrastructure here, no matter how noble its purpose, is in part a monument to the egos of its architects. In that respect, today's aqueducts and clinics aren't so different from the Mayan temples or Catholic cathedrals once erected in this country.

"Look, Malia." Ben puts his hand atop mine. "I feel weird about quitting, too. I love this place." He turns toward the point. "I never thought I'd leave early. But things happen. That two-year target is just an arbitrary number."

"I know," I admit. "Still, it's hard to swallow—leaving now, with the country in ruins. I mean, we came here to help, didn't we?"

Ben sighs. "No matter what, we'd have to have left our sites in worse shape than we found them. What were we supposed to do with four or five months? Other than miss each other and be miserable?"

I nod. Everything Ben says makes sense. But it's like one of those riddles where you have to push one person in front of a bus in order to save all the passengers: The act in itself is simply too unpalatable.

"Should we have stopped him today?" Ben spears a tiny piece of cured fish with the toothpick and slips it into his mouth. "Should we have said something before they signed those papers?"

It's our first stab at the elephant in the room.

"I don't know," I say. "I keep telling myself that it's not about Pelo so much as Don Miguel. We don't want to mess with his life, right?"

"Sure," Ben says. "But is he better off heading to the States to sweep floors? Is that worth more than his land?"

I pick at the label on my bottle and try to take the long view on Pelo's land deal. Is he any different from the other gringo opportunists who've been coming here for years? They say Sir Francis Drake founded the port of La Libertad, on his way to California. Surely, he came in search of gold and plunder. Who are Ben and I to stop this long tradition?

On the other hand, I can't help but think of Hawaiian history. An uncle on my mother's side has ties to the sovereignty movement—a subject that's become as taboo in my presence as the details of my mother's final years. He often describes island lands as "stolen" by haole missionaries and entrepreneurs. In fact, most of those land deals happened like the one we watched today—with cryptic documents, a stack of money, and a desperate, misled seller. They weren't fair or honest, but they were *legal*, in the strict sense of the word. That was all that they were. Would I have put my foot down against the generals and the sugar barons had I been alive a hundred years ago?

"I hope that swell gets here soon," Ben says.

"If it exists at all," I add.

Back at the hotel, Pelochucho sits in that same rebar and rubber band easy chair outside his room. "There you are!" He holds a big Regia bottle between his knees. "I didn't know what happened to you guys."

"We went to get a beer," Ben says. "You hungry? We could all order dinner."

"Actually, I need you to do something for me."

"What's that?" Suspicion cuts through my voice.

Pelochucho stands up and reaches deep into the cargo pocket of his board shorts. "I need a little cholly."

"A little what?" I ask.

Ben looks over his shoulder.

"Cholly. A little white, a little blow. Some fucking cocaine, all right?"

"So get Peseta to do that!" I'm outraged.

"I don't want Peseta to do it. I'm paying you guys to do stuff for me. Paying you well, actually."

Ben is unruffled. He stands up and takes the money from Pelo's hand. "You know they sell it in those newsprint packets here, right? They're usually a little more than a gram."

"Is that enough to get me two?" Pelochucho asks.

Ben nods. "Should be."

Still furious, I keep silent. Ben is streetwise; he'll be okay. More than anything, this is insulting. I suspect Pelo—consciously or not—set up this errand as petty revenge for my criticism of his hotel plan.

"I'll be right back," Ben says. "Malia, could you see what Kristy has for food? Maybe order me something?"

He kisses me good-bye, then leaves the hotel.

I find Kristy in the kitchen and ask her about dinner. She has some ripe plantains and hard cheese. I order plates of both, along with beans. She seems in good spirits tonight.

Pelochucho materializes over my shoulder. "*Hola*, Kristy."

I take a step back.

He places his empty Regia on the counter, then walks into the kitchen and takes two more bottles out the refrigerator. "*Dos más, mi amor.*"

Kristy blushes at the pet name.

"Cheers." Pelo thrusts one of the bottles into my hand. I'd not realized it was meant for me. "Shall we sit?" He gestures at a table in the dining room.

The beer is cold and tasty. Kristy chops plantains and heats oil a few meters away.

"I appreciate you guys helping me out today," Pelochucho says, "and sticking around to do it. Seriously."

"Pelo," I say. "All that stuff about the hillside and your hotel plans—I didn't say it to be a bitch. It's a big deal."

"I know." He sighs and takes a gulp. "I'd hoped this project would be quick and easy. I've got a lot of capital tied up in another Seattle deal right now. I'll have to go more slowly, invest more dough."

"I'm not sure it's about that," I say. "It's not so much a money thing as a land thing."

He turns to me, incredulous. "There's got to be a way to make it work, right? If you throw enough cash at it?"

His question reminds me of a documentary I saw years ago, about a bunch of rich people trying to climb Mount Everest, and what a disaster it turned out to be for them and all the Sherpa guides they'd hired.

"Pelo, don't take this the wrong way, but just because you've got money, that doesn't mean you get to surf every wave, or climb every mountain."

He takes a long sip of his beer but keeps his eyes locked on mine. "You're going to sit here and tell me that—with ample time and materials—you couldn't figure out a way to build on that spot? That it's totally impossible?" He shakes his head. "Some engineer," he mutters, then goes for another sip.

I shrug. An angry, competitive itch creeps up my spine. My brain spins in a direction it hasn't gone for weeks. "If it *had* to be done, it would take at least two retaining walls on that hillside, with surface and subsurface drains." Blueprints take shape in my mind's eye. The image of that fatal, preventable landslide in Santa Tecla still looms in a neglected part of my memory. I feel a bit drunk with the possibilities. "The building itself would need footings poured directly onto the bedrock, however deep that is. And even though it's expensive here, you'd have to frame it all with wood."

Pelochucho grins and slaps his hands together. "Now we're talking!"

"The interesting thing about a large building right there is the roof. You'd want to catch every drop of rain, to keep it from washing away the hillside. If you hooked your gutters up to a big-enough cistern, you'd have all your water needs taken care of. You might have more than enough."

"We can fill the pool!" Pelo says.

"I was thinking of offering some to your new neighbors, actually."

"Sure," he says. "That's cool, too."

"After the retaining walls and the pilings, you'd want to start planting that hillside." I take a sip of beer. "It'd be best to do some windbreaks and live barriers right away, then bring in saplings. Stuff with complex root systems that'll hold the hillside together, absorb all the excess water. You might even get some fruit."

"You should stick around, Chinita!" Pelo says. "Help me out with this."

"No thanks." I shake my head. "That's the best way to do it, but I still think it's a bad idea. Just move the damn building to the other side of the ridge."

His mouth twists up, as if he's tasting something sour. Before he can respond, Ben walks in and joins us.

"Here you go." Ben drops two thin newspaper envelopes on the table. "It was cheaper than I thought. You've got some change coming."

"Keep it," Pelochucho says. He grabs the packets off the table, as if ashamed, and shoves them into his shorts. His eyes linger on Kristy, who plates up my meal.

"Nice one, Chuck Norris. Thanks." Pelo stands. "Stop by after dinner if you want to party." He seems to be inviting Ben and not me.

Pelo takes the beer and the coke off to his room. Kristy drops heaping plates in front of Ben and me, a stack of re-toasted tortillas and a dish of salt in the center of the table. We ask for glasses and share the Regia.

The food is delicious. The plantains are sweet and crisp, a perfect counterpoint to the salty cheese and liquefied beans. Like so many Salvadoran suppers, it is a meal meant to be eaten without utensils, with only the torn pieces of corn tortillas. It could've been eaten without teeth.

As usual, I finish before Ben. He grins at me as I mop the last bit of the beans off the plate.

"Don't take this the wrong way, Malia." Ben puts a fist in

front of his mouth. "But have you ever been checked out for a tapeworm?"

I laugh. "If that's what I have, then I've had it all my life." I pop the final bite into my mouth.

"Was your mom skinny?" Ben asks.

I swallow. "She is in most of the pictures, and the couple times I saw her in the flesh." Ben knows this isn't a subject I'm comfortable with. "Let's hope that's all I inherited from her."

We ask Kristy to start us a new tab, and to put this dinner on it.

I follow Ben out of the dining room. Without discussing it, he passes by the expensive wing and knocks on Pelo's door.

"Who is it?"

"It's us," Ben says.

The door swings open.

"Come on in," Pelochucho says. "You want some blow?" A rolled-up American bill hangs between his first two fingers like a cigarette.

Pelo has taken the one piece of art off the wall: a framed picture of a flying dove with flowing Spanish script that reads. *If you love something, set it free. If it comes back to you, it's yours forever. If it doesn't, it never was.* He's cut his cocaine on the glass of the frame. The powder forms a few rough lines. A credit card covers the dove's head. I strain my eyes to read Pelo's real name but can't quite make it out.

"No thanks," Ben says. "I'm beat. Just wanted to say good night. Any plans for tomorrow? Looks like you'll be sleeping in."

Pelo lets out a small laugh, then pulls a chair up to the table with the picture. "I want to get some waves," he says. "This flat shit is getting old." He leans over the dove and snorts up one thick white line.

"All right, then," Ben says. "See you in the morning."

"Close that on the way out, would you?"

I've had a long day, and spent hours in the sun. It comes as a huge relief that Ben has no interest in staying up and doing lines with Pelo. We go to bed with tired eyes and full stomachs. I hope we'll wake up to this rumored swell, not so much for the surf, but so Ben and I can sooner sever ties with Pelochucho and be on our way.

12

A year and a half ago, I followed Ben out the gate of La Posada. We wore swimsuits and sandals, surfboards under our arms. Ben carried a grocery sack with his tobacco, a lighter, and a couple of *refrescos*—sugary Day-Glo drinks sold in clear plastic Baggies.

"Where are we going?" I asked. This was only my second or third stay in La Libertad. I didn't understand why we weren't sticking around to surf the point.

"A little spot up the coast." Ben kept walking.

In the west end of town, we passed local women with buckets of masa atop their heads, coming from the mill. We crossed the small bridge that seemed to form an unofficial city limit. At the far side of it, Ben stopped walking.

"Do you have bus fare?" I asked.

"No need." With his surfboard and grocery bag in one arm, Ben stuck his other hand out into the road, thumb extended.

I took a couple of steps off into the shoulder. Several cars passed without stopping or slowing down. For a few minutes, there was no traffic. Then another wave of vehicles. Again, nobody paid us any mind.

"Here." I held my board out in Ben's direction. "Take this for a second."

Ben took my board with his free hand and switched places with me.

Suddenly self-conscious in board shorts and a bikini top, I crossed my arms over my chest and waited while a rattling pickup full of bananas rolled by. Next a crowded sedan passed. I began to wonder what I'd been thinking—offering to handle this. Finally, I spied a newish double-cab pickup coming our way, with only a driver aboard, and what looked like a logo on the door.

I took a step closer to the road, stood up straight, stuck my thumb out far, and put my other hand on my hip. My midriff felt long and exposed, like something hanging from a hook. The driver and I made eye contact; his gaze drifted downward as he gave me the once-over. The truck pulled off a few yards ahead of us. Ben ran out from the shoulder and we both jogged for it. I climbed into the bed and took the boards from Ben one by one. He hopped in, then tapped twice on the top of the cab.

"Wow," Ben said once we were rolling. "I guess it pays to be a girl in El Salvador sometimes."

I rolled my eyes. "Rarely." But despite the brush-off, I was surprised by my own actions. I'd never done anything quite like that before—flagging down a ride, leveraging my femininity. This was still early in our honeymoon phase. Perhaps I hoped to impress him with my boldness. Perhaps I felt emboldened by his presence.

The drive was beautiful. It still seems to me that the best way to see this country is from the back of a fast-moving pickup. Ben pointed out Sunzal as we wound around the bluffs above it. He told me about the thriving parking space and *palapa* industry along the sandy beach at Majahual—so popular with merrymakers from the capital. From a distance, we saw the private club at Atami, where who knew what kind of secret shorelines were off-limits to nonmembers.

Before long, Ben tapped on the cab and the truck slowed. Along a desolate stretch of the Litoral, we disembarked and thanked the driver.

"Where are we?" I asked.

"It's called Kilometer Ninety-nine, because of that sign." Ben pointed to a highway marker up the road that read K 99. "This way."

I followed him down a dirt road heading seaward off the highway. It ended on a sandy beach within a protected cove. A rocky point—shorter than Punta Roca, but made up of the same kind of black stones—stretched out before us. There wasn't much swell that day, but we stood and watched a midsize set break. Nobody was around, let alone in the water. Ben buried our flip-flops and his grocery bag under a stack of rocks near the end of the road.

We paddled out and traded waves. The water felt cleaner this far from any port or city. Out in the lineup, I turned back several times to look at the landscape. This was during the rainy season; all the surrounding hills were lush and green. From the water, it was hard to make out any signs of civilization. Unless a car drove by, I couldn't even see the road. Back then, I had no idea that Don Miguel and his neighbors were up there on the hillside. From the water, the view was too foreshortened even to see their cornfields.

Once the wind picked up, we paddled back to shore. Ben went to find the bag he'd hidden under the stones. I gathered my leash and wrapped it around my fins.

"Ah!" Ben screamed.

I turned and watched as he brushed one hand with the other.

"Fire ants!" He held one of the plastic *refresco* bags by the corner, swatting at it with his free hand. Ants bit his toes; he lifted his foot and brushed at them.

I collapsed to the sand, laughing.

For several more seconds, he did an aggravated dance of arm wagging and body slapping. Finally, he ran down to the ocean with a *refresco* bag in each fist and dunked them into the salt water. My eyes were teary with laughter.

After a minute of rinsing in the surf, he joined me on the sand.

"I'm sorry," I said, still chuckling. "But that was hilarious."

"Here." He smiled and handed me one of the bright-colored bags. "I hope you like *refresco*."

We bit off the plastic corners and sucked at the sugary liquid now spiked with seawater. Ben rolled a cigarette and we passed it back and forth.

"Do me a favor," Ben said. "Don't tell anyone about this spot."

"No problem," I said. "Is it a secret?"

He shrugged. "This whole coast will change eventually. The waves are too good. I'd rather not be the one who speeds it up. Does that make sense?"

"Yes," I said. "I know exactly what you mean." I turned and looked back down into the secluded cove. "We should camp here sometime. We've got all the gear. There's nobody around."

Ben shook his head. "You don't want to be near this spot at night. This is where they bring in the cocaine that gets made into rocks back in town."

My jaw dropped. I turned back to the ocean. "They bring it in by boat?"

Ben nodded. "That's the rumor at least. All the old-timers say never to come around here after dark. You don't want to see something that you shouldn't."

"Good enough for me," I said.

We walked up to the road and hitched a ride back to La Libertad.

13

Again the next morning, we wake early and walk to the steps. Something's changed. Though the surf isn't good, it's not entirely flat, either. An abnormal wind pattern whips the sea toward the land, raising small waves that look almost rideable.

"A little bump." Ben stares at the point.

"Hope this isn't the swell that Pelochucho flew in for," I say.

A black beetle—big and round as a Ping-Pong ball—buzzes past us and bounces off one of the columns alongside the steps. It hovers like a radio-controlled toy, one whose pilot needs more flying lessons.

"Watch." Ben stands. "A guy in my village taught me this one."

With one hand, he snatches the insect in midair. The buzzing stops short. Ben's back is to me, but it looks as if he's about to eat the bug. I stand up to see.

Ben turns around and puts his face in front of mine, cheeks puffed out. We stare each other in the eye for a second. Then he opens his mouth and the beetle flies out.

I can't stop myself from grinning. "Good one," I admit.

"Thanks." Ben spits on the ground.

Back at La Posada, Pelochucho crosses the courtyard with an armload of his own luggage.

"What are you doing?" I wonder if he isn't moving out—heading home or off to camp on his newly purchased land.

"Just changing rooms." He dumps the load inside the bedroom next to ours.

"You're moving into the cheap wing?" Perhaps his stack of bills isn't as bottomless as he's made it out to be.

He emerges from the new room, sunglasses down over bloodshot eyes. "I'm a little over budget," he says. "No big deal."

I almost ask if we should expect our hundred bucks today.

"There's some kind of a wind swell out there," Ben says. "Not big, but maybe worth paddling out. I'm thinking it might break a little cleaner down at Sunzal."

"Yeah?" Pelo looks surprised. "Sounds like a plan. Give me a second to finish up here."

Ben helps him roll the surfboard coffin across the courtyard. I wait by the dining room.

Crackito, youngest of the local addicts, shuffles past La Posada's gate. Thirteen or fourteen, he's barely bigger than Nora. He holds his hand out toward me and mutters, "A coin?"

Kristy stands at the stove and scowls, ready to stop him if he tries to enter.

"Wait." I take a piece of sweet bread from the glass case on the counter, signal Kristy to put it on my tab, and walk over to Crackito.

"Eat it," I say. "Now." If he carries it off, there's a chance he'll sell it for a few cents or trade it for a hit off another kid's pipe.

He rolls his eyes, then devours the sugary breakfast in four bites. As I walk back toward the Jeep, I can feel Kristy's gaze hardening unhappily into my back.

On the drive, Pelochucho and Ben pass a thick joint back and forth. I lie prone across the plywood shelf, crowded in with our three surfboards, trying to find a little fresh air amid the pot smoke. Pelo brought along a flawless brand-name board. It looks as though it's never been surfed.

Ben parks at a friendly restaurant-hotel and asks the owner to watch the car for us. Straight away, we see that Sunzal was the right decision.

The beach is a long expanse of black sand at the base of a cliff. In addition to the consistent waves, it's one of the more beautiful spots in this part of the country. A panoramic shot of it opens the classic John Milius surf feature *Big Wednesday*. At one end stands a rock formation known as "the pig"— though I've never been able to find a porcine shape in it, from any angle. Sunzal had a heyday in the seventies as a kind of hippie camp, covered in tents full of gringo surfers and expats. All that ended with the war.

We walk from our parking spot out toward the break. The tide has dropped in the hour since our surf check. The waves still aren't huge, but they're standing up nicely here, definitely workable. And nobody else is out. With the black sand and the solitude, this spot could pass for Hawai'i—a country beach perhaps, on one of the neighbor islands.

"Looks fun," Ben says.

"Yeah."

The three of us enter. Pelochucho lags behind.

Ben and I trade waves on the outside. They aren't anything to write home about—a solid drop, one punchy section, then a soft shoulder—but we enjoy it. So often when surfing in El Salvador, the waves justify the means. But at this spot, simply being in the water is a privilege. Morning sun shines over our shoulders as we look out to the horizon. Flocks of pelicans skim the ocean surface.

A bigger set rolls in and we scramble for the outside. Out of position for either of the first two waves, Ben dashes for the third. I watch as he drops in, does his bottom turn, and finds the trim. He pumps up a bit of speed and cuts back to the curl once the wave fattens.

Of the two of us, most people likely consider me the better surfer. Ben started in his high school years and could practice only during a short and fickle North Carolina swell season. I switched to surfing from boogie boarding when I was eleven or twelve, and lived within walking distance of Oahu's south shore—which has waves almost year-round. Certainly, I'm lighter on my feet than Ben, able to put a bit more spring into my turns.

But I like the way Ben surfs. His style is unadorned and functional. Even though his ass sometimes sticks out, he always keeps his center of gravity low, his turns close to the pocket. Perhaps it's the result of learning in those East Coast beach breaks, where he had to snatch rides from the closed-out waves before they collapsed.

I watch his backlit figure rise above the crest as he makes one last turn. He kicks out, then paddles toward me.

Where would you go right now if you could travel anywhere? What would you do with all the money in the world? I often wonder what Alex or Courtney—or any of those other volunteers, really—might say if asked that question. They'd laugh, mutter something about a vacation. They might speak of expensive foods or sex fantasies, a party they could imagine throwing.

But if you ask those same questions of a surfer—especially a surfer who's traveled even a little—you'll get specifics: beaches, breaks, countries, proper nouns. You might hear some half-baked idea like Pelo's, about a hotel or other business, but what they're truly talking about is waves, a commodity that is both priceless and free, that can only be bartered for days and years of your life.

If you knew you'd die tomorrow, how would you spend today? Ben and I could've answered that question with one verb. Could you? Could Alex? Could my father? It sometimes feels like a horrible burden to me: living each hour with the knowledge of what you'd rather be doing, the wave you might be riding.

"Good set," Ben says once he's within earshot.

"It's beautiful out here." Sitting up on my board, I hold my arms out to either side.

"Right?" As if reading my thoughts, he says, "Think about how many spots like this we'll see. I mean, this country is tiny and crowded, and still there're new waves around every corner. Imagine Chile, or Peru. They've got point breaks down there that have never been surfed before."

I smile at the very idea. I spent most of my life on a small island, where every beach is known and named, has some cabal of locals claiming ownership. The thought of so much uncluttered coast is beyond my imagination. Add to that the inland places we'll go—Machu Picchu, the Amazon, Patagonia. It's more of the world than I ever expected to see.

I turn toward land to check on Pelochucho, and finally catch a glimpse of him between crests. He's far away from us, close to shore. I still have no memory of ever having met him before this week. For a moment, I wonder if he can even surf.

The next set is the biggest yet. I take the first wave and manage to string together several sections, riding it all the way to the inside and landing a little floater on the final bit. I surface with a giddy smile, hoping Pelochucho might have seen the maneuver.

I look around but can't find him anywhere.

At last, I turn to the beach. There on the sand, Pelo stands beside his board. He puts his hands up over his forehead and then out in front of his face. His feet stumble in a clumsy circle. Something is wrong. I ride whitewater on my belly, then paddle hard for the shore. Once on my feet, I get a good look at him and nearly faint.

Blood gushes everywhere. It's all over Pelo and his new surfboard and the sand. He holds his hands up in the air and looks around, trying to see out of one blood-covered eye.

"Here I am, Pelochucho," I say.

He turns toward my voice. A flap of his eyebrow and forehead hang down over his face. The socket is a swollen, bloody mess. I'm not sure if the eyeball is still in there. I look around for it on the sand, lift his board and check underneath. Nothing.

"I don't feel so good," he says. "I want to get in the shade."

I leave the boards on the black sand and lead him by the arm. Two teenage boys point and wince as they pass us. How did this happen in such small waves? With two fingers in my mouth, I whistle hard for Ben, who's still out in the lineup. Soon enough, he sees us and paddles in. Pelo and I continue toward the car.

"What happened?" I finally think to ask Pelo.

"I rode the shore break in too far, caught the nose of my own board."

"Okay. Ben will be here soon. Promise me one thing. Promise me you won't look at yourself in the mirror." I'm convinced he'll pass out if he does.

"I promise."

As we reach the Jeep, Ben catches up and winces at the sight of Pelo's eye. "You look like shit," he says. "Let's get you to a doctor."

He takes a towel from the car and makes Pelochucho press it against his head.

"I feel sick," Pelo says.

"Ben, what about our boards?" I point up the beach, where Pelo and I left them.

Ben does an awkward dance of indecision on the driver's side of the Jeep. Finally, he asks the restaurant owner if she can send a child to retrieve our boards, and if she'll look after them, maybe until tomorrow. She nods. I climb onto the plywood shelf. Ben shuts the back gate at my feet.

On the drive, Pelochucho sits in the passenger seat and pukes out the window. All along the roadside sit camps of families recently rendered homeless by the earthquake, living under tents and shelters of black plastic. I lie flat upon the rack, feeling the moisture from my swimsuit soak into the plywood, trying to stay still enough to avoid splinters. Traces of

Pelo's vomit rush back in through the window and splatter me. Bile stings my eyes. Ben drives fast.

In San Salvador, we see a sign that says TWENTY-FOUR HOUR EMERGENCY CARE. The three of us walk inside and find a receptionist seated at a desk. She fills in blanks on a document and doesn't look up. Ben and I each take one of Pelo's armpits.

"Excuse me!" Ben says at last. "There's an emergency here."

"Have a seat." She gestures toward some chairs along the far wall of the office.

"I'm not having a seat. This guy needs medical attention." Ben's Spanish is extra fluent.

"All right." She sighs. "Go down this street until you get to a woman selling fried chicken. Then take a left and go two more blocks, until you see a fireworks stand. Right after that, there's a clinic where they take emergencies like yours."

We must look like a ridiculous three-headed monster: soaking wet, no shoes, covered in blood and puke, wearing only our still-wet bathing suits. Pelo's head wobbles atop his body like a child's toy. The locals must think we're three drunks coming from a fight as we amble through the labyrinthine hospital-market district in the midday heat.

At the next clinic, they give us an important-looking piece of paper and directions to yet another location. At this third place, a doctor has Pelo lie across a table and places a special cloth over his face. It has a hole that exposes his injured eye. The doctor cleans the wound. Pelochucho groans and squirms with the pain. It's hard to watch.

"Do you mind if I step outside?" I whisper to Ben.

He hands me the car key. "There's tobacco in the console. Roll a smoke if you like."

On the street, everyone stares at me in my bikini. Old women mutter their judgment. Young boys giggle.

I look through the car for a sarong but find only the bloody towel. In the passenger seat, I sit and smoke one of Ben's rollies.

A kid in rags approaches the window. He holds his palm out flat and says, "One coin?" My hand goes instinctively to the side of my thigh, but find no pants, no pocket, much less any money there. I have no cash at all. Not for this kid. Not for lunch. Not for Pelochucho's stitches or anything else.

Once the cigarette is done, I fast-walk to the hospital doors, eyes forward, ignoring the stares of onlookers. The piece of wire in the sole of my sandal scrapes against the pavement.

Back inside, they've set up a couple of chairs for Ben and me. On the walls are eye charts and mirrors. Racks of eyeglass frames line the shelves. From the ceiling hang instruments used to measure vision. Pelo's surgeon seems to be an optometrist.

A beautiful Salvadoran nurse assists. Judging by her dress, she must also be the receptionist. Bracelets dangle from her wrists as she passes the doctor sutures and clamps. Her nails are long and polished. Neither of them wears rubber gloves.

I stand up, walk to the table, and look over the doctor's shoulder. He complains about how much sand is in the wound, as if there's something I can do about it. With a crescent-shaped needle, he stitches up the internal tissue. Each time the doctor goes to insert it, I whisper "Breathe out" to Pelochucho.

The doctor seems to enjoy the fact that I'm watching. I look up from the surgery at one point to see a framed painting on the back wall, done in dark velvet. It's a picture of a surgeon in the OR. Jesus Christ—who bears an uncanny resemblance to the actual Chuck Norris—stands behind him, looking over his shoulder, guiding his hand. With a gasp, I realize that I'm standing right behind this surgeon the way that Jesus is in the painting. I sit back down beside Ben.

Soon, the doctor announces that he's finished and writes out prescriptions. The nurse takes the cloth off Pelo's face and tapes a thick bandage over his eye.

Somebody must've seen gringos and figured we could afford first-class treatment. They lead us to a private room, with a bed, an easy chair, an air-conditioning unit, and a bathroom.

"Pelo," Ben whispers, "we should clean you up before you sleep."

Pelochucho nods and stumbles into the bathroom. He takes a second to undo his drawstring, then lets his board shorts fall to the ground.

The bathroom has a small concrete cistern with a faucet, a drain in the floor, and a wide-bottomed bowl for bucket bathing. Pelo looks confused. Ben opens the water tap and picks up the bowl. Finally understanding, Pelochucho sits on the tiles and hugs his knees. Ben dumps bucketfuls of water over him, careful to keep the eye bandage dry.

I can say with my right hand across my heart that I'll never forget the image of Pelochucho naked on that bathroom floor. His body folds itself up and trembles from the cold water. He brings his forearms together under his chin and opens his hands like a flower. It's a gesture akin to both prayer and pleading—not unlike the fruit vendor's expression in the minutes after the quake. I'm not sure if he's enjoying the bath or hating it. He might be crying; I can't tell. But it's clear to me, in that moment, just what a thin and porous layer it is that separates every single one of us from such a state—a frantic and filthy mess of blood, tears, and torn flesh.

Pelo opens up his posture some, once adjusted to the water's chill. His dick sticks against his inner thigh. I try not to stare, but his is the first uncircumcised adult penis I've ever seen. It looks unfinished. Some odd rush of blood forms a lump near the end, as though it's a snake that has just swallowed a rodent. With his one good eye, Pelo catches me staring. I turn and step outside of the bathroom.

A nurse brings in soap, toilet paper, a towel, and a pair of blue hospital pants that might've fit Pelochucho when he was ten. Now they come just past his knees. I have half a mind to ask if she has any clothes for me to change into. Pelo falls asleep immediately, his feet twitching against the rail of the bed. The nurse returns with paperwork. Ben and I make up all of Pelochucho's information while he sleeps. We guess his birthday, estimate his age, invent his real name.

Figuring he'll sleep for a while, Ben and I leave the room in search of lunch.

In the market, a vendor sells soup from a blackened pot. She has a table and three chairs set up under a blue tarp. Long bones stick out of our bowls. Oil forms egg-shaped bubbles at the surface. We slurp down a broth of leaves and potatoes.

"This is not cool," I say, stirring my soup.

"What's not cool?"

"None of this is cool. Pelo's eye. The fucking earthquake. Quitting the Peace Corps. This isn't how it was supposed to be." My eyes tingle with the beginnings of tears. It feels as if today's events are the exclamation point on a boldface message from the universe.

"What are you talking about? This doesn't have anything to do with the quake. Pelo got speared in the eye. That's all. It's just bad timing."

I try my best to compose myself. "The Hawaiian language has this word: *kuleana*. There's no exact translation. It implies rights or property, but also responsibility. It means your calling or your duty. The idea is that you can't have ownership without stewardship, that they're not separate; they're one and the same."

The truth is, I'd never before used the word *kuleana* in relation to my own life. But in the past few days, the notion keeps bobbing up in my mind—with Pelochucho and his land, with Cara Sucia and the aqueduct, with the refugee camps and the mass graves. I'm not sure what my duty is anymore, but I'm convinced I've been a bad steward of it.

"Ben, I know that we have the right to leave El Salvador." I look him in the eye. "But that doesn't make it the responsible thing to do."

"No offense," Ben says, "but I'm starting to think my *kuleana* is in South America already."

We both turn and stare at our soup.

"Do we need money to pay for this?" I mean the hospital bill, but the question could just as easily apply to lunch.

"Those bills he gave us yesterday are still here." Ben pats the cargo pocket of his trunks. "I forgot about them until we were out in the water."

I stir my soup and slurp cautiously at the too-hot broth. The vendor adds tortillas to the stack on the table. She glares at me—in my bathing suit—as if I'm naked.

"Sweetheart, listen." Ben puts his hand out on the table, palm up.

I lay my own hand inside his.

"We're gonna be okay," he says.

Back in the hospital room, Pelo snores hard. He looks horrible. One side of the bandage hangs off by the tape. His eye is swollen shut. It'll probably stay that way for days. A ragged scar will now run from the bridge of his nose up through his forehead.

I lean into Ben's shoulder. He wraps one arm all the way around me.

A nurse comes in and checks on Pelo. She tells us that only one visitor can stay overnight, and empties the garbage bin on her way out.

"Why don't you take the car back to La Posada, mind the fort and get changed? I'll stay." Ben pulls the thin cushions off the single chair and lays them on the floor. "You should probably hit the road before it gets too late."

"Right." Driving at night in El Salvador is considered a matter of taking your life into your own hands.

"Take one of these, in case you need gas or something." He reaches inside the pocket of his shorts and hands me a moist hundred-dollar bill.

Ben and I kiss good-bye. He's become oddly calm, whereas I still shake with nerves and adrenaline.

"Good-bye, Pelochucho." He moves slightly as I touch his forehead. I tuck the bill into the top of my bathing suit and turn back to Ben. "I'll be here first thing tomorrow morning."

"Drive safe."

"I will."

"Malia." Ben stops me with a stare. "I know you're having second thoughts. I feel awful about it. Maybe I should've given you more time . . . to decide to quit and everything. I'm sorry if I rushed you."

"It was my decision," I admit. "Don't feel bad."

"The thing is, it's kind of a done deal now. We can't go back to being volunteers, even if we wanted to."

"I know." He's right, of course. "I'm just venting. I'll be okay."

"See you tomorrow."

We exchange another kiss good-bye.

14

I've never learned the layout of San Salvador, beyond the Peace Corps office, the hostels and bars popular with volunteers, and the bus terminal for La Lib. Ben, born with a superhuman sense of direction, has done most of the driving since we've owned the car.

I have a hell of a time making it out of the hospital district, then straight away get stuck in a traffic jam on one of the city's bigger arteries. In a cloud of carbon monoxide, I watch boys run between cars with tiny boxes of chewing gum, chanting *"Chicle, chicle, chicle,"* as if trying for a cadence that will put the motorists into a buying mood.

At the next light, a man in a clown costume and greasy makeup scrapes a Popsicle stick along a ribbed metal flashlight and mutters lyrics. After each verse, he holds out his palm and collects donations.

A boy in a bright orange vest walks past with a stack of daily newspapers. The headline is, once again, about the Monkey-Faced Baby. This is a local legend that surfaced in the wake of the earthquake. It has several variations, but most of them involve a baby born at a hospital somewhere near Zacatecoluca. The newborn had a mature primate face: full head of hair, a big set of yellow teeth. The delivering doctor took one look at it and said, "This is the ugliest thing I've ever seen in my life!" The baby then opened its eyes and, in perfect Spanish, said, "If you think I'm ugly, wait until you see what happens on the thirteenth of February." The second those words were spoken, the baby died.

Local news media ran with the story. They interviewed a series of frazzled subjects and so-called experts—doctors, witches, geologists, and clergy—about the potential implications of the Monkey-Faced Baby's prophecy.

Many people buy the paper. The vendor does a better business than the flashlight clown.

I have no idea where I am. The eye-level afternoon sun gives way to dusk. It occurs to me that I might be inching along in the wrong direction. Traffic speeds up at last. I recognize the tall pink monolith of the Hotel Intercontinental looming above the rest of the block.

I'm at Metrocentro, a shopping district near La Estancia—the cheap hotel where Peace Corps volunteers stay. An appealing plan B materializes inside my mind: Why not go by the hotel and see if I know anybody? Maybe I can borrow some clothes. It might be nice to stay one last night in the city, have a few drinks perhaps. If nothing else, it'll save me hours of driving.

Once the seed of this idea is planted, it grows into a wishful tree within minutes. I take a right onto Boulevard de Los Heroes, a street that I finally know my way around on, then turn left at the Esso station and enter the neighborhood.

A teenager in a mismatched hat and uniform shirt carries a shotgun and approaches as I park. He smiles and tries not to stare at my bathing suit. I ask him to keep an eye on the car for me. He nods.

At the doorway to La Estancia, gringos fill two couches in the main room, their faces illuminated by the television screen. My pupils dilate, desperate to recognize someone.

"Malia?" I hear my name before I can make anybody out. "Is that you?"

"Courtney!" I'm so happy to hear her voice. "Do you have some clothes I could borrow? I've had a really bad day." As I say it, I realize how true it is. My body is chilled and chicken-skinned, still speckled with salt, vomit, blood, and diesel exhaust.

"Come on, honey." Courtney rises and wraps me up in a tight hug. The warm softness of her feels reassuring. With an arm around my shoulders, she leads me toward the back bedrooms. By a few seconds, she may have saved me from a pathetic crying breakdown in front of everyone else. "Let's get you cleaned up."

We enter the bedroom she shares with several others. I tell her the story of Pelochucho's injury and the hospital, how I couldn't find my way back.

Courtney's maternal instincts come into full bloom. She's much bigger than I am, but she doesn't hesitate to root through the backpacks of rookie volunteers in search of clothes. We come up with a wrap skirt and white tank top only slightly too loose. I take a shower and wash my hair with Courtney's fragrant American shampoo. Niña Ana—the owner of the hotel—is able to change my hundred-dollar bill and reserve me a bed for the night.

Once I'm clean and dressed, Courtney fetches two beers from the refrigerator.

"*Salud.*" We clang the aluminum together.

"So." Courtney swallows beer and grins. "You up for going out tonight? A bunch of us are heading to the Zona Rosa."

I'd come here hoping for a quiet evening in. But after a few sips of beer, I feel a second wind. This could be my last night in this town, after all, the last time Courtney and I will get to go out together.

I dry my bathing suit in Niña Ana's oven, and put it on under my borrowed clothes. I stuff the bikini top full of Salvadoran bills. A caravan of yellow taxis arrives and carries us off to San Salvador's best attempt at a posh nightlife district.

The Barra Española is a long woody room one story above street level. I always thought of it as expensive, a place to go on special occasions. But these volunteers see it fit for a Wednesday night out. They all order drinks and light up cigarettes, forming little circles of three to four throughout the space, going from one conversation to another in search of the most interesting chatter, the funniest jokes, the cutest boy or girl.

Courtney orders each of us a beer and a shot of tequila. I feel in high spirits all of a sudden: clean, surrounded by friends, my hair smelling of tropical fruits. This is like the good-bye party I never thought to have.

"To your trip." Courtney raises her shot glass.

The tequila goes down with a soothing, medicinal burn.

"Are you excited?" she asks.

"Of course." I take a sip of beer. "I'm ready for a change of scenery." My mind summons up the images that Ben has mentioned so many times: tossing that stone into the ocean at the Tierra del Fuego, ice and glaciers in the background.

"I hear that," Courtney says. "I'm so fucking glad to be in the capital right now, I can't even tell you."

"What are you doing here? Just hanging out?"

"I wish. I got to the Estancia right before you did. I had meetings at the embassy all day today."

"Meetings?" The fact that Courtney never works is a running joke between us; I figured she'd be even more checked out now, with so little time left on her service. "Are you busy these days?"

"Totally." She signals the bartender for another round, then looks me in the eye. "There is so much money pouring into this country right now; it's insane. I've already got funding for two hundred latrines. I could probably get a water system if we could find a damn source that wasn't contaminated."

"This is coming from the embassy, this money?" None of it makes any sense. Securing funding for a new project often took years—and might be the work of more than one volunteer's tenure.

"Partly them, partly other countries. To be honest, I don't know where it's all coming from. But it's not like it used to be." She lifts the beer bottle to her lips.

I take one of the bills from out of my top and lay it on the bar.

"Thing is, they gave us all those temporary plastic houses, and I got them distributed and set up in a heartbeat. Now I'm on their rock-star list. If you can spend their money fast, you'll get more of it. That's the way it works now."

"That's crazy." I truly don't understand. "It would take me months to get an extra piece of pipe if we came up short on my project."

"You don't get it, Malia. Back then, we were doing *development*. We're in the *relief* business now, like it or not. No more twenty-year time lines. It's about hit it and quit it."

"Is that sustainable?" I hadn't used the *s* word in earnest since training.

"Pfftt." She rolls her eyes. "It's handouts, plain and simple. Some of the shit's downright dishonest. This latrine money is earmarked for families that lost theirs in the quake, but I'm giving them to everyone. Do I feel bad about it? Hell no. The donors don't understand how it is where the rubber meets the road." She is almost breathless as she pauses to take another sip. "And this will be over soon. Some volcano or tidal wave will happen somewhere else next month and the sympathy dollars will move on."

I nod, feeling bad for having doubted Courtney's work ethic.

"To be honest, I like the relief angle better," she continues. "It's less frustrating, more cut-and-dry. Give people shelter, food, water, medicine—basic human needs—and don't pretend to do more, you know? All that 'teach a man to fish' crap they sold us in training will drive you crazy, if you let it."

"Is this happening with a lot of volunteers?" I'm interested in a way I never thought I'd be again, after seeing that mess of metal pipes scattered about the jungle.

"With the ones who can read the writing on the wall. A lot of these guys are doing the same as I am." She looks over my shoulder and takes a visual inventory of the others in our party.

"That's amazing." Maybe I was wrong. Maybe we could've repaired that aqueduct. It might've even happened quickly, if all this money has indeed been loosened up.

"You know who played it smart was Alex." Courtney isn't finished. "He saw the big picture—beyond his site. He'll be traveling the world soon, disaster to disaster. Red Cross people wait decades to get the kind of experience he's getting now."

It's true. Christ, and with my education and experience, I'm more qualified for this line of work than either of them. Maybe there are options that Ben and I haven't considered; maybe it isn't as simple as staying or going.

"Speak of the devil." Courtney again looks beyond my shoulder. "Look who's here!" She stands up off her stool.

I turn around and see Alex, who's once again wearing long sleeves in a town way too hot for them.

We each give him a hug and kiss on the cheek.

"What are you doing here?" he asks me.

"Long story."

"It's her *despedida*!" Courtney slams the empty beer bottle on the bar and orders a round for the three of us.

"Where's Ben?" Alex asks.

"At the hospital."

"Oh my God."

"No, it's not like that. We had to drive somebody else in. Ben's just keeping company."

Alex nods but still looks confused. Perhaps he hoped for a different set of reasons to find me here without Ben.

"I didn't expect to see you," I admit.

Alex shrugs. "I live here now."

"Courtney was telling me how much things have changed. She says you played your cards right."

He accepts the shot and beer as Courtney passes them to him.

The three of us drink and talk for a while. I relate our rush to the hospital. Alex tells the story of a local newscaster who gave a ten-minute on-air tirade, explaining how such a thing as the Monkey-Faced Baby was impossible. He's not been seen on television since. Courtney's laugh grows louder.

It reminds me of our training days. On the balcony of Courtney's host family's house, the three of us used to make warm cocktails from cheap local vodka mixed with rehydration salts. Those were good times—before Alex and I hooked up, before his suicide attempt, before the earthquake. It was a brief era of harmless flirtation, not just with Alex but also with new friends, a new lifestyle, with the country itself.

I suddenly wonder if that house—the only two-story building in that village—still stands. I don't ask.

One of the other volunteers we came with touches Courtney on the shoulder. "We're going to the *subterráneo*."

Courtney nods and finishes her beer. "Let's go."

I follow our crew of relative strangers out into the now-cooler San Salvador night. Well-dressed urbanites stand in doorways, shouting into cell phones. Shining SUVs piloted by drunks swerve upon the road. And in front of every home or business stands the requisite teenager with a shotgun.

I don't know our destination, but it isn't unusual for new nightclubs to come and go in this district. Many are the half-baked business ideas from the sons and daughters of El Salvador's ruling elite. They have the capital and connections to get them started but lack the skills or discipline to keep them open.

We come to a stairway entrance. Ecstatic to see so many white girls, the doorman waves us all in at once. The *oomp-*

chick of the techno music makes conversation nearly impossible. The gringas instantly have Salvadoran dance partners competing for their attention. Courtney drags Alex out to the floor.

Suddenly exhausted, I find a stool at the bar. I ask for a rum and Coke, hoping the caffeine and sugar might grant me a second wind. I smile at the sight of Courtney and Alex on the dance floor, making a joke of the music, doing exaggerated disco moves.

After the first song, Alex begs off. A Salvadoran suitor approaches Courtney. Alex comes over and signals the barmaid for one of whatever I'm having.

While she makes his cocktail, Alex takes a pack of cigarettes from his pocket and holds it out toward me. He lights one for each of us. I suck a few drags and hold the cigarette close to my mouth, like I'm underwater and the cotton filter is the tip of my snorkel.

"It's good to see you," I say.

"Good to see you, too." His voice strains against the music.

"I'm happy you've done so well."

He lets out a lungful of smoke. "I found a niche, is all. To be honest, I'm more surprised by you. Don't take this the wrong way, but I never pictured you as the type to follow any guy anywhere."

I look to the floor, use my flip-flop to smother out a bit of ash. "It's not like that. Ben didn't push me."

Alex shrugs. "I haven't talked to you. All I know is that you quit to go on this surf trip with him."

I take a long drag and gather my thoughts. "If you can imagine staring at that mess of pipes right after the quake. On the one hand, it was sort of my life's work—if you can call twenty-three years a life. But it wasn't about my wasted time. It was more about all those broken promises, about the hopes I'd let run wild." I stop and take another drink.

He nods.

"It all felt like a joke. Like, who was I to pretend I could help them? I barely knew them. I can't even take care of myself."

"I get it," Alex says.

"I don't mean to be a downer, but all of it hit me at once: all the trees we cut down to lay that pipe, all the crops we'd dug out, the river we'd eventually dry up, and the way that it was truly just a tiny bandage on this country's wounds. You know the kind of water issues El Salvador will have in twenty years? The root of every single problem here is overpopulation. With this aqueduct—it's big and impressive and the people are excited about it—but all it's going to do is cut down infant mortality for a couple generations, let the population grow exponentially, and send thousands more into the fray once the shit really hits the fan."

I'm drunk and gushing, the way Courtney was earlier, but from a different point of view. Somehow, Alex seems to follow every single word.

"I know exactly what you mean."

"Maybe it sounds like a cop-out. But all of a sudden, trying to save people's lives felt . . . it felt a lot like trying to kill them." I swallow and hope for some spark of articulation. "Even pretending to have any sort of control over life and death felt weird to me."

"I think about that all the time." Alex lays his pack of cigarettes on the bar and lights another. "Especially when we're distributing medicine or blankets or something. All these tall men in uniform, forcing a bunch of families in rags to line up—it reminds me of a scene from a Holocaust movie or something."

I've never spoken to anybody about these thoughts. I've never quite understood them myself.

"Exactly," I say. "After that, I couldn't be a volunteer of any kind. I felt like a fraud for having been one at all. I just wanted to surf."

"Good for you."

"Fuck off." I figure that for sarcasm.

"I'm serious. I slit my wrists once I started thinking that way. If I knew how to surf, it might've turned out better." It's the first time he's ever mentioned his suicide attempt to me.

"I'll teach you one of these days." I raise my empty glass to ask if he wants another.

He holds up a vertical palm. "Let's get out of here, shall we?"

"Good idea." I've nearly lost my voice from competing with the music.

On the way out, I make eye contact with Courtney, who stops dancing long enough to offer a disapproving gaze. I start to shrug, but I'm pulled up the stairs by a hand that holds mine. We walk down the street, passing by men with guns at first, then beggars and supine drunks as we make our way to lower-rent neighborhoods. I smoke another cigarette.

As we enter Alex's apartment, it's dark but for a streetlamp that lets in dull yellow light through a front window. Keys jangle onto a counter. Hands materialize at my waist. When his face first leans in toward mine, I do turn away—aware that something isn't right.

"Stop," I whisper.

Alex pulls his head back for a second, then leans in again.

Between the alcohol and the memories of nights spent with

him in this city, I can't seem to stop it. The kissing feels natural—down to the prickle of his sharp stubble. For a moment, it feels as if this is all just a dreamy revisiting of an episode from our past.

The borrowed tank top comes off over my head. As he stretches and pulls at my bikini, the Salvadoran bills tucked into it fall to the floor. My eyes adjust to the dark room. Bent forward, Alex places his lips on one of my shadowy nipples. He kisses it and then bares his teeth for a gentle bite. I remember this habit of his, but I never liked it. His face is like sandpaper against my breast. One of his hands moves upward along the inside of my thigh.

We collapse onto his bed, which is in the same room, tucked in a corner far too dark for us to see each other. The second he's inside me, I can't remember how he got there. His breath burns hot against my shoulder. One of his hands cups the lowest vertebra of my spine.

It's not until then that I sober up enough to think of Ben, to realize that there's a word for what I'm doing right now, and that word is *cheating*.

But sex with Alex was always a peculiar brand of satisfaction spiked with shame, a baring of desperate and vulnerable parts. There was never talking, no communication of any kind. He was prone to acts of teeth and fingernails that stopped just short of violence. We were used to feeling embarrassed, awkward, even a little appalled in the aftermath. And it always felt inevitable somehow—like those kernels of suffering were a key part of pleasure, like love couldn't exist without a smattering of cruelty.

I buck hard against him. All of his weight presses down on a spot just below my navel. We grind against each other with force, like we want to get this over with, want to exorcise some specter of the love between us because we're sick of it haunting our waking lives.

Once it's finished, I lie there in his arms. A wave of guilt and self-loathing looms ahead, jacking up along my mental reef and threatening to break. I hope it will back off for a few more hours, so I can at least get some sleep.

15

In the first few months of my service—before I ever met Ben, before I ever saw La Libertad, before I'd done a lick of work on the water project—I took a weekend trip with Alex. We stayed at a cabin high in the mountains of Morazán, and went to the Museum of the Revolution. It was staffed by former guerillas and displayed the weapons and equipment that they had used and that had been used against them. Pieces of shrapnel were on display with stamps that read MADE IN TEXAS. The biggest exhibit was devoted to Radio Venceremos, the underground radio network that formed the backbone of the Farabundo Martí National Liberation Front. Behind glass stood a re-creation of a studio room with some of the original transmission equipment. Outside, a bomb crater was roped off, alongside a disarmed version of the U.S.-made bomb that had formed it.

"I want to go to El Mozote after this," Alex told me. We hadn't said much in this somber place.

"Where's that?"

"It's a small town near here, the site of the worst massacre of the war."

I nodded, a little disconcerted that this was what he wanted to see.

"I read a book about it," Alex explained.

At the village of El Mozote, site of the worst tragedy in modern Latin American history, I followed Alex to the town square. We came upon the memorial—four black silhouettes cut from iron, two adults and two children, all four of them hand in hand. They stood on a stone pedestal, which bore a plaque that read THEY HAVE NOT DIED: THEY ARE WITH US, WITH YOU, AND WITH ALL OF HUMANITY.

"What were you doing in 1981?" I asked Alex.

"I was four," he said. "That's when my parents finished the house I grew up in. I don't remember that, but there's a little plate by the door with the date engraved on it."

"What happened here?" I asked.

He turned away from the memorial and looked out at the town. "News of a big offensive had gotten around."

It was as if he'd memorized passages from whatever book he'd read.

"One of the local men—the store owner, I think—sent word

to all the villages and provinces that there would soon be heavy fighting. He told the women and children to come here to the town, where they'd be safer."

Alex took a few steps down one of the dirt streets along the plaza and looked up at the houses. "All of the homes were crowded with people, family and friends who'd come in from the campo, frightened strangers needing shelter."

I followed him as he took more steps down the block, my arms crossed in front of my chest. A mountain breeze blew cool air against our skin.

"Then the Atlacatl showed up."

"Who?"

"The Atlacatl. They were a battalion trained by our government, at the School of the Americas. This bloodthirsty asshole named Monterrosa was in charge."

"What does that mean, Atlacatl?"

"The name comes from an indigenous warrior who fought against the Spanish conquest. Before the war, he was a kind of folk hero for the country."

"They might've named the money after him." I swallowed and noticed that my hands were trembling. "Instead of Columbus."

"Now that name only means murder," Alex went on. "So they found all these civilians, but no guerillas. They ordered everybody out of the houses and had them lie down on the ground. They stuck machine guns at the backs of their heads and asked stupid questions about the Frente. Then they made everyone lock themselves in their houses, and said that anybody who stepped outside would be shot. The next day, all the people were dragged to the plaza again. Men were separated from women and children and locked up in groups. Most were in the church." He pointed at the empty lot that was now right beside us. A little fence surrounded it, a stone pedestal with a plaque in the center.

I thought of Niña Tere. Had she seen anything like this? Did she hear about it on Radio Venceremos, perhaps?

"The men were first," he continued. "The soldiers went ahead with their bullshit interrogation, then moved on to torturing and killing, while the wives and children screamed from inside the locked buildings. That took most of the morning. Around noon, they switched to the women. Girls were raped and then shot down. The little children were the last."

The sides of my eyes grew moist. I clenched my teeth and breathed out through my nostrils.

"They burned down the buildings. When the first reports came out, our government denied it. Reagan called it 'communist propaganda.'"

"Men." I spat out the word as though it had a bad taste. "Men with guns killing women and kids."

I put my hand out and Alex took hold of it. We each squeezed hard. With my other hand, I brushed away the beginnings of tears. He put his arm around me and turned back to the iron silhouettes on the memorial. We shared an embrace there, in the middle of the town square. My face pressed into Alex's chest. I looked up, past the bullet-riddled houses and into the hills beyond. El Salvador's beauty and terror spread itself out in ridges and wrinkles all the way to the horizon.

Though it was barely twenty years old, I was dumb enough to believe that this atrocity was never to be repeated. I saw this as a dark age from which this nation was emerging.

But more than anything, as I stood there in that killing field with the boy I loved, I felt the exquisite sensation of my ego slipping momentarily away. For a second, I wasn't the hero of my own drama, but just a bit player in something bigger and much more meaningful. Looking back now, it fills me with an odd sense of guilt—like we were indulging in some creepy form of tragedy tourism.

I pulled Alex even closer to me and rubbed my hand up and down his spine. Clouds moved in from the east. History sprouted up all around us like the blades of tall grass. That was one thing about being Alex's girlfriend: It always felt important.

16

Morning sunlight shines through the sole window in Alex's room. His slender arms still wrap around me. For the first time, I see the scars along his wrist. They are many, done in a haphazard mess—as random a series of lines as those galvanized pipes scattered down my riverbed. What did I expect—a single deep and decisive cut on each arm? I run my fingers along the raised mounds of flesh, as though they are a kind of Braille and I can tease a meaning out of them if I concentrate. My mind's eye tries to picture Alex in the act. Was he uncertain? Could he barely bring himself to make the deepest cut? I allow myself to wonder: Did he ever mean to go through with it? Or was this a desperate plea for attention—a cry for help, as they say?

Alex stirs as my fingers touch the scar tissue. He wakes with a series of jolts and shudders—another habit I remember well from our days as a couple but do not miss.

I climb out of bed and dress in the things I've left scattered about the floor: bikini, borrowed clothes, dime-store rubber sandals.

"Malia." Alex rises and sits up on the bed. "I'm sorry."

For a second, I wonder if I can lay the blame on his shoulders. Can I compose a version of last night in which I was drunk and he took advantage? I try that out for half a second but can't sell it even to myself.

"It's my fault." I pick the bills up off the floor and stuff them back into my bikini top. "I have to go," I tell him, without any real idea what time it is.

"You don't have to go, Malia." The pink marks on his forearm look like their own odd form of clothing. "That's the one thing you should get straight in your mind: You do *not* have to go."

"Good-bye." I leave the apartment without a kiss or hug.

It takes a while to find the car. The gate of the Estancia is visible a few doors from my parking spot. I look down at my skirt and top, knowing I should return them. But then I recall Courtney's disappointed parting glance last night, and I can't bring myself to face her.

As I pull the door handle on the Jeep, I realize that I don't have a choice: She's got my keys.

Luckily, Niña Ana is up and buzzes me in. She has a habit of boiling tap water and then cooling it in the fridge for her guests. I take out one glass bottle and drink the entire thing in a series of bubbling gulps. Gingerly, I push open the door to Courtney's room.

Inside, half a dozen bodies lie across the mattresses in various states of drooling, snoring, hungover slumber. Courtney's things are arranged upon a folding chair by her bed. Searching underneath a couple layers of clothes, I find my car keys tucked inside her shoe.

So they don't jingle, I wrap my fingers tightly around the keys and make my way to the door.

"That was a shitty move you pulled last night." Courtney's voice shocks me so much, I put a hand over my heart.

"Jesus, you scared the hell out of me." I speak softly, hoping not to wake this roomful of sleepers.

"Sorry." Her eyes hardly open. Her head turns slightly upward off the pillow. "Just thought you should know."

I want her on my side. So often, she's been my confidante in times like these. "I fucked up last night," I say. "Cut me a little slack."

"You can't have your cake and eat it, too, Malia."

A grumble comes from a body in one of the other beds.

"I know," I whisper. "I'm a little confused about things. . . ."

"Try not to mess with too many other lives while you figure it out, okay?"

I don't have a response to that. Why is she being so cruel? "Courtney, did you . . . Were you hoping that you and Alex might . . . ?"

"Would you all shut the fuck up, please?" bellows a voice I don't recognize.

Courtney doesn't answer me.

"Is that what this is about?" I suppose the better part of my interest is pure curiosity. But another part, from a deeper and darker place, feels that she's violated some unwritten code. It's true that I'm with someone else and all, and technically on my way out of this country. But Alex is my ex. And Courtney is my best female friend. There's some sort of rule against that, isn't there?

"That's not even the point, Malia."

"Shut up!" The same sleeper throws a pillow, which lands near my feet.

It occurs to me that I might not see Courtney again for a long time, years even. "Thanks for everything you did for me yesterday. You're a good friend and you're right: I messed up. I hope you'll forgive me." I leave the room, grateful that nobody asked me to return the borrowed clothes.

Traffic is light for a weekday morning. Large н signs point the way to the hospital. Young boys carry tins of Spanish olive oil between the cars at every stoplight. The oil was Spain's primary form of aid to their former colony in the wake of the earthquake. It's given out in shelters and refugee camps. Nobody in this country knows what to do with the stuff. It smokes too much to fry with. Teenagers sell gallons of it for pennies. Salvadoran cooks often dump the expensive oil out upon the ground so that they can use the sturdy tins for something else.

Luckily, there's a parking spot close to the building where I left Ben and Pelochucho. I buy sweet bread from a cart outside.

"You look like shit," Ben says to me.

"I didn't sleep well. Brought you some food." I hold out the bag of baked goods, hoping its aroma might mask the smell of cigarette smoke, that the cigarette smoke might mask the smell of sex.

Pelochucho stirs, says hello, and bites into one of the sugar-encrusted rolls.

"How was the floor?" I ask Ben, looking down at his make-shift pile of cushions.

"Not so bad." He shrugs. "I was tired."

"And the patient?" I ask Pelo.

"Ready to get the hell out of here." His mouth is full of eggy dough.

"You smell like cigarettes," Ben says.

"I smoked some on the drive."

He nods but doesn't look convinced.

Checking out of the hospital takes longer than expected. Ben and I leave Pelo in the room and sort things out with the clerks at the front desk. They give us syringes and a vial of antibiotics to inject into Pelochucho's ass, as well as spare bandages and an eye patch. Ben hands over the rest of his money—everything we "earned" from Pelo yesterday. That barely covers the bill.

Again, I ride in the plywood storage space. It's uncomfortable, but I'm thankful not to have to make conversation. My hangover reaches fever pitch on the ride back as we descend toward the coast. It brings gallons of guilt along with it. In one long evening and a short bit of morning, I've lost two of my closest friends in this country, and managed to cheat on Ben in the bargain. I keep thinking of Alex's last words to me, about not needing to leave, and Courtney's accusation that I want to have my cake and eat it, too. It's true: I want to go south and surf, to leave behind the ruins of this place and get some waves, to see Patagonia and toss those stones Ben's always talking about into the sea. But I also want to stay and set things right, to help heal El Salvador and make my father proud. The two possibilities wrestle with each other inside my mind. I wonder if my Hawaiian ancestors had a way of choosing between competing *kuleana*. Perhaps those were simpler times. In the end, I decide the best thing is to convince Ben to leave as soon as possible. At least that way, my indecision can't cause any more trouble.

The more I commit to it, the more it seems that all my problems stem from our still being in this country. Indeed, we've stayed in El Salvador just a couple days too long. I worry that now Ben will feel obliged to stick around and take care of Pelochucho.

The engine cuts off. We're back in La Posada. I want to speak with Ben about our departure, but I need to get cleaned up and have a nap first, maybe a beer as well.

Ben comes around and opens the back for me. Pelochucho works his way out of the passenger seat in a jerky, one-eyed hobble, his legs still stiff from so many hours in bed. Kristy runs over the second she sees his bandages and helps him to the room. Pelo explains the accident with Spanglish and hand gestures.

"I'm dying for a shower." I climb off the plywood platform.

"Wait," Ben says. "What's that?" He points toward our bedroom.

"What are you talking about?"

"The window."

My eyes follow the invisible line extending from his index

finger. Our single bedroom window is a louver—a screenless series of glass slats operated from inside by a crank. And at the bottom left-hand corner, where Ben points, two of the slats have been pushed inward and lie cockeyed on the rack.

"Where's the key?" Ben feels the pocket of his shorts.

"I don't have it," I say.

"Fuck!" Ben walks over to the window and sticks his hand through the space made by the moved louvers. "How is this possible? Motherfuckers came in here during broad daylight?" He cups his hand around his mouth. "Kristy!" he shouts.

"Ben, stop," I say. "I think it happened last night."

He squints, confused. "You didn't hear anything? You didn't notice it this morning?"

"It's not like that." I swallow. "I didn't come back here. I stayed in the capital."

This information only confuses him more. "Why?"

"I got lost. I went in circles in the traffic. It was getting dark. Then I saw Boulevard de los Heroes and drove to the Estancia. Courtney was there."

He turns toward the window and studies the breached panes of glass. "Why didn't you tell me?"

"I don't know." I sift through the memory of our morning conversation, reconsidering what was a lie and what was merely an omission. "It never came up."

"'Never came up'?" Anger swells inside his voice. He takes a few steps toward me. "What about the drive?"

"What?"

"You said you smoked cigarettes on the drive. But there was no drive."

"Did I say that? I'm sorry. We went out. I'm not sure why I didn't mention it. I didn't think you needed to know."

"What the hell is that supposed to mean?" The jealous streak that Ben always warned me about takes over the microphone. His hands clasp my upper arms. Pupils swiveling within the now-round whites, his eyes lock onto mine. "What is going on? Is there something you're not telling me?"

"No!" It isn't hard to act offended, especially with a stiff thumb pressing into my biceps. Though my answer isn't quite true, it feels like the best option, given the circumstances.

Ben doesn't speak, just holds me tighter in his hands. With our faces so close together, both of us breathing hard, me making my best doe eyes, there's something dirty about the whole exchange—a scene from a bad porno film.

"I was with my friends," I say, a statement that is marginally true—at least they were still my friends when the evening started. "All I wanted was a night out with some of the other volunteers. I had fun." The explanation is for myself as much as for Ben. That's all I meant for last night to be. And it was nearly a success, but for one big mistake toward the end.

He releases me and takes a couple steps backward, holding his hands away from his body, fingers splayed, like they're sharp objects to be handled with care. He turns his head to the side and nods, then closes his eyes.

"I'm sorry." Ben sticks a hand into each armpit and squeezes them there. "I'm so sorry, Malia." He looks up at me with a furrowed brow. "I trust you. I swear I do."

"It's okay," I say.

Though I'd never admit it, Ben's jealousy is something I find oddly endearing. Among my small circle of college friends, and even more so among the volunteers here, couples are so often changing places, people playing musical lovers. There are jokes about it, as if it's no big deal. This is the first time I've seen Ben get so far out of control, and it did scare me, so much so that I felt compelled to lie. But at least he takes our relationship seriously.

"Let's find that fucking key." Ben opens the door to the Jeep and rifles though the console. I walk over to the bedroom window and look inside. The bedside table is directly below. Several items are still upon it: a tube of sunscreen, a half-used bar of surf wax. But I don't see the woven wallet that I bought in Guatemala last year.

"It's gone," I whisper to myself. "It's gone."

Ben finds the key and works the door open. Inside, he kneels down, peeks under the bed, picks up pillows, then sheets, tosses them in the air.

I follow him into the room. My purse is tucked inside my backpack in the far corner. I check it, but I already know I won't find what I'm looking for. "They got my wallet," I tell Ben.

"Are you sure?" His face reddens. He digs his arms into the top of his backpack up to the elbows.

"Positive."

He throws a few things into the air, opens and closes a couple zippered compartments. "Fuck! They got my bank card."

Ben runs out of the room. I follow. He puts his elbows on the hood of the Jeep and buries his face in his hands. "What was in your wallet?" he finally asks.

"The airfare cash, all my bank stuff," I say. "And my passport." To myself, I recall the Red Cross business card Alex gave me at the Peace Corps office; it was in there as well.

Ben makes a guttural draining sound. "Fuck." He covers his face with his hands. I wonder if he might be crying. After a couple seconds of that, he stands up straight. He shakes his head first and then his whole body, like a dog drying off.

The shaking stops and he sighs. "My passport is still in the car. You should get on the phone. Call the bank first. Maybe Jim knows somebody we can talk to at the embassy. I'll go find Peseta."

I didn't expect him to regain composure so quickly. "Okay." I struggle to do the same.

In the neighboring room, Pelochucho lies like a starfish across his bed, the fan going full blast and shaking in its mount. Kristy stands in his doorway, looking in.

"The poor thing," she says.

"He'll be fine." I put my hand on her shoulder. "We should close this and let him rest."

She steps back and I pull the door shut.

I spend nearly an hour at the public phone office. The bank passes me from one employee to the next. Without my passport, they can't confirm that it's my account. I fail to get a hold put on it. Nobody will even tell me the balance.

Jim is nice enough, but he reminds me that since I'm a private citizen traveling in this country, there isn't much he can do beyond point me in the right direction.

He gives me the number of a kind woman named Elaine from the embassy. At first, she talks as if we can sort the passport out in a few days. But she is mistaken, speaking of an emergency document that would be good for only one month. I explain our trip, the fact that we're planning to travel for several months.

"I see. You'll need a full-fledged passport, then."

"That's right," I say.

"I'm afraid that will be more difficult."

"It will?"

"Yes. As you can probably guess, the embassy is a little overextended at the moment. Under normal circumstances, we might issue emergency passports for as long as a year, but the ambassador has passed some blanket policies since the earthquake. Now they're all for one month, period."

I sigh audibly into the receiver.

Elaine seems to register my frustration. "Sorry about this. The black-market value of a U.S. passport has gone through the roof recently. They've had to crack down."

"I didn't sell my passport," I say.

"Of course not. I didn't mean to imply any such thing. Still, issuing new ones is not taken lightly these days."

I tell myself to stay calm, that she's trying to help. "So, what's my best bet here?"

"You should make an appointment immediately and fill out the paperwork. Do you have a photocopy of your lost passport?"

"No," I say, though I'd been told many times that making a copy was a good idea.

"Bring in whatever documents you have. We'll start the process right away. But I must warn you: It could take weeks."

I swallow her facts as best I can, hoping that Ben is having more luck with a street-level approach than I've had with the bureaucratic one.

"Shall I make you an appointment for tomorrow morning?"

"Yes, please."

Elaine urges me to keep my spirits up and says good-bye.

The phone's old bell lets out a droning ring once I hang it up. In my mind, I tally up what time it is in Honolulu. There's nothing I'd like more than to hear my father's voice right now. But what would I tell him? That I'd abandoned the aqueduct he thought so much of? That I accidentally sabotaged the surf trip I'd left it for? That I might've just lost thousands of dollars, much of which wasn't my own—on account of a drunken infidelity?

Back at La Posada, I ask Kristy for my day's first cup of coffee. She brings out a mug of hot milk and a jar of instant mix. As I stir black crystals into the cup, all sorts of ideas brew through my mind. Could I conceivably sneak my way past every single border in South America? I've known others to skip through here and there, mostly volunteers who hadn't taken vacation days on their way home from Guatemala or Honduras.

But Ben and I are looking at a lot of borders, and we'll have to get on a plane eventually, to somewhere. Plus, we no longer have any real budget.

I look up from my coffee and see Ben in the street with Peseta. Their conversation turns heated. Peseta shrugs and Ben nods. After a couple more words, they bump fists and Peseta takes off. Ben comes in to join me. I signal Kristy for another cup of coffee.

"How'd it go on your end?" Ben sits down.

"Not great. They've got an emergency option, but it's only good for a month. A whole new passport is more complicated. I have to go to the embassy tomorrow. This could take weeks."

"Shit."

"How about your approach?"

He sighs. "I told Peseta I'd pay for the passport and the bank cards. He isn't too hopeful. He says most of the crackheads burn the documents straight away when they steal a wallet—so they won't be caught with them later. With an American passport, there's some chance they might hold on to it. Especially in the case of yours, because . . ." Ben pauses.

"Because I'm brown," I say, finishing the sentence for him. "A Salvadoran girl might use it to sneak through immigration—if she looked enough like me—without even changing the photo." I realize it as I say it.

"Right," Ben says. "But that sort of thing is a little sophisticated for the rank-and-file sneak thieves. Which means there's a chance your passport is still around, waiting for a buyer."

Kristy brings out a tray with another mug of warm milk. We are silent as Ben fixes his coffee.

"You need to call the bank. They might put a hold on your account."

"I did that," Ben says. "But the balance shows there are only a few bucks left."

"What? They can't take your cash without the PIN number."

"That's right." Ben sighed and looked at the spot where Peseta had been standing. "But apparently they used the debit option and bought stuff with just a signature. It takes more time, but still."

"Shit." I hadn't thought of that. "So the thieves must've been on a spending spree for the last twelve hours or so."

"More likely the thief passed the cards on to somebody else, somebody with wheels. Anyplace that was open, they bought shit from it."

"What do we do now?" I ask. The outlook for my own bank account isn't good.

"I'm not sure." He extends his hand across the table and touches mine. "We'll figure something out."

For a few minutes, we sit in silence and drink our coffee. I want to ask if our trip is still on. How little money would be too little?

"I'll run out to Sunzal real quick." Ben takes a final sip and puts down the mug.

"Why?" I ask.

"To get the boards." He stands up.

I'd forgotten all about them.

Ben waves as he drives out of La Posada. Though it isn't even noon, I ask Kristy for a beer, hoping to keep this hangover at bay long enough to hold my thoughts together. I drink it fast and then brush my teeth in the sink by the shared bathrooms.

"Chinita!" Kristy pokes her head out of the office, her hand held over the mouthpiece of the phone. "For you."

I'm still rinsing toothpaste foam from my mouth. "One moment." I spit in the sink, then cross the courtyard.

Kristy hands me the phone, cord stretched out through the office door.

"Hello?"

"Does everyone know you as 'Chinita' in that town?"

"You shouldn't call me here, Alex."

"I just wanted to say I'm sorry about last night."

"We had too much to drink and we fucked," I say. "That's all it was. I'd like to be able to blame you for it, but that's not how it happened."

"Can I see you again?"

"Look, Alex, I'm in a relationship, a serious one. We've got plans." The word *plans* feels like a punch to the stomach after the events of this morning.

"Will you tell him?"

"Tell Ben? About last night? I don't think he'd take it too well." I neglect to mention our jealous exchange a couple hours earlier. I look down at my arms. Twin black dots—the size of nickels—form at the base of each bicep in the spots where Ben pressed his thumbs.

"That's probably for the best," Alex says. "It's not about him, after all."

"It's not about anything. I feel shitty not telling him, but it isn't worth ruining our trip." I leave off the fact that my carelessness—combined with some crackhead's cunning—might already have ruined the trip.

"I'm with you," he says.

"Look, Alex. I have to go."

"You don't have to go, Malia."

"I do, actually. Ben will be back any minute, and we've got some stuff to deal with here."

"I don't mean right now," he goes on. "I mean period. You don't have to leave El Salvador. I understand your reasons. You can, obviously. But don't act as if you have no choice. That may be the only thing I learned from going to D.C., then coming back here. I didn't think I could face it: Salvador, El Vado, the Peace Corps, anything. But the truth is, nobody cares. People have their own problems."

I hear the distinct rattle of our Jeep's engine coming down the street. "Alex, I have to hang up now."

"Come see me if you can, please."

"Good-bye."

I hang up the phone and take a few steps out into the courtyard. Ben pulls in and parks. Once he climbs out of the Jeep, he sticks his index finger in his mouth and then holds it straight up above his head. "The wind still hasn't picked up," he says. "Might as well go surfing."

Ben and I set out into a hapless sea. We don't bother with the point, opting instead for the shorter beach break on the inside, the surf spot the locals call La Paz.

A couple small sets roll in after we paddle out. I get a workable section right off the bat and land a little floater before it closes. For a moment, I have that rare and wonderful sense that surfing can redeem the rest of this mess. My feet hit the deck, and for one fleeting instant my bank account and my passport don't exist. Two turns into a moderately punchy face, and I can see myself from a distance, from years in the future; today's problems look small and silly—a funny story told over cocktails. That feeling lasts less than a second, then fizzles out with the white water.

After twenty minutes or so, the wind picks up and the surf turns to crap. We stubbornly sit on our boards, hoping that a fluke wave might line up, waiting for that same elusive sense of redemption.

Bobbing up and down in the blown-out sea, with the midday sun now reflecting so hard off the water that I have to squint, things finally catch up with me. I internalize the accusations that Courtney hurled my way. I think of my mother again. Once she'd cheated on my father and left us, at least she left for good. She didn't lie about it—as far as I know. And she didn't come back and try to be a wife or parent every so often. Maybe she deserves some credit for that.

The shame washes over me along with the residual indecision and a slight sense that I ought to tell Ben what happened. For a second, I fear I might drown in all of it.

"This sucks," I shout to Ben, and paddle for shore.

———

I rinse off. Ben gathers the medical supplies and enters Pelo-chucho's room. In my sarong, I go to the doorway and watch as Pelo lowers his board shorts and exposes the uppermost inches of his white ass.

"Easy," Ben says, then sticks the needle in.

I wonder if Ben has ever done this before. He looks like a pro. Beyond tired, I walk back to our own room. The sun is still high in the early-afternoon sky. I shut the door, turn on the fan, take off my sarong, and lie down across the bed. For a few minutes, I enjoy the cold, quick air against my naked skin.

I wake up feeling drugged, barely able to open my eyes. It takes a second to remember where I am. I paw at the bed beside me, surprised not to find a male body there.

In the hastily wrapped sarong, I have a peek out the door. It's dusk. The sun will be setting soon. Ben sits at a table in the kitchen, a Regia and a glass set before him. He waves when he sees me. I put on some proper clothes and go to join him. The metal wire of my flip-flop scrapes against the tiles of the dining room.

"How'd it get so late?" My voice is deep and froggy.

"You were out like a light." He stands up and grabs me a glass from behind the counter. I pour myself a beer from the big amber bottle.

Ben reaches into the cargo pocket of his board shorts. "Got you a new wallet," he says.

Before me, he places a leather square with the image of Che Guevara burned into it, along with the words ¡HASTA LA VIC-TORIA SIEMPRE!

"Where'd you get this?" I pick up the gift. It's still stiff and smells of the tanning process.

"The jewelry lady stopped by. It was either Che or the Virgin Mary."

"Tough choice." I grin. "Thank you." I love it. It's sweet of him. And while we're prone to joke about Che's misunderstood iconography, I find the image and the mythology comforting at that moment: a handful of men with ideals and bird rifles taking on the strongest military in the world, their faith and their struggle. *Until victory always!*

"I am sorry," Ben says. "About before. I shouldn't have . . . grabbed you like that."

"No, you shouldn't have," I say. "But it's been a messed-up day. I forgive you."

"It's my Irish side," he says. "My grandmother used to say that Irishmen treat women and horses the exact same way." He takes a sip of beer.

"How's that?"

"They worship both, but they expect both to suffer constantly and gracefully."

"I was expecting something more R-rated," I say. "How's Pelochucho?"

"He's fine. Sleeping. I was bored out here with nobody to talk to."

"Has he mentioned anything about the hospital bills?"

"Yeah, he paid me back." Ben nods and points at the Che wallet. "That's all we have in the world."

I look inside. There's a little over four hundred American dollars.

"You hungry?" Ben asks.

"Starving." All I've eaten today is the sweet bread at the hospital.

A couple doors down, a woman cooks *pupusas* on a porta-ble gas grill. She wraps them in brown paper, along with plas-tic bags of spicy pickled cabbage and red tomato sauce. We take them back to the hotel and open more beer.

Once the food is finished, we carry our bottles up to the roof. Ben takes out his pouch of Dutch tobacco and a newspa-per bundle of the local brown weed. He rolls a spliff. Opting out on the pot, I make myself a thin cigarette. The ocean is still and sounds like a dog's whimper. It laps gently upon the shore, as if afraid it might do harm to the land.

"No waves," Ben says with a dry mouth.

"Not one."

We're silent for a minute, sharing only the mild sucking and puffing sounds of smoking.

"Can I ask you something?" The quiet night turns me con-templative. "Why do you love surfing so much?"

"It's fun," Ben says, trying to brush the question off. "What's not to love?"

"I know it's fun." I won't let him off that easy. "Lots of things are fun. But why surfing? Why you?"

He holds the spliff upward and inspects the cherry. "I come from a family of—for lack of a better term—tough guys. My dad, my uncles, my older brother: They've all been marines, high school football stars, that sort of thing."

I pay attention, never having heard him say much on this subject. "Obviously, I'm the hippie in the bunch, right? And I'd never make it in the military—could never stand some asshole shouting at me, or, God forbid, to shoot anyone. Even the team sports thing was too much."

I take a long gulp of beer.

"But when you're a boy and you're raised by guys like that, they presume you're a pussy—too scared for all that physical stuff. For me, surfing—especially in North Carolina, where I learned, with the only real waves coming in as storms and all—was a way for me to have adventures, to test myself."

"Did it work?" I can't say the next sentence with a straight face. "Did it prove to your dad that you're not a pussy?" The suppressed laughter bursts at the sides of my mouth.

Ben smiles at the silliness of the question. "It's not like that. My dad, my brothers, they'll never get it. But yeah, it gives me peace of mind. I know I'm not afraid. That's enough. In a sense, I like that they don't understand it. After all, I don't get any of the stuff they're into." Ben tops his beer glass off, relieved to be finished with his explanation. "What about you?" he asks. "What do you love about surfing?"

I shrug, wishing I'd prepared a response before starting this. "Most of all, I like that it's an end in itself, you know? That it's not a means to an end."

"How so?"

The cigarette feels hot in my fingers. "Speaking of families, my father's family is . . . we'd say *pake* in Hawai'i. That word technically means Chinese, but it's used for anyone who's frugal and thrifty. You met my dad; he's very disciplined. Everything is about getting ahead, or helping the next generation get ahead. It's sort of admirable. My grandparents were plantation workers, and my grandfather managed to save up and start his own business. Now my dad runs it, and it's successful. He raised me by himself, of course. Sent me to private school. But there's no stopping to enjoy it, no indulgence. It's all profit and loss."

Ben furrows his brow.

"With surfing, I like that there's no earning or spending involved. Waves aren't an investment in something else to come. There's no past or future—only the moment at hand."

He licks a finger and wets one side of the spliff.

"I get hard work and sacrifice and everything; it's not like I'm lazy." I'm having a hard time expressing myself. "But people like my father, or Alex, for that matter . . . it's as if they see life as one big suffering contest, you know? That's like the only measure of character for them."

I stop talking. The two of us stare out at the dark ocean.

"I've got a bad feeling about this passport thing," I confess.

"Want me to go with you tomorrow?"

"No." I didn't even think of that, but it's kind of him to ask. "It'll be a shitty day. No reason for both of us to go through it." I almost add that it's my fault, but figure that much is obvious. "It's probably better if you look after Pelochucho."

Ben puts the still-burning spliff down in an upturned jar lid on the cinder block we use as a table. "I got to piss; be right back."

His steps are slow and heavy down the stairs. As it had a few hours ago in the water, the swelling shame surges again and comes after me. I want a crude time machine that can go back one day and fix all the mistakes I made. I can live with the guilt over what happened with Alex. But this burglary stuff was stupid, and it's ruined Ben's surf trip, this dream he's been looking forward to for years.

I have to fix it. Maybe it's all the beer, or maybe it's simply the lack of a better idea, but something emboldens me. It's absurd: We know the exact location of whichever crackhead stole our stuff, or where he'll be coming back and forth from at least.

I slip down the staircase. From the bathroom comes the sound of piss splashing water. The gate is still open. Kristy's light is on.

I leave La Posada and head out into the streets. Walking around this town alone after dark is something I know better than to do.

The crack house is only a couple blocks away, a nondescript two-story building. It fared well through the earthquake. Its white exterior looks newly painted; the trim and front door shine bright red.

I stop on the far side of the street and stare at the crimson door. Somebody inside will know who took my wallet. It must've caused a spike in sales, the greatest binge in some lucky addict's career. I will demand only the passport back; the money will be long gone. That's reasonable, isn't it? Perhaps the thieves will even thank me, the way that gunmen often do on the buses here if handed a particularly large sum. I'm not some tourist; I'm La Chinita, after all. That has to count for something.

As logical as I tell myself that this plan is, I can't quite cross that street. I hear low chatter and the inkling of what sounds like choral music coming from inside. A taste like bile and pennies rises in the back of my throat.

"Chinita! ¿Qué haces?" I hear my nickname in a barbed voice. It's Peseta. "What are you doing? Have you gone crazy?"

"I want my passport back. I don't care about the money. Somebody here must have it or know who has it. Come with me."

"You don't understand." Peseta carries a white paper bag spotted with grease. It smells of fried food. I've never seen him eat before. He puts his body between mine and the crack house.

"I need that passport," I say.

"Chinita, trust me on this. You can't go in there. Please."

I look over his shoulder at the red door—the final thin

membrane that separates the surfers and the crackheads in this town. It's a Pandora's box of trouble and change that I'm both attracted to and repulsed by all at once. My eyes turn back to Peseta. He seems sincere. This is the only interaction I've had with him that carries no trace of a hustle. Perhaps he doesn't want me killed just because then he'd lose my spare coins.

After a few more seconds, I exhale and realize that I don't have the guts. I'm *only* La Chinita—that's all I'll ever be here.

"Malia? What the fuck?" The second I've made the decision, I hear Ben's voice.

"Chuck Norris, do something about your girl. She's acting crazy." Peseta appeals directly to him, as if I'm incapable of reason.

"Malia." Ben puts his arm around me. "Let's go. Goddamn, you gave me a scare."

After we've walked a few blocks, I swallow my pride and say, "I'm sorry."

"It's all right," Ben says. "It's not a big deal."

"I screwed up all our plans."

"We'll figure something out." We enter La Posada. He leads me to the bedroom and sits me down on the bed.

"The money was easy come and easy go." Ben takes a seat beside me. "We're safe. We're together. That's what's important."

My chin starts to quiver. I can't quite look up at Ben.

"I love you, Malia." He rubs a circle into my back.

I wipe at my eyes with the hem of my shirt. "I love you, too."

We lie down, but between the long nap and the adrenaline rush, I toss and turn for hours.

Finally slipping into the twilight stage right before full

sleep, I'm awakened by a bang and then a grunt from the room next door. Immediately, my thoughts leap back to my first night in La Lib.

"Ben!" I shake him. "Somebody's in Pelochucho's room!" My voice is a hissing whisper.

"What? Huh?" He forces himself up onto his elbows.

"Fucking crackheads. They know Pelo's hurt." In that insane logic that could only occur in La Libertad, I feel that this is unfair, outside of the rules somehow.

Another bang comes through the wall, then a third, lighter one. The sounds settle into a rhythm. Ben's expression goes from concern to mischief. He lies back down. "Don't worry about it." He shuts his eyes. "It's not fucking crackheads; it's only fucking."

I listen closer and hear coos and moans in a female voice. "But . . . Pelochucho? How? With whom?" My first thoughts are of prostitutes.

"Kristy," Ben whispers.

"For real?" How have I been denied such a juicy bit of gossip? "Since when?"

"Apparently, it all started the last time Pelo was down here. I guess it got weird when he left. She fell for him more than he realized, hoped he might take her back to the States. He wasn't sure what would happen on this trip." Ben closes his eyes and turns over to one side. "Now we know."

I lie there silent beside him. On the other side of a few thin inches of wood and plaster, Kristy and Pelochucho fuck away. As Ben and I grow more silent, I can make out everything.

"*Te quiero. Te quiero. Te quiero,*" she purrs over and over— that Spanish phrase that means both to love and to want, a word that never can be satisfied.

It goes on and on, prolonged perhaps by all the pills that Pelo took for the pain. Ben snores beside me. I listen to the lovemaking a while longer, with a feeling I finally recognize as envy. My own bed feels tainted with the betrayal I committed, the jealousy Ben showed, and the half-truths I used to cover it up.

I hardly get any sleep at all.

17

Three weeks after my trip to El Mozote with Alex, there was a swearing-in ceremony for a new group of volunteers. These were always a big deal; everyone went to the capital for the weekend, attended a party at the embassy, got to dress up and eat fancy hors d'oeuvres.

I was busy with my health census and wasn't able to travel to San Salvador until the day of the ceremony. It had been a while since I'd left Cara Sucia, and I looked forward to blowing off steam.

I went straight to the Peace Corps office to pick up my mail and drop off some paperwork. Courtney came and found me in the volunteer lounge.

"Did you just get here?" she asked. Her face was white.

"Yeah. A few minutes ago. What's up?"

"We need to talk."

Courtney led me out of the office to the parking lot, lit up a cigarette, and said, "What's going on with you and Alex?"

"What do you mean?" I shrugged. "I figured I'd see him today. I paged him, asking him to find us a room."

"Did something happen between you guys?"

"No. We had a nice trip to the mountains a few weeks ago. That's the last time I saw him. Why?"

"He was attached to one of the new girls last night," Courtney said. "They were, like, all over each other at the bar."

"Seriously? Alex?" At first, I thought this must be some sort of misunderstanding.

She looked at the ground and blew out smoke. "Everybody was watching them. They were practically making out on the dance floor. It was gross."

"Is he staying at the Estancia?" I asked.

Courtney shrugged.

I left the office and headed straight to the taxi stand at the Hotel Princessa. The driver quoted me a price for where I wanted to go; I handed him nearly double the amount, asking to please get me there as fast as possible.

The taxi seemed to go eighty miles an hour from the second I shut the door. I should've felt terror at the run red lights, the weaving through lanes, and the near-misses. But my heart was so full of anger that I had no space left for fear. A trip that took an hour plus by bus was over in a few minutes.

Other guests sat on the front patio, drinking coffee, so I had no trouble getting into the hotel. I opened the door to two other bedrooms before I finally found Alex—in a shared room with three twin beds, all of them occupied, him in the center one.

What I hadn't expected to find was that new volunteer, still tangled up in Alex's arms. The two of them turned to face me. Oddly, the thing that unnerved me the most was that she was also Asian. She pulled the covers up to her shoulders; I glared at her from the doorway.

"Hi, Malia." Alex was remarkably calm. "Did you just get here?"

"Shut up. You're an asshole; you know that? I never want to see you again."

"Okay," he said. "I guess I didn't realize you thought of our relationship as an exclusive thing."

"You had to pull this in front of all my friends? Is this, like, your thing?" I literally shivered in disgust. "You know, you try to come off as this dark, brooding, smart guy—but the truth is, you're just a jerk."

He nodded, as if agreeing.

I left the room, took a bus to El Centro, bought a bottle of cheap vodka, then found my connection out to Cara Sucia. At that point, the project hadn't yet broken ground. I hadn't yet discovered Ben or La Lib. I drank vodka by candlelight in my little house that night, listening to sad songs on my tape deck, wondering if there was any place for me in this country.

Not long after, Courtney sent me a letter explaining that the new volunteer from Alex's bed had quit and gone home after a few days in the campo. That news gave me a smug, superior feeling that I carried around for weeks.

18

Roosters crow me awake. Thin streaks of sunlight enter through the bedroom window. I shower and brush my teeth. By the time I'm dressed and ready for the embassy, Ben and Pelo sit in the dining room, eating breakfast.

Pelochucho's eye patch has inspired them to talk like pirates: "Arr, after breakfast, Captain Pelo be needin' another shot of antibiotics in me arse, arr!" I wonder how long that will last.

Short on time, I grab a piece of sweet bread from the case on the counter and ask Kristy for coffee.

"¡Qué guapa!" Kristy says to me. I'm wearing a khaki skirt and white top with a collar, an outfit reserved for meetings and embassy functions. She's not used to seeing me in anything but bathing suits and sarongs.

"What are you so dressed up for?" Pelo asks. "I figured you guys would be itching to get out of here by now."

I roll my eyes. "We can't leave. Not after what happened yesterday." Though it's unfair, I do hold Pelochucho partly to blame. His presence, his injury, his insistence that we stick around in the first place, they all conspired to put me in the position to lose my passport—and to sleep with Alex.

"Hey." Pelo looks back and forth between Ben and me with his one good eye. "You two don't have to stay here just to take care of me. I'll be okay."

"It's not that, Pelo." Ben lays his fork on his empty plate. "The night before last, our room got ripped off. We lost a lot of money. Malia's passport is gone."

"For real?" Pelo lets his mouth hang open. "That sucks."

Kristy sets my coffee on the table.

Pelochucho leans back in his chair. "That was a shitty day for everybody, wasn't it?"

"She's headed to the embassy to see about a new passport," Ben says.

I take a seat and burn my mouth on the first sip of coffee.

"Hey, listen." Pelo lowers his voice. "If you guys want to make some quick dough, there is a way—with your Jeep, I mean."

"What are you talking about?" Ben asks.

"Just do a midnight run." Pelo shrugs. "It takes only a couple hours. You'll probably make back more than you lost. Last time I was here, this South African dude did three or four of them without a hiccup. I rode along for one."

I hold the coffee cup halfway up to my mouth. "You mean . . . drugs?"

Pelo nods. "The bales that come up on the boats. The guys from the crack house are always hiring runners."

Ben furrows his brow. "Bringing it from the cove at K Ninety-nine back to town here?" His index finger makes a journey from one side of the table to the other.

"Exactly." Pelo nods. "Frankly, I'm surprised you guys haven't done one yet. You could fit four or five bales in the back of that thing, and you've got four-wheel drive. If you want, I'll set it up. We could split the money three ways."

"Are you insane?" I say. "Absolutely not. I can't believe we're even talking about this."

Ben looks at me. After a second, he nods.

"Hey." Pelo holds up his palms. "It was just an idea." He rises and walks off to his own room.

A second of silence passes. Finally, Ben says, "Crazy, huh?"

I snort out a halfhearted laugh, then finish the coffee.

"You'd better get going," Ben says.

"Want anything from the capital?" I consider asking Ben if he needs more of his Dutch rolling tobacco, though I don't truly want to drive across town and buy it at the Hotel Intercontinental.

He shakes his head. "Malia," he says, "good luck today."

"Thanks." I slow down my slurping long enough to look him in the eye.

"But don't worry. If it takes days, it takes days. If it takes months, it takes months." He puts a hand on my knee. "We'll be okay."

I nod and smile, though I lack his optimism. And this is just the passport issue; we still have no idea how to solve our money problems.

———

The drive feels therapeutic—the morning air still cool, dramatic sunlight upon the trees and the recent ruins of adobe walls, my hair and collar flapping in the wind. Rising uphill and inland, I feel in control of things for the first time in days.

The outskirts of the capital gather on both sides of the road. The last time I saw this part of the city was in the aftermath of the earthquake, from the back of that pickup—the traffic, the looters, elephants and giraffes running around cars, the dust clouds rising up like some unnatural kind of weather. I know now that it was a 7.7 on the Richter scale. Over nine hundred were killed, thousands more injured. Encampments of homeless refugees line all the highways. And here I am, worried about trivial things like lost money and a single drunken indiscretion. I tell myself to keep my problems in perspective.

El Salvador's American embassy is a sprawling cross between a campus and a fortress—larger than any of the Salvadoran government's own buildings and enclosed by a three-story concrete wall. It's located to the west of the city, and there are rumors that it was built atop an old Mayan temple, that thousands of artifacts were uncovered and disposed of during its construction.

I find street parking on a nearby block, gather my purse, and lock the car.

The line has already formed. Each day, thousands of Salvadorans queue up for their visa interviews—a three-minute ordeal in which someone from the lowest tier of State Department underlings examines their bank balances, asks a few questions in passable Spanish, crushes their dreams, and calls in the next applicant.

Armed Wackenhut security guards watch the embassy's

perimeter. I approach the closest one and say, "Excuse me. I have an appointment with—"

"There's the line," he shoots back.

"No, you don't understand." I try to show him my slip of paper with Elaine's name and number. "I spoke to her on the phone."

He looks away, as if our exchange is over, as if my taxes don't pay his salary.

I extend the paper toward his face. He puts both hands upon his shotgun.

"The line!" he shouts.

"I'm not here for a visa!" But I've given up on him already. I walk off to find someone more accommodating.

At the next corner, I approach a slightly kinder-looking guard.

"Excuse me." I hold out the paper. "I need to get inside. I have an appointment."

"The line." He points with his lips, careful not to make eye contact.

"You don't understand."

"Go get in line."

He points with his finger this time, as if I've not seen the long worm of humanity inching its way forward and extending for several city blocks. In spite of myself, I turn and look in the direction of his hand gestures. I suddenly feel at one with all those people—having lost my home and livelihood in the earthquake, lacking the documentation required to enter Fortress America. Could it be that I'm the one who's wrong? Is the line where I belong?

"I don't need a visa," I say, snapping out of it. "I'm an American citizen."

"You don't look American," he says.

"I'm Asian-American."

He stares at me as if I've invented the term. "Passport?"

"I lost it; that's why I'm here." I take out the other documents I've brought: my Hawai'i driver's license, a copy of my Social Security card, the ID that the Peace Corps issued me but which did little good.

Finally, he sighs and presses a button on the radio strapped to his chest.

While the Wackenhut speaks in a color/number code, I look out at the visa line again. There—not for fortune, not for grace, not even for race—but for a few official documents go I.

The guard gives a version of my story to whoever listens on the other end. He describes me as a "Hawaiian-Oriental type of lady"—as if those labels disqualify me as authentically American.

"Her name?" The voice comes back over the radio.

I give my full name. The guard struggles to pronounce it.

The voice crackles on the radio. "Send her in."

I'm sent through a metal detector and directed to American Citizen Services. In the waiting room, I'm given a number and shown a seat. After several minutes, the woman I spoke to on the phone the day before, Elaine, comes and finds me. She shows me into a white-walled, windowless room lit by fluorescent tubes. We sit at either end of a table. I'm a little concerned that the wire in my sandal might scrape the nice floor. On the wall behind Elaine hangs a series of corny patriotic photos in frames: Mount Rushmore, the Washington, D.C., skyline, a screeching bald eagle.

"All right, fill this out." She hands me a clipboard with a form several pages long. "What do you have for documentation?"

I show her the same cards and papers that I showed the guard outside. She chuckles at my Che wallet.

"Let me make a copy of these." She leaves the room.

I spend some time alone with the form, the clipboard, and a pen bearing the State Department seal. What should I put down as my address? I've used the Peace Corps office for so long. I can't even remember my father's street number in Honolulu. What is the mailing address for La Posada?

Elaine reenters the room a few minutes later. Her heels click hard against the tile floor.

"So you're a Peace Corps volunteer?" she asks.

"I was," I say.

"Good for you. I served in Tonga, years ago."

The idea of Peace Corps volunteers in Tonga sounds funny to me. I knew lots of Tongans growing up. But I nod and smile, feigning interest, doing my best to establish some sort of rapport.

"Did you just close your service?" she asks.

"ET'd, actually." It's the first time I've uttered the Peace Corps code for quitting.

"Oh." Elaine doesn't seem to know how to respond. "I'm sorry."

"You shouldn't be sorry," I say. "It made sense. The project I was working on, it was destroyed by the earthquake. I had only a few months left. The handwriting was on the wall, you know."

She nods. "And now what?"

"Surfing," I say.

"Right." She raises my driver's license to study it. "You're from Hawai'i, aren't you?"

"My boyfriend and I planned to go to South America. We hoped to spend a year or so."

"That sounds wonderful."

I nod. "The trip of a lifetime. But we were robbed the night before last. Now, I'm not sure we'll make it."

Neither of us speaks. I drop the pen on the table and the sound echoes like thunder.

"So." I try not to come off as desperate. "How long do you think this will take?"

"This paperwork has to be sent to Washington for processing, and then the passport must be shipped back. It could be a while. And as you know, the embassy has other priorities at the moment."

I study the screeching eagle in the photo behind her. "Can I ask you something?"

"Of course."

"Is it exciting to be working here right now, with the earthquake and all? Do you enjoy it?"

She sighs. "It's less boring than my last post; that's for sure. But it's frustrating as well. And stressful. There's more at stake, I suppose, more chance for success and for failure."

"Right." It seems a stupid question almost as soon as I've asked it. "Remember what you told me yesterday, about the emergency passport to fly back home?"

"Yes." She looks puzzled. "The one-month option. The one that you weren't interested in?"

"Out of curiosity, how long would one of those take to process?"

"Not long. Could be the same day." She cocks her head to one side, perhaps considering whether I'm a quitter at surfing and traveling as much as at Peace Corps work. "Is that something you might want to pursue?"

"Just curious is all." In truth, this is the first time I've seriously considered simply going back to Hawai'i. "I look forward to hearing from you."

"Malia." She says my name sternly as I rise to leave. "I'm sure you'll get to South America someday."

Outside the embassy's tall white walls, I pause and stare at the visa line. It isn't hard to imagine a Mayan temple standing on this spot. An entire caste of disposable laborers already lines up. Well-fed guards stand over them, looking superior. And the high priests are hidden somewhere inside, along with their cryptic means of receiving orders from their far-off gods.

I try, with a strain like a mental push-up, to put myself in the place of those poor Salvadorans in the line, to appreciate the couple hundred dollars I have left, the car, the father in the States who could send me more money—if I could only bring myself to ask. I could even walk back inside the embassy, opt for the temporary permission, and return to the United States within the week.

Back at the Jeep, the clock on the dashboard shows that it's still early. I don't feel like returning to La Lib just yet, to pass another waveless day waiting for my future to start. Without deciding to, I find myself crossing town. Traffic is light at this time of the morning. Within a few minutes, I come to the familiar stretch of Boulevard de los Heroes and find a parking spot in Metrocentro's ample lot.

Across the boulevard, inside the Hotel Intercontinental, I buy Ben the rolling tobacco he didn't ask for. I walk up a nearby side street into a residential neighborhood. It's a place I've been to only one other time—the night before last. My feet seem to find it on instinct, by sense of smell. Soon enough, I'm standing at the front gate of Alex's apartment.

But why? I regret what happened between us two nights ago. I truly do. Still, Alex has been a big part of my life here. I need to close this chapter in a satisfying way, not with a hurried hungover exit.

Also, one part of me wants to know what he meant about my staying here, and about the job that he wanted to offer me last week. Even if my mind is made up, even if I have chosen Ben and our epic trip, I should at least know what that decision means, what my options are, or were.

Too nervous to ring the bell, I stand outside for a span of several minutes. I break open the sack of Dutch tobacco meant as a gift for Ben. With shaking hands, I roll a too-loose, too-damp cigarette and smoke it there on the sidewalk. The sound of a high-pitched pan flute startles me. The flutist turns out to be a man with a mobile knife-sharpening cart. He rolls past and stares, curious as to what I'm doing here, whom I'm waiting for.

Finally, light-headed from the tobacco and an empty stomach, I ring the buzzer beside Alex's name.

"¿Quien es?" I hear through the intercom.

"Alex? It's me, Malia."

There's a pause. "Hold on a second. I'm coming down."

Though it's late morning, Alex looks as though he's just awakened—which shouldn't be a shock, considering his schedule.

"You want to come up?" he manages to say.

"Yeah."

He's already made a pot of coffee, so we spend the first few minutes fussing over spoons and cups and milk and sugar. Alex wears only the sweatpant shorts he's slept in. The scars along his arms are visible but look less striking to me now.

"So," I say once both of us have our coffees and are seated—me on the bed, Alex on the single plastic chair at his multipurpose table. "No work today?"

He shrugs. "We're trying to rotate our days off throughout the week, so services don't dry up on Saturday and Sunday. I've been spending a lot of nights in Zacatecoluca."

"Do you like it?" I ask.

"Zacatecoluca?"

"No, the job. The lifestyle."

He looks into his coffee mug. "I don't stop to think about whether or not I like it very often. But I suppose that I do, yes. It's busy, you know. The work is valued."

"That's good. You seem happier now, compared to before." I catch myself staring at his forearms and will my eyes back to his face. "At first, when they sent you back down here from D.C., I was a little outraged."

He brings his coffee mug up to his lips and holds it there.

"I didn't think it was responsible to send somebody in your . . . your condition straight back after a few weeks of therapy."

"Maybe they shouldn't have." Alex lowers the cup and forces a smile.

"But now it seems like a perfect fit."

"I suppose that's true." His eyebrows rise. "My 'condition' is probably best described as depression."

It's the first time I've heard him use that word.

"The doctors, they see it differently from the way I do. But I've always felt that at the heart of it was an inability to pretend."

He pauses and looks about the room, as if the words he wants are written on the walls or ceiling.

"To pretend what?" I ask.

"Ever since I was a teenager, I've seen everything in life as a sort of slow, senseless withering toward death. People who are happier than I am—at least it feels this way—are able to pretend that's not the case, or maybe they forget or ignore it long enough to function."

I'm not sure what to say to that. His tone is calm and measured.

"With the job I have now, I don't feel I have to pretend anymore. The fallen villages and the refugee camps, they're exactly what I believed the human condition to be all along. It's as if some sort of veil or tinted glass is finally removed from my vision—some layer of distortion that I always knew was there. Don't get me wrong: It's nice to bring food, and medicine, and clothing. But honestly, I feel like my real job is simply to witness it all. To confirm that this is the state of the world. To ignore nothing, and deny nothing."

And in that instant, his Red Cross job seems as selfish and indulgent as surfing. "I'm glad that works for you."

"The more I think about it, the more I'm convinced that some of our ideas behind development and aid are flawed. It's sort of a twentieth-century construct that we do good works as a means to an end. Before that, people did them as charity, as penance. It was a way to get into heaven, or to gain enlightenment. It was about you, the giver, not about the receiving end. I'm not sure we've adapted so well to the secular, results-oriented version."

"Maybe not." Some of what he says rings true, but I'm in no mood for his philosophical musings.

He smiles and puts his coffee cup down on the table. "It's good to see you, Malia. I didn't want our final good-bye to be that morning a couple days ago."

"Neither did I." My stomach feels dry and cavernous.

Alex refreshes both our coffees.

"Do you remember what you said at the Peace Corps office last week?" I ask.

"I said good-bye." He puts the now-empty coffeepot on the table.

"Before that. You mentioned that the Red Cross needs engineers. That I'd be perfect for the job. That was why you came looking for me, right?" I take a sip from the warm cup.

"I guess I remember saying something like that."

"Is it still an option?" My question comes out sheepishly. I try to picture it. Could I do relief work long enough to cash up for both Ben and me? How many months might that take?

"A job? For you?" He looks surprised. "Not exactly. I mean, we've gotten a lot of people in place since then."

"A lot of engineers? People who speak the language? Who have experience in the sort of water systems that were crushed?" My voice turns loud and defensive.

"Look." He holds his palms up, as if to say, *Don't shoot.* "Something could come along; that's always a possibility. But things are different now."

"It was like five days ago you told me this."

"That morning at the office, I tried to find you because of a rumor that you were about to terminate your service. I was convinced I could sort out a situation for you like mine— working with the Red Cross for a few months until your service was up, then come aboard officially."

"So, why not come aboard now?"

"Because you quit, Malia!"

I don't have a response for him.

In a lower tone, he continues: "It doesn't mean anything to me—two or three months, one acronym instead of another— but the bosses take that stuff seriously."

Whether or not this is true, it makes me feel small.

"What's all this about anyway? Aren't you going to South America? What happened to your trip?"

I let out a deep breath and look at the floor. "I lost my passport, and all our money. That night I spent here with you, somebody broke into our hotel room and ripped us off." I emphasize the *here* and the *you,* hoping he might see this as his problem, too.

"Fuck." Alex winces and bares his teeth. "I'm sorry. Have you been to the embassy?"

"Of course. They're working on it, but it could take weeks."

"So this job is, what, the consolation prize or something?"

"It's not like that." I have no patience for his judgment. "I want to know what my options are. You offered me something once, not so long ago. I came to see if the offer was still good."

He looks down at the floor and sighs. "I don't think that's the right attitude for this sort of work, to be honest."

"What attitude?"

"You know, a plan B kind of thing. You need to be committed for this relief stuff."

"Don't lecture me, Alex." After all, he was the one who spent nearly two years getting sick, hardly working at all.

His face goes blank. He's clearly content with his moral high ground. That one squiggly vein along his temple throbs.

"Well." I stand up. "I guess this is good-bye."

"Good-bye, Malia." We share an insincere embrace. As I leave his apartment, I realize that this is, in fact, a worse farewell than the hungover walk of shame I performed two days prior.

At the Pollo Campero in Metrocentro, I use a big chunk of my remaining money to buy two boxes of fried chicken.

On the way out of the neighborhood, I get stuck in an awful traffic jam. The Jeep inches along the Boulevard of Heroes for over an hour, avoiding vendors, beggars, and clowns. A window-washer boy practically throws himself under the wheels before I hand over a coin. All the papers feature the Monkey-Faced Baby above the fold. The needle on the gas gauge leans dangerously toward empty. I feel something like a nervous breakdown creeping its way up my spine. Is there an eject button I could press to launch me high above this car and this country and parachute me someplace safer? If I took a razor to my own forearms, might I wake up in a hospital bed, with concerned professionals hovering about, a passport, an important job, and an apartment in the city? What might it take to finally get something like that—a sense of purpose?

The traffic untangles, and I find a gas station on the outskirts of the city. I fill up the tank and buy a six-pack. It's almost noon. I still don't feel any desire to return to La Lib. Instead, I head down a less-traveled route south of the city, through Los Planes de Renderos, past Panchimalco. Two beers later, I find myself on the old, familiar road to Cara Sucia.

The village looks quiet, as though the residents are all busy working. I wonder if I'm the only one in this country with nothing to do all day long. I park alongside Niña Tere's house, hide the other beers under the passenger seat, and take out one of the boxes of fried chicken.

"Niña Tere?" I call out at the doorless entrance to her house. Rambo barks and howls from inside. Has he already forgotten my scent and come to think of me as a stranger?

"¿Sí?" she calls back from the kitchen.

"It's me: Malia. I came to visit you."

"Come in! Sit down!" She emerges from the kitchen and finds a rag to dry her wet hands.

"I brought Campero," I say.

We go inside and take seats at the wooden table with the red oilcloth.

"I thought you'd be gone by now," she says. "Down in South America or someplace."

"Soon," I say. "Not quite yet. There's been a little problem with my passport. But I'll sort it out."

She is back out of her seat, fetching us plates and utensils, reheating some of this morning's tortillas in the kitchen. I smell beans boiling over a wood fire and realize I'd rather have her home cooking than the fried chicken.

"How are you, Niña Tere?" I ask.

"You know—fighting for our beans, like always." She drops a plastic plate and a fork in front of my place and hers.

"Right." I bite into a drumstick. Grease soaks my fingertips and the sides of my mouth. I swallow the first bite and ask, "Where's Nora?"

"School." Niña Tere uses her lips to point back in the direction I've just come from.

I take a visual inventory of this house, where I spent so much of my time in the past two years. This table is not only where we ate our meals but where Niña Tere showed me how to make tamales and *pupusas*. There's a spot out back where we roasted cashews from the trees in her little parcel down the valley, the cistern where we all washed our clothes. The level of the water is low, and the cistern itself is partially covered by a sheet of corrugated metal. Above it, a single pipe with a water tap stands erect, like a rigid cobra waiting to strike. It was the responsibility of each householder to run the pipe from the street to his or her house. Many had already done so before the earthquake hit.

"How's the water situation?" I reach into the box for a thigh.

"Bad as ever." Niña Tere tosses her chicken bones at Rambo, who catches them midair, chews, and swallows. "We've been washing in Santa Cruz. The mayor sends a truck every so often; they fill a barrel or two for each family."

I follow suit with the bones—tossing them to Rambo, who stands at attention by our table—and recall the burden of living here during the dry season.

"They say there's a lot of money coming into El Salvador these days," I tell her. "Other countries are donating. Maybe they'll finish the project."

"Maybe." She sighs. "Until then, we'll keep on as usual."

"Niña Tere." I put my chicken down. "Are you upset with me for leaving when I did? For not staying to fix the aqueduct?"

"Upset with you?" She covers her mouth and laughs. "Don't be ridiculous, child. What could you have done? Reversed the earthquake?"

"I didn't want to, you know, to abandon the community."

"Abandon nothing! You spent two years with us. And for what? You didn't need the water. You have a house in Hawai'i with water that runs hot and cold, do you not?"

"That's true," I admit.

"The community was lucky to have you."

From outside the house comes the sound of a southbound bus. The *cobrador* calls out a destination and rattles his coins. Rambo abandons his post at the side of our table and barks his way toward the entrance.

"Nora!" Niña Tere calls out before she's even turned the corner. "Look who's here."

"Niña Malia!" Nora rushes in and hugs me where I sit. In

her starchy school uniform and backpack, she presses her cheek against my shoulder.

I struggle to return the embrace without getting chicken grease all over the white of her blouse. Rambo paces anxious circles around the dirt floor.

"Run and change your clothes," Niña Tere orders. "Then come and have some chicken."

Nora does as she's told.

"She looks even bigger than last time," I say.

"That one." Niña Tere rolls her eyes. "She grows each day. I fear she'll be taller than you even."

Nora emerges from the bedroom in her normal clothes: a plain green skirt, a secondhand American T-shirt—I'M A TOYS-"R"-US KID! written across the front—and rubber sandals. Niña Tere fetches her a plate and utensils. I pick up one of the retoasted tortillas, blistered black from its second turn on the *comal*.

"Niña Malia, have you come back to stay?" Nora asks.

Her question is innocent enough, but it rips open a gaping hole inside my gut, despite the big greasy meal.

"No, Nora," I say. "I've come here to visit one last time before I go."

"You're still going to South America?"

I pause for a few seconds. "That's right." I nearly add "Someday," the way that Elaine had hours earlier.

"Be careful," she says.

"I will."

Niña Tere rejoins us. "Isn't this nice? Niña Malia brought you Campero."

"Yes." Nora's fingers shine with the oil from the chicken. "But I'd rather she stayed here for good."

Once again, this is likely the last time I'll be inside this house, the last meal I'll ever eat here. There will be no plaque or framed diploma to commemorate my exit. It'll be as simple as walking away.

Though there is plenty more chicken in the box, we all stop eating. After a minute or so without conversation, Niña Tere finally says, "What heat, no?"

"What heat," I repeat, taking the weather talk as a sign. I let out a long breath and say, "Well, it's time for me to go."

"So soon!" Niña Tere feigns surprise and starts to pack up the chicken box.

"You keep that," I say.

"Are you sure?"

"Absolutely." I stand, and they do the same. Nora hugs me around the waist, the way those unfamiliar children did during the earthquake. Niña Tere pats my shoulder.

"Take care of yourself," she says.

We repeat our good-byes, while Rambo whines nervously in the background.

A local farmer, Don Chavelo, walks uphill as I exit. We exchange a little wave. He looks confused at the sight of me. I turn the key in the ignition and stare at the other houses in Cara Sucia. Across the street, Felix's cross still stands in the courtyard, though the flowers upon it are now all brown and withered. I consider going over and offering my condolences to his grandmother, telling her good-bye, but I can't quite make the walk.

For nearly two years, my subconscious prophecy about leaving this place involved triumph, running water in every house. Somehow, I can't settle for less. Whether or not it's my fault, this alternative feels too much like failure.

As I leave town, I see other men I once ordered around in

the hills not far from here, while they built what I thought of then as my life's work. I see my hubris and helplessness measured out in several more worthless water taps hovering above empty cisterns.

And while I do feel personal disappointment as I drive out of Cara Sucia, I can't convince myself that it makes much difference. My project wouldn't have resurrected this fallen country. It would have offered only a small measure of comfort to one tiny village within a badly broken nation. More than anything, it was a way to convince myself that—for a little while—I wasn't making things worse.

19

Ben swings in the hammock outside our room, a Salvadoran newspaper on his lap.

"Want some chicken?" I climb out of the car and set the second box on the hood.

Ben stands. "That took a while." His voice is studded with suspicion.

"I went by Cara Sucia on the way back." I remind myself that this is nothing to be ashamed of. "How are the waves?"

Ben gives a thumbs-down, then reaches for the Campero box.

"I got you this." I take the rolling tobacco out of my purse and place it on the hood.

"Thanks." Hands full of chicken, Ben lets the pouch lie there.

"Any news from Peseta?" I ask.

"Yeah. Somebody put newspaper between Crackito's toes while he was asleep on the seawall, then lit it on fire and ran away. Poor kid woke up with burning feet and fell down onto the rocks." Ben manages to suppress a chuckle at the cruel prank. He takes a bite.

"I meant about my passport." I pick up the tobacco and roll a cigarette, hoping Ben won't notice that the pouch has already been opened.

"No." He covers his full mouth with a hand. "Haven't heard anything about that."

I find a plastic lighter on the windowsill and light up.

"You don't want any chicken?" Ben sits back down in the hammock.

"I already ate."

A flush sounds from the shared toilets. Pelochucho emerges from one of the stalls, both his eye patch and his big sunglasses on, that same faded surf magazine tucked under one arm. "Do I smell Campero?"

"Help yourself." I gesture toward the box.

"So, Chinita." Without washing his hands, Pelo takes out a drumstick and bites into it. "We need to talk."

"Let me guess," I say. "You're broke."

"There is a sense in which that's true." Pelo holds the chicken leg before his mouth like a microphone. "You know, during Donald Trump's divorce, he went walking with his daughter in Manhattan and they passed this homeless man. Trump whispered into the little girl's ear, 'Sweetie, that man has ten billion dollars more than Daddy does.'"

"Is this a parable or something?" I ask.

"Because of all the debt, you know. But who would you want to switch places with?" Pelo takes a bite of chicken. He looks back and forth between Ben and me, perhaps worried that we might choose the homeless man.

"The point is"—Pelo waves his free hand in a circle, erasing the story from an imaginary blackboard—"in this day and age, it's not about how much money you have, but about how nimbly you can move that money through space and time."

"Pelo, no offense," I say, "but what does this have to do with us?"

"I went online today," he says. "I've got some investors who sound interested in the surf resort. A while back, I sent out a few queries—mostly to be polite to some guys I know, returning favors and whatnot. I never expected to have help."

"Congratulations," I say. "Please be careful. And when did you start calling it a resort?"

"I told them about your concerns. They're not trying to cut corners. They want to do this right." He points his now nearly meatless chicken bone at me. "They're interested in you, Chinita."

I shrug. "Interested?"

"It would be a consulting position. You could come up with your own title—environmental engineer or sustainable development officer—whatever's best for your résumé."

"Have you lost your mind?"

"This would not be like before." Pelo lets the bone hang limp between his fingers. "You'd be an expert, not a gofer. No stupid errands, nothing like that. And I wouldn't be the one paying you. Your contract would be through the LLC we're setting up. I want to call it SalvaCorp. What kind of salary are you thinking? Does a grand a week sound okay?"

"Wait." I'm confused. "So I'd consult on this thing, but who'd have the final say? I mean, if my input is 'Don't build on that hillside,' will your people listen?"

"They want to do it like you said the other night—with the walls and the gutters and the planted hillside and everything."

Both Ben and Pelo stare at me, anxious for a response.

"Hold on a minute." I take a seat beside Ben in the hammock and slow my thoughts. "What's the time line here? We're trying to go on a trip."

"No worries." Pelochucho looks inside the chicken box. "We could write this arrangement up for something like a six- to eight-week commitment, then go month to month after that. And once you leave, we can stay in touch through e-mail or phone. Hell, if there's anything that's super important, we'll fly you in from Chile or Peru or wherever. That's a no-brainer."

Ben and I steal a glance at each other. He raises his eyebrows.

"I'd like to get your input on some other possibilities, too. Have you seen this?" Pelo takes that same old surf magazine out from under his arm and waves it at us. "I want a piece of this Wild East thing. Do you two know anything about boats?"

"No," I reply before Ben has a chance to. "El Cuco—the Wild East or whatever—it's different." Ben and I took a hitchhiking expedition out there last Semana Santa. We camped right at the base of one of the points and paid a local family for our meals and water. "There's not much there."

"There's waves." Pelo pulls out a chicken breast, takes one bite out of it, then throws it back into the box. "That's good enough for me."

"It's far away. From everything. They've got serious squatters' rights laws in this country, you know."

"We'd have to hire a caretaker. Are you guys sure you don't

have any capital you want to put into this?" He points at the magazine.

"Pelo, that issue is like six months old."

"Exactly. From before the quake, right? It's a buyer's market— now more than ever."

"People lost their homes," I say. "People died. Can you think of anything else besides how desperate they might be to sell their land?"

"Again with the high-and-mighty routine." He rolls his one good eye. "You gotta understand, Chinita: Surfing is the new golf. And you can't build a point break in Palm fucking Springs. This is happening. You can watch from the sidelines or get into the game."

Ben stays silent, still seated in the hammock.

"Shit. I'm not as bad as some of the players," Pelo mutters. "Have you heard about that Florida kid down in Nicaragua? Dude was dynamiting the reef to give the waves better shape."

Ben speaks up at last. "Guys, could we maybe stick to the K Ninety-nine thing? That's all that's really on the table right now, isn't it?"

"Absolutely!" Pelo puts the magazine down on the hood of the Jeep. "As usual, Chuck Norris is the voice of reason. The K Ninety-nine surf resort is a green light. Everything else is pie in the sky."

Both of them turn their eyes toward me.

"What do you say, Chinita?" Pelo takes his bit-into chicken breast back out of the box. He rips off a piece of white meat and sticks it inside his mouth. "Hang around. Make a little jing. Wait for your passport. Hold that hillside together for future generations. Give some free rainwater to some poor families. It's a good deal."

The two of them stare at me, waiting. Working for Pelo got

us into this mess. Ben might not see it that way, but staying here to help him out was where things started to go wrong, the original mistake from which all our other mistakes sprang.

"I don't know," I say. "It doesn't feel right."

Ben lets out an exasperated sigh. "I need a beer." He walks off toward the kitchen, flip-flops slapping extra hard against the ground.

"I'm not into the whole high-end surf tourism thing." I mean the explanation for Ben, but Pelochucho is the only one left to hear it.

Pelo takes a step closer to me. He raises his sunglasses up so that his one good eye and his cloth eye patch are both exposed. Once Ben is out of earshot, Pelo lowers his voice and says, "Chinita, who is Alex?"

I look up. My tongue turns dry and thick inside my mouth. "He's my ex-boyfriend."

"Oh yeah." Pelo giggles. "Little blast from the past, huh?"

I hear the top pop off a bottle. Across the courtyard, Ben stands by the kitchen. He lifts the full Regia to his lips and takes the first big gulp.

"What are you talking about?"

"Your phone call yesterday. I happened to be in Kristy's bedroom at the time."

I look over his shoulder. Always empty during waking hours, Kristy's tiny bedroom is alongside the office, a few feet from where I stood speaking into the phone.

"Nothing happened," I say.

Pelo puts a hand up over his mouth. "You got drunk and fucked this guy. You didn't tell Ben." He squints. "Nothing?"

Over by the kitchen, Ben wipes his lips with his forearm, then starts back toward us.

"Why are you saying this?" I ask Pelo in a whisper.

"I want your help with this resort thing; that's all. It's a good option—for all of us. I'm happy to keep a secret, for a friend. I'm less inclined to do that for somebody who turns her nose up at all my ideas."

Furious, I stare into his one good eye. He takes a couple steps backward as Ben approaches.

"So," Ben says. "What do we do now?"

Pelo lowers his shades. A second of tense silence passes.

"I'm in." I keep my eyes on the reflective surface of Pelochucho's sunglasses. "I can commit to three weeks for now—that should be time enough to get my passport. We can go week by week after that."

"Yes!" Pelochucho holds his fists up in triumph. He high-fives Ben and me.

I feel decent for a moment or two. Perhaps I can engineer my way out of the errors of the past couple days. I can salvage our budget and rescue our trip. Maybe I can finally save one little corner of El Salvador, too, resurrect a single eroding hillside in a nation densely packed with them. It's no Red Cross, but it's something. Still, I loathe the idea of working for Pelochucho and his investor friends.

"All right." Pelo grins. "I'll get back online and see what we can hammer out. We should know the details by tomorrow."

"I'm going to check the surf," I say.

Still in my embassy clothes, I walk out to the shore and sit on the stone steps. There isn't much to see. The ocean is blown out, no inkling of a swell. Two stray dogs—one white and one dark brown—wade out into the water as if to bathe.

Once I finally turn away from the ocean, I see Crackito limping toward me.

"*Una moneda?*" He holds out his hand and looks as if he doesn't remember me.

The rumors about the burning-foot prank are true. His face bears scratches and a bruise. Black spots and a single red blister cover the favored foot.

First, I think about the spare pieces of cold chicken back at the hotel. But after a second, I reach into my pocket and pull out a handful of coins. For once, I don't care what he does with them.

Before Crackito can take off, Ben comes to join us.

"Do you see that?" he asks Crackito in Spanish.

"See what?"

"Blowfish, right there." Ben points. "On the beach."

Both Crackito and I scan the shoreline. Finally, I see it: a bloated purple fish with short, sharp spines extended, lying among the shells and seaweed at the tide line.

"C'mon," Ben says to Crackito. "Let's throw rocks at it."

The boy hesitates for a second, the coins in his pocket pulling him to that white-and-red house up the street.

"C'mon!" Ben insists.

The two of them go down to the beach. Ben uses his foot to draw a couple of lines in the sand. He picks up the swollen fish by the tail, drops it behind one of the lines. Both of them gather a handful of smooth black rocks.

I see Peseta making his rounds on the street near our hotel. I turn and whistle, make a motion for him to come closer.

He pauses, perhaps still weary of me after our late-night encounter at the crack house. But in the end, he walks over, his too-big sandals shuffling against the pavement.

"Chinita," he says. "What's shaking?"

Ben and Crackito begin their game. The two of them take

turns chucking rocks from behind their baseline at the blow-fish several yards away. Crackito has a furious pitcher-on-the-mound-style windup. Ben's is a smooth and casual underarm throw. The two wet dogs come out of the water and watch, excited by the flying stones. They wag their tails and bark at the impacts.

"You still have that doctor friend?" I ask Peseta.

"Of course," he says. "You need something?"

"Valium." I take a bill from out of my Che wallet and hand it to him. "Can you bring it to La Posada?" I can't handle another sleepless night.

"No problem." Peseta puts the money inside his fist and takes off down the street.

A squishing sound comes from the beach. Crackito giggles in triumph. Ben claps and offers his congratulations, raises the little boy's hand up in the air like a prizefighter's. It's the first time I've ever seen Crackito smile. It makes him look exactly like the child that he is.

Pelochucho disappears for the rest of the afternoon. We guess that he's either at the Internet café or the telephone office.

Peseta never shows up with my Valium. I struggle to get to sleep, while Ben snores at my side. In my mind, I curse Peseta for ripping me off, and berate myself for being gullible enough to trust him.

While I lay awake, my mind spins on a whole separate wheel. Is there any way out of working for Pelo on this ridiculous resort idea? If I bail, he'll tell Ben about my night with Alex, and who knows how Ben might react. But where will it end? Can I trust Pelochucho to let me go once I have some traveling money and a new passport in hand? What's to stop him from further blackmail, from forcing me to stay longer and help develop new properties out in the Wild East?

I roll over and study Ben's sleeping body in the darkness. A part of me wants to shake him awake and confess right then. Maybe he'll be too tired to freak out. So much of the time, I don't mind Ben's jealous streak. It seems a more than forgivable fault. But at the moment, it is utterly inconvenient.

20

It was Courtney who first gave me the news about Alex. She somehow found the number for La Posada.

That was about eight months ago. My aqueduct was in full swing, and I was enjoying a slow weekend at La Lib. Ben and I had made love in the afternoon and he'd fallen asleep. I'd tried to nap as well, but a dream kept waking me: A giant snake, big as a freight train, slithered up beside my sleeping body. I'd lie still and play dead; then the snake would move on. But each time it started on its way, I'd shudder from fear and wake up.

"Chinita." A hesitant knock came at the door. Kristy rarely bothered us in our rooms. I'd heard the telephone ring a few seconds before. It must be important, I thought.

"*Momentito.*" I wrapped a sarong around my torso and tied it behind my back. Ben didn't stir. Outside the room, my eyes constricted against the sun.

Kristy crossed the courtyard. I followed several paces behind.

The phone cord stretched from the office out to the patio in front of Kristy's room. I took the call there.

"*Sí,*" I said, still groggy.

"Malia? Is that you? Are you sitting down?"

"Courtney? What's up?"

"Sit down, Malia."

The only way to get a chair was to put the phone down and fetch one from the dining room—too much trouble. I waited a second, then lied and said I was sitting.

"It's about Alex," she said.

"What about him?"

Outside the gate, Peseta walked by, scanning the street for some sort of action to get into—travelers in search of accommodation, surfers in search of drugs, any brand of honest-enough hustle that might result in a few coins.

"Alex hurt himself," Courtney said.

"Is he all right?" Finally, I woke up; the tragedy reel played through my mind. This was long before the earthquake, so it was informed mainly by images from television and film: hospital rooms with their beeping machines, bent-up car bumpers, swirling red and blue lights.

"They say he'll be okay." She exhaled hard, so that it came through the phone as static. "He lost a lot of blood."

I grew more confused. What exactly had happened to him? Kristy's broom scraped across the floor behind me.

"It's weird, because nobody knows what they can or cannot tell us. But the rumor is that he's got some bad scars."

Peseta passed again, looking impatient.

"Courtney." My heart thumped inside my chest. "I don't understand. What happened?"

"It was some kind of razor knife, apparently."

"Alex got stabbed?" As I pronounced the *a* in *stabbed*, my bedroom door opened across the courtyard. I saw Ben stretch his arms above his head and yawn.

"His wrists, Malia." Courtney spoke as if this should all have been obvious to me by now. "Alex tried to kill himself."

My vision went grainy and out of focus. I put my hand on the wall to keep my balance. "Where?" I asked.

"It happened in his site, but somebody found him."

Ben crossed the courtyard toward me. Our eyes met and his expression turned somber.

"Like I said," Courtney went on, "it's all rumors and speculation right now. But they say a woman there put tourniquets on his arms and called for help."

Doña Carmen. I knew her. In a sense, she was to Alex what Niña Tere was to me. During the war, I'm sure she'd stopped the bleeding of hundreds of hurt guerillas, but this sort of wound was almost certainly new to her.

"Holy fuck," I said.

Ben stood beside me now. He put a hand on my back.

"They're sending him to D.C. tonight. It's a medical evacuation."

"I see." I wanted to get off the phone. "I guess I'll send an e-mail. That's probably the best way to get in touch with him."

"Probably. Like I said, a lot of what I told you is rumors, so don't quote me, okay?"

"Right. Thanks for calling." My legs wobbled as I reached inside the office and hung up the phone.

"What the hell happened?" Ben held his arms out at his sides, as if ready to catch me.

"Alex tried to kill himself."

"Jesus." Ben winced. "He all right?"

I shrugged. "They're sending him to D.C., to see the shrinks and all."

"Chuck Norris!" an obnoxious teenage crackhead known as Marlboro hollered as he walked past. He used two hands to make that in-and-out gesture symbolizing sex—for no discernible reason.

"Let's get some privacy," Ben said. "How about the roof?"

Ben rolled a joint while we sat and watched the sea. The wind had died down and the point looked fun, but I couldn't bring myself even to talk about surfing.

I got much more stoned than was my custom, and tried to figure out what my emotions were, exactly. I'd not looked back since Alex and I broke up. He was a great confidant in training— able to be sarcastic and brutally honest about the Peace Corps. Along with Courtney, the three of us gave one another a break from the relentless optimism and political correctness. I'd always found Alex smart and interesting. He'd been a classics major in college, and was well read—full of references to Shakespeare, mythology, and the Bible.

But as a boyfriend, he'd been a heavy burden. It was hard to read his sentiments and navigate his moods. His awkward good-byes often left me feeling guilty and confused until the next time we saw each other. Socially, he was two-faced. The life of the party one moment—cracking jokes and telling stories. But if he felt the least bit intimidated, he'd retreat into a shy and judgmental shell—not speaking for hours on end. And then there was the fact that he'd cheated on me with that girl who was only here for a heartbeat—something I never forgave him for. We hadn't spoken since.

"Can I ask you something?" Ben studied the nearly spent joint in his hand.

"What?"

"Do you think he'll come back down here?"

I shrugged. "He's got his family right there in D.C. It wouldn't be hard to stay."

"What might be better for him, do you think?"

"I don't know," I said. "Guess it depends on how the therapy goes."

Ben pinched the last of the joint, gave it one more pull, then set it down and left it to burn itself out.

"This would all be easier to handle if we were in the States," I said. "I tried to talk about suicide with Niña Tere after the news about that Estonian chess master who jumped out a window. It was like we couldn't understand each other. She kept thinking he'd fallen or gone crazy. All these Salvadorans who've been through hell—the war, refugee camps, trips through the desert on the way north—it's like killing yourself doesn't even exist in this culture."

"Funny," Ben said. "I feel like this country has made me understand suicide for the first time."

"How's that?" I asked him.

"It helps to compare us to plants."

"Plants?"

"Yeah. Plants have this thing called the root-shoot ratio, which keeps them balanced. If they can't get enough sun or air, they grow more shoots. If they need more soil nutrients, they grow more roots. If there's not enough nutrients to be had, they let part of the roots die, and sort of cauterize them."

"What does this have to do with suicide?"

"You've said yourself that overpopulation is the source of all this country's problems—all humanity's, in a sense. We don't have enough resources, too little light and air. Try to think of people not so much as individuals but as one big organism—a field of grass or something. Then it makes more sense. Killing off some of the new growth gives room to the rest."

In spite of all my mixed emotions, I didn't like to hear Alex spoken of this way. "Human beings aren't fucking grass."

Ben shrugged. "It's not how we prefer to think, that's for sure. We like to see ourselves as wolves out on the frontier or something, not connected to any other species, free to go wherever. Eat what we kill."

The conversation's new direction looked like it might lead us into an argument. I said nothing more.

Months later, a rumor floated around among the Peace Corps volunteers that on the morning of his incident, Alex had spotted a man from his village having sex with a neighbor's goat. The story went that Alex thought of the goat as sort of a favorite animal—one he fed scraps to and watched children play with from his backyard. The man was apparently some cruel drunk coming down from a bender—a man Alex loathed.

It was a story that traveled fast and grew well known. Darkly funny, memorable, and with something of a causal relationship to the suicide, it was perfect. As far as I knew, Alex neither confirmed nor denied it. I was certain it was complete bullshit.

Most likely, he invented the bestiality anecdote while in D.C. He probably didn't lie to the therapists, but the story must have been useful for fending off the curious volunteers

from other countries who wanted to know why he was there—
and could see the scars along his forearms.

At any rate, he came back to El Salvador six weeks later,
joking about the fact that he'd been declared "not a threat to
himself or others" by the psychiatrist, as if that was funny.

21

We sleep in later than usual. I wake and find myself wrapped up in Ben's arms, my body stiff and starting to sweat.

Ben is half-awake as well. Once he feels me stir, he tightens his arms around my torso. We move toward each other until I'm lying on the inside of a tight spoon. Ben's whiskers tickle the side of my neck.

As the sun rises, a few dogs bark, along with the crowing of the odd rooster and other birdsong. One pink ray shoots in from between the louvers and illuminates the dust particles levitating about our bedroom.

Ben speaks in a throaty morning voice. "Malia, we're going to be all right."

I sigh. At that moment, I feel more inclined than ever to tell him about the other night with Alex. I believe he'll forgive me, eventually. But I'm terrified of another confrontation like the one we had in the wake of the robbery. If we get into any sort of fight over this, things might be said that would end the trip for good. Better to tell him, I figure, once we're out on the road—if we can still manage to make that happen. And if I can manage to keep Pelochucho quiet in the meantime.

Ben sits up a little. He leans over and looks me in the eye. "You get that, right? It doesn't matter to me how far we go, or how many months we travel. So long as we're together, it's all worth it."

I lift my head off the pillow and kiss him on the mouth.

He returns my kiss, hard, in a way he hasn't done in days. I inch my way toward him and feel his erection through the sheets. With one hand on my shoulder and another on my hip, he pulls me closer. For a moment, I believe what Ben just said: We will be all right.

Still in a semblance of a spoon position, we grind against each other for another minute. Ben licks his first two fingers, puts them on my hip bone, then walks them inward and down. I spread my knees. Ben breathes into my ear, thrusts his hips forward. I reach between my legs and am just about to guide him inside. Then we hear it.

A piercing beep sounds first. It's followed by the slow rumble of a diesel engine. I sit up straight, afraid that a semi is about to plow into our bedroom. Ben sits up as well.

"What is that?" he asks.

I shrug, then stand and wrap a sarong around myself. Ben fumbles into his board shorts. We open the door and find an enormous flatbed truck backing into the courtyard of La Posada.

The *beep-beep-beep* of its reverse gear makes it hard to hear anything else. Pelochucho stands near the back, giving hand signals to the driver. Kristy watches by the counter, a broom in her hands. Her face can't hide her concern. Did she give Pelo permission for this? What might the owners say, on the off chance they stop by? Surely, Don Adán and his wife would not be pleased to see their establishment turned into a bodega—storing supplies for a competing business.

"What the hell's going on?" Ben shouts into my ear.

"Materials, I guess. For Pelo's hotel."

Once the rear of the truck is only a few short yards away from us, the beeping stops. Two workers step out of the cab and untie the twine from bundles of rebar and stacks of cement bags. It all feels oddly familiar, like an inside-out version of the deliveries that once arrived at my bodega in the hills above Cara Sucia.

"Morning!" Pelochucho shouts once he sees us.

"You're storing stuff here?" I ask.

"Better this than out at the job site, don't you think? Here it's all locked up. We can keep an eye on it."

Ben yawns.

Pelo shows the laborers where to stack the cement. He wants it under the hotel's overhang, which won't be easy.

"Make sure they don't block our car in," Ben says. Nobody but me listens.

"He's probably hoping we'll ferry most of the stuff over in the Jeep," I say. "It takes four-wheel drive to get up that hill."

I go back inside our bedroom and put on a pair of cutoff jeans and a tank top. By the time I emerge, the truck's engine is back on. Ben is in the kitchen with Kristy.

"Congratulations!" Pelo screams over the noise. "You're an

environmental impact consultant." He shoves a stack of still-warm fax pages into my chest. "That's your title, by the way. We want to say we hired one of those. Sign and date the last page, put your Social Security number here, and we'll be good to go."

"You need to give me a little time," I say. The document is at least ten dense pages.

"Some time?" Pelo looks shocked.

Ben returns from the kitchen with two cups of coffee. He hands one to me, then takes a seat in the hammock.

"This is all happening fast, Pelo. Can I read through this? Think it over?"

Behind him, the truck has shut off. Pelo's helpers stack the cement way too high. It's turning into a tower even taller than they are.

"Some time?" Pelo says again. "I mean, sure. We're on a schedule, but okay. I guess."

I nod, open the door to our bedroom, and am about to slip inside.

Pelo keeps talking. "Hey, Norris? Who is Alex?"

"What?" Ben asks.

I turn back around.

"Do you know somebody named Alex?"

"He's a Peace Corps guy who works for the Red Cross now. Malia used to date him." Ben looks over his shoulder and steals a glance at me.

I shrug.

"But he doesn't hang out here. Ever," Ben says. "Why do you ask?"

"No reason." Pelo waves his hand through the air. "I must've heard you guys talking about him or something."

"Give me a second," I say in a stern voice, staring straight at Pelo, "to read this over. Would you do that for me?"

He smiles. "Of course."

"By the way, that stack of cement is getting awful high. You'll need a ladder to undo it."

Pelo turns around. "Shit!" He runs over to his workers and hollers, "Stop! Wait! ¡Muy alto!"

Inside the bedroom, I do my best to give the contract a quick read. Its legalese is just as indecipherable as the document I signed in Jim's office to end my Peace Corps service. At least the money and the time commitment are both what Pelo promised yesterday. I take a deep breath and sign my name.

Back outside, the truck pulls away in a cloud of dust. Ben has taken his coffee up to the roof. I knock on Pelo's door.

He answers it without saying a word.

"Here you go." I hand the contract to him.

"Excellent." He takes it and drops it on his bed. "Listen, we need to get out to Ninety-nine today. Could you run me by the Internet café first?"

I swallow and remind myself that this is what I signed up for, that I'm doing it for Ben and me. That our trip is worth it.

"Let's go," I say.

He smiles, holds up one finger, then steps back into his bedroom. I wait in the doorway while Pelo puts on a collared shirt. On the bed, he pops open a fake-leather briefcase I've not seen before and throws in my contract, along with some other documents.

"Glad we're getting an early start, Chinita." He opens the small drawer inside his night table. "We've got a lot to do today."

From the drawer, he takes out a half-open newspaper envelope—one of the cocaine packets. He dips his room key into the powder and holds a white clump out toward me. "Eye-opener?" he offers.

"No thanks," I say.

Pelo shrugs, then snorts the whole clump up one nostril. A yellowish chunk sticks to his nose hairs. "Okay," he says. "Let's fucking go."

He gives a few last-minute instructions to the men unloading the truck, then climbs into the Jeep's passenger seat. I steer carefully around the big cement stack. At La Posada's gate, I wave to Ben, who's still up on the roof.

We park on the street across from the Internet café. Pelo takes forever inside. Luckily, a woman sells *pupusas* and coffee at a stand nearby. I eat off the Jeep's hood; my coffee balances on a painted star from the New Zealand flag.

"Okay." Pelochucho bursts out of the café, a new manila folder full of paper under his arm. "Let's hit the Western Union, then off to the site."

"Western Union?" I burn my mouth on a last rushed sip of coffee, then climb into the driver's seat.

"That's right." Pelo puts the new documents inside his brief-case. "We're back in business."

I pull up in front of the well-appointed office but don't shut off the engine.

"This won't take long," he says.

Western Union recently dethroned a local service called Gigante Express as the preferred method for sending *remesas* from the States to El Salvador. Niña Tere uses the one in the capital often. I wonder what Pelo is getting cash for. More materials? Maybe he'll give me an advance against my first paycheck.

After a few minutes, he emerges from the office with his sunglasses down, the briefcase in his hand. He looks suspiciously up the street in either direction, then climbs inside.

"Let's roll."

I drive out of town. Pelo pulls a one-hitter from his pocket and packs it with some of his potent weed. "I'm sorry about that Alex comment." He lets the words out along with his first puff of pot smoke. "I don't feel great about leveraging that eavesdrop. But what can I say?" He pauses for another hit. "I'm just a born deal-maker."

He passes the still-smoldering pipe in my direction. I wave it off.

"The swell will probably be here by tomorrow. You'll get some good waves, maybe a few barrels, and this resort will practically build itself."

At the turnoff, I throw the Jeep into four-wheel drive and head uphill. Through the bumps and potholes, I maintain speed.

"Careful!" Pelo shouts as we near the top. By less than a meter, I manage to avoid driving straight into a gigantic hole in the center of the small hamlet, where we'd originally met with Don Miguel.

"Jesus," I say. "Did a bomb go off here?"

"The pool, dude." Pelo raises his sunglasses and stares into the hole. Three shirtless Salvadoran teenagers stand inside of it, swinging shovels and picks, chipping away at each of its sides.

"You can park over there, behind their truck."

I pull up in back of an old Toyota pickup, the only other vehicle around. Pelo puts his pipe and lighter into the glove compartment, checks the vanity mirror, and straightens out his eye patch.

"Let's do some work," he says.

The second we step out of the car, we're swarmed by the remaining members of the community. Half a dozen women take the lead, men and children behind them. Several hold up pieces of paper and all fight for Pelochucho's attention.

"¡Tranquilo!" Pelo waves his hands and shouts at them. He turns to me. "Chinita, I'll need you to translate."

I nod. "Go ahead."

"Please," he says. "Let's do this in an orderly fashion. Can we find a spot in the shade and sort all this out one by one?"

I do my best to translate.

An older woman whom I recognize from our last visit tugs at my arm. "We can use my house."

She leads us toward a series of adobe walls that no longer have a roof. A blue tarp is strung over the top, with help from a nearby tree, and shades the inside. Pelo and I take a seat around what appears to be the same table we sat at with Don Miguel.

"What's going on here?" I ask Pelo.

"I'm solving the problem with the hillside." He places his briefcase on the table and pops it open. "You'll like this."

The owner of the house introduces herself as Niña Gloria and sits at the table with her teenage daughter. The other families wait by the entrance to the room.

"She has her deed?" Pelo asks me, pointing to a plastic folder full of notarized papers held tight to her chest.

Not knowing the Spanish word for deed, I ask about her "housing documents." She smiles and hands them over. Pelo pushes his index finger around the lines of text, clicking his tongue inside his mouth. He then fishes a fresher document from his open briefcase.

I make out the title at the very top; it's in Spanish and means "Letter of Intention." There are several blanks throughout the main body of the text. Pelo takes a pen from his case and proceeds to copy a few names and numbers from the deed into his letter.

"Okay." He looks up. Sweat has beaded along his brow. "Tell her to look this over and check if everything is correct." He passes the paper to Niña Gloria. I relate his instructions. She holds it up to her eyes, but it's obvious she can't read. She hands the paper to her teenage daughter.

From his briefcase, Pelo produces an envelope full of hundred-dollar bills. He counts them out on the table. Niña Gloria stares wide-eyed at the currency.

"Jesus." Pelo wipes his forehead with the back of his hand. "We had to do this on the hottest fucking day of the year."

"What are we doing, exactly?" I ask.

He snaps a rubber band around what looks like a thousand dollars. "I talked to the guys at SalvaCorp about your issues with the hillside." He counts out another stack. "They got squeamish. Then somebody suggested we just buy up the whole hamlet. Move our buildings back—and upward. We'll have the kitchen and dining room on the lower floors. But the suites up top will still get the ocean view."

My first thoughts are all about engineering. I steal a look out the door, at the line of sight toward the ocean. It would work, more or less. The ground is level here at the top. Then I become human again. "You can't just displace this whole community."

Pelo dribbles air out of his lips. "Is that a joke? They're dying to sell. They're living under fucking tarps. The earthquake did most of the displacing for me."

The mother and daughter at the far end of the table sign the paper and pass it to Pelo. He smiles and hands them the stack of bills. "*Gracias.*"

I pick up the letter and have a look. "Is this even legal?" It's one single-spaced page. Niña Gloria and her daughter rise and exit.

"Legal enough." Pelo shrugs. "A lawyer friend drew it up with speed in mind. Your tip about the squatters' rights laws, that was a big help. Truth is, if they take the money and go now, and we build on this land, it'll be ours either way."

"That's not what I meant about those laws."

"*¡Próximo!*" Pelo hollers at the small crowd outside.

A younger couple enters, the man with a roll of papers cupped in his hand, the woman with a baby on her hip. Pelo smiles and extends another of his letters toward them. This time, he simply points at the blanks that need filling—perhaps guessing they are more literate, perhaps already bored with that part of the task.

"What are you paying them?" My voice quivers as I ask the question. "Like one or two fucking grand?"

He loses count of the bills and sighs, checks to see if the two understand. "Look here, Chinita. Every house, every road, every building that's ever been built in the Americas—in Hawai'i, too, for that matter—has pushed out somebody who was there first. You want all that to stop now? With me?" He scoffs and turns back to the money. "Grow up." His rubber band snaps around another grand.

"I won't help you with this."

"You don't have a choice."

"I'm only supposed to advise you on environmental impacts."

"You didn't read that contract very carefully, did you?" He turns to me. His one exposed eye is bloodshot and yellow. "This could work out, Chinita. For all of us. Don't screw it up just because you don't like my style."

"Who are you?" It's a question I've wanted to ask for days. "Are you even a real surfer? Or just a poser businessman? Are you some kind of evil spirit sent here to fuck things up for me?"

He grins harder. I wonder if he's not a new incarnation of the Monkey-Faced Baby, another mischievous prophet who is never truly right, but never truly wrong, either. Though it makes no sense, I half-suspect him of somehow stealing my passport and my money, even of purposely putting Alex and me in close-enough proximity to commit the act he now blackmails me with.

"I'm just like you, Chinita." Pelo lowers his sunglasses back down and relaxes his smile. "I'm just another drifter doing the best he can."

"You're nothing like me," I say.

"I'm not as lucky as you are, if that's what you mean." An unfamiliar note of sincerity swells in his voice. "Not as lucky as Chuck Norris or you. I don't have somebody in my life, like you guys have each other. I don't have the chance to take this trip you'll be taking. Don't have that kind of freedom." He turns his head away from mine. For a split second, I wonder if he might break down in tears.

I open my mouth, but no words come out.

"Okay, who's next here?" He turns to the man and woman seated before him.

My face feels like it could pop from all the blood pumping through it. I turn to the couple. The man slowly fills in the blanks.

"Don't do it," I say in Spanish. "It's not worth it."

The baby in his mother's arms begins to cry.

"It's a bad deal," I say, raising my voice.

"Shut the fuck up, Chinita," Pelo mutters at me. "You don't know what you're talking about." He turns to the couple, spins his finger around his ear, and says, "*Loca*"—calling me crazy.

I stand up. "I won't be part of this."

Pelo gives the couple their money and takes the letter out of their hands.

At the entrance to the house, I stare at the other families, all of them queued up with their deeds and their children in their arms. I'm reminded of what Alex said the other night, about the Red Cross lines and the atrocities they called to mind.

"Don't listen to him!" I stand outside the doorway now but point back inside the house at Pelochucho. "It's a bad deal! He's tricking you!" My head feels light. My heart flops and flutters like a headless chicken inside my chest. "Don't give up your homes!"

But my words are met mostly by confused silence. One of the men at the back of the line snuffs out a laugh and whispers, "*Chinita loca*." The pool diggers stop working and stare up out of their hole.

Trembling, I climb inside the Jeep and dig the key from my pocket. The engine turns over. The entire line looks toward me. Pelo comes to the door of the house as I shift into reverse. He raises his sunglasses and gives me a one-eyed glare. I turn my head over my shoulder and back up.

As I have so often in the past few days, I drive fast with the windows rolled down, let the wind and the sound of the engine drown everything else out, until I can almost forget about Pelo's plan and how mixed up in it I am. Who knows what sort of sick revenge he might concoct for my abandoning him there.

Back at La Posada, I park in front of the too-high stack of cement bags. Ben swings in the hammock outside our room.

My eyes are moist from all the wind on the drive. I lift up the front of my T-shirt to wipe at them. "We've got a problem," I say.

"Just one?" He sits up straight in the hammock, finds his tobacco pouch on the windowsill behind him.

"We were out there today, at K Ninety-nine. His people want to buy up all the land, turn the whole hamlet into the site for their resort."

A thin turd of tobacco takes shape between his thumbs. Ben looks up and cocks his head. "Would that help with the erosion thing?"

I shrug. "It depends. But he was getting all the families to sign over their deeds for a thousand bucks or so. I couldn't be part of it."

He nods and licks the glue edge of his rolling paper.

"So I ditched him there."

Ben's eyes widen. He stops licking, but his tongue still hangs halfway out of his mouth. "You ditched him out on K Ninety-nine?"

"That's right." I prepare myself for admonishment.

Instead, Ben laughs out loud. "Holy shit." He shakes his head. "Wish I could've seen the look on his face."

"I told the sellers that they were getting ripped off." I can't help but share a little of Ben's mischievous glee. "I screamed it."

Ben lights up his cigarette and shakes his head again.

"What do we do now?"

He shrugs. "I'm not sure. Can you stop him from buying up the rest of the parcels?"

"Doubt it. It's probably over by now."

"What's he going to do? Fire you?"

"I'm not sure he wants my help anymore. He might try to use the contract against me somehow."

"Right." Ben takes a deep inhale and lets the smoke out slowly. "Listen. Don't sweat it. Getting back here is easy. He can hitchhike or wait for a bus. I'll have a talk with him, play the good cop."

I sit down beside Ben in the hammock, take the cigarette out of his hands, and help myself to a long drag. "What about all those people losing their homes?"

Ben puts a hand on my knee. "You told them the truth; you walked away once it got uncomfortable. If everyone in the world did that all the time, it'd be a better place."

I nod, hand back his smoke.

Ben pushes off the wall so that we swing back and forth inside the hammock. "Should I grab a beer?" he asks.

"Why not wait a bit?" I put my hand on Ben's thigh. "Maybe we could pick up where we left off this morning, before we were so rudely interrupted."

Ben grins and steals a quick glance around the hotel. Still no Pelochucho. Kristy has disappeared inside the office. He climbs out of the hammock and offers me his hand. We enter our bedroom. I close the door behind me. Ben hits the switch and the fan starts up like an old airplane propeller. Already sweating in the hot room, I undo the buttons on my cutoffs and pull my shirt off over my head.

Ben rips open his Velcro fly, lets his board shorts fall to the ground, and then lies across the far side of the bed, naked and already hard. He pats a spot beside him on the mattress. We truly will pick up where we left off this morning—pretend that loud truck of building supplies never arrived. I wish we could do such a thing with even greater chunks of time—splice the present into the past and delete the bits in between.

I lie down on my side in front of Ben, in a near-fetal position. His hand runs up from the peak of my hip to the bottom of the valley formed at my waist. He cranes his neck around my shoulder and kisses my lips at a glancing angle. I turn my head to meet his. He moves his hand to just below my belly button. We stop kissing. I close my eyes as his forefinger inches farther downward.

Ben's first two fingers hold fast against me as I shudder on the bed. I squeeze his hand between my upper thighs and inch closer. His other hand strokes the top of my head.

He lowers himself next to me. I reach between my own legs, find him there, and finally we make it further than we did this morning. Ben lets out a long breath.

He moves with a gentle and circular rhythm, one that somehow falls into step with the oscillations from our fan. He wraps one arm around my shoulder, grabs my hip with the other, and pulls me even closer to him. I brace my hand against the wall and push my whole body into his. With my other hand, I grip the underside of his thigh.

Normally, I find it stupid when people make comparisons between sex and surfing. As if all sources of pleasure should be converted to some kind of universal currency, then measured against one another. But today, I see the connection. Like the barrel I had so many months ago, this session with Ben is a beautiful set of blinders. For a few moments, there is no Pelochucho, no Alex, no earthquake even. My peripheral troubles melt away like fat rendered off a bone. With all our limbs wrapped up tight, it feels as though we are indivisible, that even the worst of our secrets and jealousies won't be able to split us apart.

Once it's over, we lie limp and silent. Our bodies spread across the bed. I settle my head into the crook of Ben's armpit and run my fingers through the hair on his belly. As the minutes go by, Ben's breath slows, his chest rises and lowers less often, until I'm certain he's fallen asleep. I feel drowsy myself.

Lying beside Ben on the bed, I'm momentarily able to imagine our trip once again: waking beside each other, surfing, seeing the world. It had all been so very much within our grasp one week ago. What could I do to get back there now?

A few minutes later, Ben wakes and turns to me.

"Let's go up to the roof," he says.

"I'll meet you there," I say. "I want to shower."

Inside my preferred shower stall, I turn the single knob and open the tap all the way. Though there's no heater, the water is normally warm by this hour of the afternoon.

Once my hair is lathered up, a bang sounds from the sheet metal of the stall door.

"Yeah?" I ask.

"Hey. It's me," Ben shouts over the running water.

For a second, I wonder if he isn't about to join me inside.

"Lock the door to the bedroom when you're done, will you?"

"Okay." I hate that Ben has to remind me about the ground rules of staying in this town. I rinse my hair and shut the water off. Back in our room, I dry off and get dressed.

The long day's last light clings like rust to the edges of a worn-out sky. Smoke rises in columns off the burning sugarcane fields to the east. Mariachi bands start up in the restaurants by the point. On the roof, Ben sits in his usual plastic chair, staring out to sea, two canned beers at his feet.

"No waves?" I ask.

"No waves." He passes me one of the beer cans he's brought up, his stare still stuck to the ocean.

My thoughts pace a circle through my mind's front yard, still contemplating Pelo's contract, our trip, even the temporary visa option. My eyes cast out across the Pacific, and I wonder which way it is to Honolulu.

"By the way," he says. "I spoke to Peseta again, while you were gone."

"Oh yeah?" I say. "More funny stories of torturing kids?"

"I mean about your passport."

"Right." I feel instantly sorry for the remark. "What did he say?"

"He doesn't think it's any of the usual suspects. Nobody's been flashing money or anything like that."

"That's weird," I say. "Maybe they're playing it safe."

"I don't know," Ben says. "I think we might've jumped to conclusions."

I take a big sip from my can. A kind of dreadful emptiness overwhelms my stomach, a feeling that can't be erased, not with beer or anything else. No matter what, I have to get out from under Pelochucho's thumb. That much is clear.

"Ben," I say. The beer can grows woefully light inside my hand. "I have something to tell you."

He seems to know that this means bad news and keeps his eyes on the ocean. "What's that?"

"I didn't stay at La Estancia the other night while you were in the hospital." I look at the side of his face.

He brings the beer can up to his lips and then down again, the red fur on his cheeks rising and lowering in a tight swallow. "Is that right?"

"I was with Alex." As I say it, I wonder if maybe I've overestimated how much of a surprise this will be for Ben.

"You fuck him?" he asks.

"Yeah." I turn my eyes away from his. Tears dump down my cheeks in a quick, watery way, as if from spicy food or chemical drops.

"I see." He takes the last sip from his beer can and then crushes it inside his fist. "You go visit him yesterday?"

"Yes," I admit. "I had to say good-bye. The other morning was weird."

"What about the embassy? Did you even go there?"

"What?" I'm taken aback. Perhaps I shouldn't be. "Yes, of course."

"So the lost passport, that's true, right? That really happened? That's not some other lie meant to get you out of this fucking surf trip"—he raises his voice, still staring out to sea—"which you wanted to come on in the first fucking place! And which you can bail on, at any time, just by saying so! It's your fucking life!"

I'm suddenly a child, screamed at by a well-intentioned but exasperated parent.

"My passport got stolen," I manage to say.

"Sorry to yell," Ben says.

I wonder if he's suspected such a thing all along, or if my one confession has led to a viral breeding of jealousy and paranoia that's taken over his entire mind in the last minute or so. My eyes are on the concrete roof below our feet, but I can feel his gaze settle upon me.

"Does Pelo know about this?"

"Pelo? What?" It's the last question I expect from him.

"That whole song and dance outside our room this morning. 'Do you know somebody named Alex?' Blah-blah-blah . . . Is this what that was about? Am I the last person in El Salvador not to know who my girlfriend is screwing?"

My head does a cross between a shake and a nod. "No. Well, yes. That's nothing. He heard me talk to Alex on the phone."

"You've been talking to Alex on the phone?"

"He called here; I blew him off." This all seems so tangential to the real reasons Ben should be mad at me. "That part is no big deal, seriously. But I did sleep with him that night you were in the hospital. We were drunk. A lot of weird emotions were going around. I'm sorry."

"Look at me, Malia."

I wipe at the sides of my now-puffy eyes with a trembling finger and turn toward him.

"I forgive you." He's not yelling anymore. He is impossibly calm.

"What?" Somehow, this is not at all the response I anticipated.

Ben rolls his eyes. "That's right. If you want to be with Alex,
if you want to stay in this country, if you want to bail on our
plan and on us, then you'll have to decide it for yourself. You're
going to have to pick up your bag and walk out. I'm not going
to push you away." His chest rises in a hard breath. "Frankly, I
think it's pretty lame that you'd put me in that position."

My chin goes rubbery. The crying jag gets a second wind.
Is Ben right? Did I confess only to force one of my doors
closed, be made to either stay or go? I can't bring myself to tell
him about Pelo's blackmail. I don't want him to think that's
the only reason I came clean.

"That isn't what I want. I want to go to South America with
you. I'm just scared that it won't happen."

"I need to be away from you for a little while," Ben says.
"Can you handle that?"

I nod, careful not to ask him for more understanding than
I deserve.

Ben goes down the stairs. I let myself cry in a way I'd not
wanted to in front of him—with deep, wheezing, self-pitying
gasps. The bedroom door slams. A second later, a vehicle enters
La Posada. I rise to have a look, and see a pickup full of shirtless young men. It's the pool diggers. Pelochucho hops out of
the truck. I step back from the edge of the roof so that he won't
see me.

I can't quite make out their words over the sound of the truck
pulling away, but Ben and Pelo greet each other, then walk out.
The rough shuffle of their rubber soles sounds against the street
outside.

I stay on the roof for a while and watch the rest of the

sunset—a clear-skyed affair of purple and orange that seems to mock me with all its beauty. Once it's over, I go downstairs and wipe my eyes and nose with a handkerchief. Thankfully, Ben left his tobacco and I can pass the time with smoking and hand-rolling.

Neither Ben nor Pelo returns to the hotel. Perhaps they're drinking together and speaking ill of me, of all women. Perhaps they'll visit the whorehouse. The very thought unnerves me.

A whistle sounds from the street. I see Peseta outside; he's not allowed to enter the courtyard unless he has potential guests in tow. He makes a gesture for me to come over.

I walk toward him, not sure what he wants.

"Take this." He looks from side to side on the street, then hands me a small prescription bottle. "Sorry it took so long. My friend was out of town." I nearly forgot about the Valium.

"Thank you," I say, feeling ashamed for my suspicions the night before.

"And this." He holds a few coins on the flat of his palm.

"What's that?" I ask.

"Your change."

I pick a couple of the coins off his hand, then say, "You keep the rest."

He nods and walks off.

I cross the courtyard, enter the bedroom, and swallow two of the pills. The drugs take effect in an instant. I try to confine my body to one side of the bed, hoping that Ben still wants to share it with me.

22

"Can I meet my mommy?" It was the last time I'd ever mention her so casually. My father had made lunch, then served us each a dish of ice cream. I must've been nine at the time.

His spoon jangled inside the empty bowl. With a hard exhale, he rose and carried all our dishes to the sink.

"Put your good shoes on," he said. "I'll make a phone call."

Together, we took a silent drive. Up the Pali Highway and over the Koʻolaus, we passed through clouds and a minute or two of rain. On the other side of the tunnels, the sky cleared. We had a view of the Windward Coast, looking down at both the Kaneohe and Kailua bays, the narrow spit of land between them. Though my young eyes must have traveled that road before, it would be my first lasting memory of that high panorama.

My father parked the car along a street in Kailua town and we climbed out. I followed him to the front door of the house, not understanding why we were there, and too scared to ask.

An older haole woman answered the doorbell. She was fat, with falsely red hair, wearing a frowsy muumuu. My jaw dropped open once I saw her, incredulous that she could be a possible relative of mine.

My father spoke to this woman in tones too hushed for me to understand.

She smiled and said, "Malia?" in a louder voice. "Come on in."

I looked to my father for confirmation. He nodded.

We followed the woman into her house.

"My baby!"

I was blindsided by another woman and smothered inside a tight embrace. The arms that wrapped around me smelled of mint and smoke.

"You've gotten so big." The words were muffled into my shoulder.

I didn't see my mother's face until she let go and held me out at arm's length.

"You look just like me," she said.

This wasn't true, but it made a nine-year-old me happy. She was pretty: dark skin, defined features, long, wavy hair. She wore all black clothes, including a small military-looking hat, which seemed stylish to me at that time. Behind her stood that older haole woman, along with a man I presumed was the woman's husband.

"I'm your mama." She smiled hard, grinding a piece of gum between her back molars.

"Pleased to meet you," I said.

The other adults all laughed aloud.

My mother put her hands on my shoulders and looked up at my father, who stood behind me. "Can I be with her alone for a minute or two?"

I turned around to face him as well.

He nodded, not having spoken a word aloud since we'd entered.

My mother led me to a covered carport at the side of the house. She closed the door and leaned over my shoulder, placed her head next to mine. "Look!" She pointed with her index finger. "See that gecko?" The dark outline of a lizard shone against the off-white of the patio table.

"Watch this," my mother whispered. With three quick paces, she crept up toward the table. Her flattened hand slapped down upon the lizard's rear half. "See that!" she shouted.

I joined her at the table. The lizard ran away in a jerking blur.

"Look at the tail." My mother pointed with her other hand. "He let it go!"

On the table, the small black length of reptile flesh—now free of the body—squirmed and twisted, forming curlicues and sidewinders. I squealed with delight.

My mother let out a loud, cackling laugh. She swept the tail away with the back of her hand and put an ashtray and cigarettes down on the table. "Have a seat."

There was a refrigerator out in the carport, and she opened two Coca-Colas—a treat my father never allowed me. She smoked cigarettes while we talked, the gum grinding in her mouth the entire time. I remember seeing the name Kools printed on her cigarette pack. For years afterward, I thought that was a Hawaiian word.

She asked me unremarkable questions about school and hobbies, how often I saw my Tutu, her mother. If anything underhanded went on—any attempt to get dirt on my father or how he raised me, to leverage any kind of custody for herself—it was too subtle for me to notice.

I don't remember the substance of the conversation so much as the soda and the cigarettes. But toward the end, she scooted her chair a bit closer to mine and put a hand on my knee.

"Listen to me, Malia. This is important." Once she stopped smiling, thick lines showed at the sides of her face. "You'll hear bad things about me as you grow up. Plenty of them are true; I've made mistakes. But keep this in mind: I love you very much, and I do the best I can. Okay?"

I nodded. She took me back inside and we said our goodbyes.

I didn't know it at the time, but the haoles were a couple of evangelical Christians who had met my mother through a church. She'd enjoyed a short period of recovery while staying with them. I never understood how my father knew that she was there, especially at the moment I asked to meet her.

That was the last time we spoke of her in my father's house. The rest I picked up from rumors, eavesdropping, and a few candid questions at Tutu's.

My father was good about keeping my mother's mother in

my life. I often spent Sundays and holidays in her Makiki home, eating big meals and visiting with uncles and cousins I knew moderately well. During middle school and high school, Tutu came to all of my volleyball games, and cheered louder than any parent.

In hindsight, my understanding is that my mother was a full-time alcoholic, and opportunistic in her use of other drugs, depending on the company she kept. My father supported her initial attempts to beat the disease. The final reason for my parents' split, according to Tutu, was not addiction, but infidelity. My mother ran off with another man not long after I was born. Tutu described him as "one haole motorcycle man." To my younger mind, that description conjured up an image of a part-human, part-machine lover straight out of science fiction—some bionic Caucasian cyborg with chrome arms and wheels for legs, able to steal my mother away faster than anyone could stop him. They spent time together on the mainland but eventually split up. My mother went back to Hawai'i, but not back to her husband and child.

I'm almost certain that I spotted her a couple of times in my teenage years. Once was on my way back from surfing in Waikiki. Obviously drunk, a woman cackled loud near the far end of Kalakaua Street. I turned and saw a leathery-skinned, red-eyed Hawaiian lady. She hung from the arm of a shirtless haole with an ugly handlebar mustache. I was with friends, on our way back to the zoo parking lot, and insisted we cross the street.

The last time was downtown, near the bus stop on Fort Street. I saw a woman sitting on the sidewalk, her back to one of the storefronts, lifting her head and then dropping it back down to her knees. She was older—her hair a tangled mess, lines so deep in the skin of her face that they looked like they'd been etched there with a chisel. She wore rubber flip-flops. Her toenails were long, yellow, and crooked.

I considered approaching her, maybe saying hello. For most of my youth, I'd been angry and resentful over her abandonment. Those emotions left me once I saw her in that state. What I felt then was pity, followed by something more like repulsion, or fear. I told myself that it wasn't her at all—just another homeless woman. Again, I walked away and caught the bus elsewhere.

She died the summer before I went to college. Tutu and her side of the family tried to protect me from the details. I aggressively eavesdropped on their conversations. My uncles mentioned several times that she was found "half inside, half outside" a minivan left in Kapiolani Park. I heard that phrase repeated through closed doors and thin walls, as if there were some enigmatic explanation wrapped up inside it somewhere.

At nineteen, I took some comfort in that image: my mother half inside an icon of American domesticity and half on the street, caught between two worlds, being birthed by the automobile.

The official cause of death was listed as alcohol poisoning. As a college freshman in the months that followed, I would pay special attention to that topic during the mandatory information sessions. Almost everything I learned about it could be distilled down to this single fact: Alcohol poisoning has as much to do with copious drinking as it does with the lack of anyone close by to call for help.

My father sent me to the funeral with Tutu. Having prepared many years for the event, the family members shed few tears. Afterward, we went to the Makiki house for a long afternoon of eating and talking, less festive than normal.

My father picked me up later that night. More than any emotion related to grief or mourning, I felt excited about my first year of college, doubly ready to leave an island that suddenly seemed unbearably small.

23

In the morning, I wake feeling paralyzed, tethered to the bed. I summon the force to feel the spot beside me but can't find Ben. I close my eyes again for a long string of minutes.

The ceiling fan spins and oscillates from above. The sound of Kristy's broom scraping the tiles carries in. I rise, get dressed, and open the door. With one hand, I shade my face from the sun. Across the courtyard, Ben and Pelochucho sit in the dining room. Ben waves me over.

Still foggy and confused, I walk toward them. Has Pelo forgiven me as well? Did I only dream the events of the previous day?

"Morning, Chinita," Pelo says.

"Sit down, Malia," Ben says.

I do as I'm told. "I'm sorry," I say to both of them, "about yesterday."

"It's okay," Pelo says. "Water under the bridge. Anyway, Chuck Norris and I have come up with a way to solve all our problems."

Kristy drops a mug of hot milk and the jar of instant coffee in front of me. Ben must've ordered it on my behalf.

"Come again?"

"A midnight run," Ben says. "Out to the cove at K Ninety-nine."

"I've been talking to the guys here in town," Pelo says. "There's a shipment coming in tonight. They need a middle-man."

"What?" I ask, still confused.

"Or middlewoman, as the case may be."

"The bales," Ben explains. "The cocaine."

I look each of them in the eye and wait for a punch line. They're serious. I nod, then scoop a spoonful of instant coffee into the mug of warm milk.

"We all need the dough," Pelo says. "Buying the rest of those houses out there cost me everything I had stashed. If this hadn't come through, then I'd be sitting on a bunch of land and cement, and no cash to build with. It's perfect timing."

"We'll make all our money back," Ben says. "Pay off our tab here. As soon as your passport comes, we can get on the road."

I take a sip of coffee but don't say a word.

"And I'll tear up your contract with SalvaCorp," Pelo says. "Water under the bridge, like I said."

"It's a one-time thing." Ben isn't asking for my permission

on this. "The crack trade here is the reason our money got stolen. It's only fair we get it back through the crack trade."

That's an interesting bit of logic.

"I'll give those guys the green light, then." Pelo stands up. "Glad we had this talk. No worries about yesterday, Chinita." He heads off to the shared toilets.

I sip desperately at my coffee.

"You okay?" Ben asks.

"Okay? Yeah. It's just . . . happening fast." I'm not sure what to say. This sounds like a terrible idea. But Ben is no longer angry. After what happened with Alex, the robbery, and the way I blew the hotel job, I hardly have the right to put my foot down.

Across the courtyard, a flush sounds from the shared toilets. Pelo opens the sheet-metal door with a clang. He studies the too-high stack of cement, as if surprised to find it there.

"Do you want to get out of here for a minute?" I ask Ben. "Take a walk or something?"

It's obvious that there is no surf; we don't even bother with watching from the steps. Instead, we walk into town, heading toward the pier. La Libertad wakes up and comes to attention before our eyes, at an hour we usually spend sleeping in or surfing. Fishermen have breakfast in the alley eateries and food carts along the streets. Hotel employees mop seawater across the concrete floors of their establishments. Toothless old men—with faces so exposed to sun and wind, they look as though they've been carved from wood—repair holes in fishing nets for the millionth time.

After a couple of blocks, we come to the pier. I follow Ben out onto the raised concrete platform, several meters above the

ocean. Small wooden boats line either side, from which fishermen and their families sell their wares. Women with thick forearms and bloody aprons await customers. For a few cents extra,
they'll scale, fillet, and eviscerate the catch of the day—working
fast with a razor-sharp knife and a grooved plank for a cutting
board. The most coveted of the local catch are corvina and red
snapper. Rumors abound of fishermen coloring lesser fish with
red chalk to pass them off as snapper. Live crabs shift and wriggle
inside five-gallon buckets. Fresh scallops lay on the half shell,
carrot-colored egg sacks resting beside their flat columns of
white flesh. Tiny dried fish, like grains of rice with eyes, are sold
by the plastic bagful, mainly as a condiment for *pupusas* or
fried yucca. Vendors explicate the virtues of shark fin oil—a
sludgy, viscous yellow packed in mismatched glass bottles—as a
cure for pneumonia, headaches, and general malaise.

During our honeymoon phase, Ben and I used to come
here and buy a whole fish. He had a method of checking fresh-
ness based on the clarity of the eyes. We'd take it back to
Kristy to cook. Today, we figure she has her hands full.

"Check it out." Ben points to the far end of the pier. There,
one archaic chain winch lifts a small boat up from out of the
water. A lone fisherman—aboard a blue-and-white vessel packed
full of nets and silvery piscine flesh—hangs in midair, sus-
pended by a thick rusty chain at the bow and stern.

"I've never seen them do this before," Ben says.

"Me, neither."

The boat reaches the top, and a few other fishermen help
unload.

Ben and I walk to the rail of the pier and look down at the
calm sea below.

"Some swell, huh?" I say.

Ben shrugs. "Surfing's a way of life, you know."

The tide is out. The ocean looks at least two stories below our feet. Behind the bar at La Punta, there's an old black-and-white photo of a giant set hitting La Lib; in it, monster waves break over this end of the pier. Today, such a thing is impossible to imagine.

"Are we really going to do this?" I ask Ben, staring out at the horizon.

"You want out?" he asks gently.

"I want to go to South America with you. I want to rewind our lives to a few days ago, before we met Pelo and lost our money and everything else."

Ben nods. "Me, too. The trip—it's our dream, right? It's worth fighting for. This little errand is just a way to make it happen."

"So the ends justify the means," I say.

He nods again. We stare over at the hapless point.

"You know what's weird about all this?" I ask. "If I'd helped Pelo out with that hotel, helped him displace all those poor Salvadoran farmers, then it would've been fully legal, just as lucrative, and probably good experience on my damn résumé." I look down at the ocean. "This other plan, it's like a major sin in the eyes of the world, and the truth is, I don't feel that bad about it. Scared, sure, but not guilty."

Ben nods. "It'll happen, with or without us. Somebody will get that money. Why shouldn't it be you and me?"

"You don't think we could get into trouble? I don't like the idea of a Salvadoran jail too much."

"Malia, have you ever heard of any gringo having any problem with the police here that couldn't be solved with a twenty-dollar bill? Hell, we'll be working for the guys who give orders to all the local cops."

I nod. "It's a one-time thing, right? We get paid. We get my new passport, and then we get on our way."

"Absolutely." Ben puts a hand on my shoulder. "I'm not greedy; I just want my trip. We earned it. This town owes it to us."

Out toward the point, a lone pelican dive-bombs into the calm water with a splash, surfaces a second later, and then rises up again.

"Fuck it." I reach down and take the rubber flip-flops off my feet, tuck them between the middle and index fingers on each hand. "Let's do it." I turn around, take two steps, and dive off the pier.

The drop is greater than I anticipated, but it feels safe compared to other dives I've made back home. This is open ocean, after all—no boulders or rock shelves to negotiate.

My sandals split the water first. My body slips deep down, into a colder layer of sea, before I finally turn and paddle upward. Despite all the boat fuel and fish guts in the vicinity, the water feels amazing against my skin, like an embrace from an old friend.

I surface, sandals still on my hands. The fishermen make all sorts of chatter—some cheering, others ranting about the dangers of such a stunt. Somebody claims that a jump like that could "explode the lungs."

A grin grows across my face, bigger and giddier than any I've felt in days. Ben looks down at me and laughs. Shaking his head, he removes each of his own flip-flops.

I shout, "Do it!" from below.

Feetfirst, hands and sandals cupped around his balls, Ben jumps. To the delight and horror of the audience along the pier, he makes a giant splash just inches from me. I scream.

He surfaces with a whoop and a holler. His eyes turn big and round. With the sole of his sandal, he pushes water at me.

I squeal and splash back. Both of us laugh. Ben wraps one arm around my shoulders—dog-paddling with the other—and kisses me on the lips. Groans and giggles come from the fishmongers above.

It takes a while to reach dry land, even with the tide coming in. The flip-flops on our hands slow down the swimming. By the time we come ashore, I'm starving, and still not eager to return to La Posada. Soaking wet, we find seats at one of the food stalls near the pier, a place that sells breakfast to fishermen. I dig a few wet bills from the pocket of my cutoffs. We order beans, eggs, and fresh cream. The woman behind the counter fixes our plates and serves us tortillas but provides no utensils.

"Oh my God," Ben says.

I look up.

Walking down the street is Crackito. His feet are bare and he is wearing his too-big rags of a shirt and shorts. His entire head—hair, eyes, mouth, everything—is covered in spray paint, mostly blues and reds, a bit of glittery gold in the mix as well.

This isn't the first time I've seen the spray-painted face gag. Local kids sometimes do that to drunks who pass out in the street. But this seems far crueler—to paint someone so young and helpless.

"Poor bastard." Ben sighs. "*Niño!*" he calls to the boy, motions for him to join us.

Crackito shuffles over. Ben pulls out a stool for him to sit on, then asks the woman behind the counter for another plate. She frowns at us, not pleased to have Crackito in her establishment.

"Hungry?" Ben asks.

Crackito nods, staring down at the hands lying empty upon his lap.

"Who did this to you?" I ask.

"Nobody." Crackito shakes his head.

Once the food comes, he eats the whole plateful in seconds.

I pay the tab and give the cook a large tip. Crackito takes off his shirt and goes into the ocean to wash the paint off, scrubbing at his face and torso with handfuls of black sand. It seems to work.

"If you want to stay behind tonight, Malia, that's fine. Pelo and I can handle it."

"I said I'm in." The truth is, I can't cope with the thought of leaving Ben to do this alone.

"We'd better get back," he says.

During Peace Corps training, we had a terrifying session on security, meant to scare us into caution and prudence. The only rule I remember is this: If somebody threatens you, don't ever let yourself be moved to another location. Once the bad guys move you, things always get worse. If somebody in a ski mask puts a gun to your head and tells you to get into a car—which did happen to a volunteer in San Salvador not so long ago—scream, run, but don't get in the car. I recall that lesson now, in light of Pelo's new plan. I'm convinced our situation will keep getting worse if we take steps forward in league with him.

Though Crackito has now run along, an image from a few minutes earlier, of him in the surf, still lingers in my mind's eye—the way he scoured himself with sand and salt water, while that thick and ugly layer worked its way off. I wish I knew a similar way to scrub off some of my recent missteps.

"I'll meet you at the hotel," I say to Ben. "I want to make a phone call."

At the ANTEL office, I tell the clerk the only phone number that I still have committed to memory. In my head, I count back the time zones and figure out the hour in Honolulu.

"Hello?"

"Dad," I say. "It's me, Malia."

"Malia." He's excited. "How are you? I've been waiting to hear from you. How's the aqueduct?"

I pause so long that it becomes awkward. Then: "I don't know, Dad. I'm not working on it anymore."

"Oh," he says. "Is that right?"

"With the earthquake and all . . . it's not really a priority. I left the village."

"I see." He sounds utterly confused. "What are you doing now?"

"I'm staying at the beach, with Ben. You remember Ben? I—well, we, we're thinking about doing some traveling." I cringe as I say it, but at least the words get out of my mouth.

"Traveling?" my father says.

"Yeah, Dad. We may go to South America for a while."

"South America." He says it just above a whisper. "Do you . . . do you have the money for that?"

Another awkward pause from me. "Of course."

I'd been dreading this conversation for so long. It was meant to be a confession of a truth that my father didn't want to hear. Somehow, it's become more a mix of falsehood and omission.

My father's breath sounds like static through the phone. "It all sounds very interesting, Malia."

I feel the beginning of tears, and clench my teeth together. "It's what I want. I don't know if I'll ever have a chance like this again." That much is true.

"When do you think you might come back here, to Hawai'i?" he asks.

"I don't know," I say. "It could be a while."

"Well, well," he says. "I guess you know what you're doing." He doesn't sound confident in his own words. Perhaps he fears that I'm turning into my mother—prone to run off with strange haole men, no thoughts for family or future.

"I'm very proud of you, Malia."

That's when the tears finally get the best of me.

"All the things that you've done in that country—it's incredible."

I want to tell him about the night with Alex, about the robbery, about the fact that I walked away from that aqueduct when it might have needed me most, and about the plan for tonight—to make the money that I claimed to already have. I want some way to tell him about everything, a way that might actually make sense to him. Most of all, I wish I still had the kind of problems that my father could fix with a few words.

"I love you," he says.

"I love you, too, Dad. I need to go now, but we'll talk soon, okay?"

"Okay, Malia."

I wipe at my eyes with the hem of my T-shirt, then pay the ANTEL clerk for the call.

On the street, I take some deep breaths and try to compose myself. It's time to go back to the hotel—to find Ben and Pelo—and to go get this over with already.

24

The night is still and warm. Once outside of town, we pass no other cars. For once, I'm happy to ride in the back, lying on the plywood shelf. It makes me feel hidden somehow, safer. Ben drives slowly and cautiously. Pelo doesn't light a joint.

From the back, I'm able to make out only the odd painted rock along the side of the road. By the rising and winding of the Jeep, I can tell that we've left town.

"Simple," Pelo says in a gentle voice.

Ben grunts.

"We're like Peseta now," I say from the shelf. "Runners. Legs."

Neither of them responds.

After what feels like hours of driving, Ben slows and says, "This is it, right?"

"This is it," Pelo replies.

Ben shifts into four-wheel drive. He turns left and we bump our way down a rutted dirt road toward the beach. My hips and shoulders slide and bounce on the plywood.

"Try to get the car into those bushes," Pelo says. "Might as well be subtle."

Ben shifts in and out of reverse. We jolt forward and back a few times. Leaves brush up against my back window like the rollers in a car wash. The thin limbs scratch and groan against the Jeep. Ben cuts the engine.

"All right." Pelo exhales and cracks open his door. "Now we do the waiting thing."

A second of silence passes. Pings sound from the motor.

"Could somebody let me out of here, please," I say from the back.

Ben comes around and opens the hatch. The two of us sit on the tailgate. It's still a beautiful spot—or seems so at night. The cove is narrow and rugged, full of palms and small bushes. Two tall shoulders of land reach out on either side of us. The sea laps gently against shore. The full moon turns the landscape as bright and gray as a marble statue.

Pelo walks down to the water's edge. Ben makes a cigarette at my side, the rolling papers crinkling against his fingers. I can tell from his jerky movements and shallow breaths that he's nervous. For whatever reason, I've turned calm. It's like paddling into big surf: Once you're out there, anxiety doesn't do you any good. My problem was always deciding whether to go out in the first place.

"It's nice out here," I say.

Ben sparks up the smoke. I can hear that he's packed the tobacco too tight by the way he sucks on the tip. "It's not bad," he admits, a chattering quiver in his voice.

Pelo paces along the shore, staring out at the horizon.

I reach over and take the cigarette from Ben's hand. "Relax," I say. "We're here now. Might as well be cool."

"Right." He breathes in through his nose, then out through his mouth, and straight away becomes more composed.

"I think I hear something." Pelo sings the words like a children's song.

We go quiet. The tiny, distant buzz of an engine slowly becomes audible. It sounds like one of the lawn mowers my father used to bring home to repair. The three of us turn still and stiff. For a long span of minutes, we do nothing but listen to the buzz. It grows louder and closer, and for a moment I wonder if it might be a tiny airplane.

At last, a small craft turns the corner and becomes visible inside the cove. Ben and I rise from off the tailgate. I squint my eyes. It's impossibly small, a Zodiac, and so loaded down with cargo that it appears to be dragging below the ocean's surface rather than floating atop it.

"Take these." Ben holds up the keys to the Jeep. "Wait behind the wheel. If anything happens, start it up and bail."

I accept the keys from him but don't move. My feet feel planted to the ground. "Who are those guys?"

Two men pilot the Zodiac. Both wear handkerchiefs over their faces, like gunslingers from the Old West. Apart from that, they appear to be dressed in dirty collared shirts and baseball caps—not unlike the local campesinos.

"Colombians, I suppose," Ben says. "Or guys that work for them."

"Did they come up from Colombia in that thing?"

Ben stifles a laugh. "They must have a bigger boat out there somewhere."

"What's with the handkerchiefs?"

He shrugs. "Frankly, I'd just as soon not see anybody's face tonight."

Pelo waves his arms above his head to signal them, as if they can't see him standing there.

"Get behind the wheel," Ben says again.

This time, I do as he says.

From the driver's seat, I hear the chatter down by the water's edge. The Zodiac's engine shuts off. Feet shuffle hard against the sand. Soon, I look into the rearview mirror and see Ben and Pelo carrying a rectangular package wrapped in a grain sack and tied up with twine. They drop the first one in through the Jeep's rear door, onto the plywood deck. For a second, I fear that it won't fit inside and we'll have to find a way to disassemble that wooden shelf. But they're able to hoist it a little higher and slide it in.

"Do we need to check and see if it's real or something?" I ask as they push the bale flush against my seat back.

Pelo laughs. "You've seen too many movies, Chinita. Try trusting people once in a while."

Ben claps dust from his hands. "I'd rather we get this over with and get the fuck out of here, to be honest."

The two men from the Zodiac carry the next one. They speak Spanish to each other in an accent I can't place. One of them meets my stare through the rearview mirror and I hear him mutter the word *muchacha*. I turn my eyes away.

All four men head back to the water's edge. My mind slips into paranoia. This is the moment, I think to myself, this would be the time for them to kill both Ben and Pelo, then come back for me. Were I a Colombian thug hoping to make off with both the money and the product, to take advantage of some amateurs, now would be the time to shoot. Sweat comes coursing through the palms of my hands. Be cool, I order myself; you've seen too many movies.

Instead, the four men make one more trip and fill the Jeep. Ben and Pelo accompany the Colombians back to their boat. Once I hear their motor start, I turn the key in the ignition. Ben groans as he climbs into the back and squeezes himself around the bales. The hatch slams shut and Pelo jumps in beside me. I put the Jeep in reverse and pull out from behind the bushes. My heart throws jabs along the inside of my rib cage. We bounce our way inland up the dirt road.

"Well, that was fucking easy!" Pelo takes his one-hitter from the glove compartment.

Once on the paved road, I drive fast toward La Lib. Ben and Pelo whoop and cheer for a few minutes, passing the one-hitter back and forth like a victory cigar. Soon enough, they realize that we're not finished with our work tonight and the enthusiasm gives way to a tense and pregnant silence.

As we cross the final bridge into town, I feel my palms go sweaty once again; the taste of dirty coins rises from the back of my throat.

I drive toward the crack house and come to a stop kitty-corner from it.

I keep my eyes on the house. "So, where's the service entrance to this place?"

"Not here," Pelo says.

"Excuse me?" I turn to him.

"This run, it's not for these guys. It's not their shit."

Ben speaks from the back. "What the fuck are you talking about, Pelo?"

"The deal I made, for this stuff, it's with some other guys. Don't worry; it's only a couple blocks away."

"You made a deal with some other drug dealers?" My voice rises and my breath grows short.

"So what?" Pelo shrugs. "What's wrong with a little competition? That's good for any market."

"This isn't some business-school exercise, Pelo." I can't believe what is happening. "It's a monopoly. A hostile one."

"Malia." Ben reaches forward and touches my shoulder. "Maybe we shouldn't sit here discussing this."

Across the intersection, the red door to the crack house opens a hair. A head sticks halfway out. I put the car in gear and drive around the corner.

"I don't know what you guys are freaking out about. It's not like it's any of their business."

"All cocaine in this town is their business," Ben says. "This is fucked."

"Look. Let's just make this drop and get paid," Pelo says. "If anybody gives us any trouble, we'll go to the police. We won't be the ones holding all the shit. It's not like we'll have anything to worry about."

I let out a heavy sigh.

"Pelo," Ben says. "Those guys from the crack house run the police."

That shuts everybody up for a second.

"Ben." I find his face in the rearview mirror. "What are we going to do? We can't drive around all night with a car full of coke."

"I know." He sighs, then pauses for a few seconds. "Maybe we ought to go ahead and drop the load with Pelo's people. Then pray that the shit storm falls on them, not us."

"Where is this place?" I can't even look at Pelo's face. The anger I feel for him is hot and blinding, like my own personal sun.

"Take a left," he says sheepishly.

After a couple more directions, we come to a blue house, where a couple of guys are sitting on the front stoop. They both stand as we approach.

I shift into neutral, then turn to Pelo. "Get out and get our money. If they don't kill you, then they can come for the product. The engine stays on. I stay behind the wheel."

"Right." Pelo opens his door. "What's the Spanish word for engine again? Never mind." He gets out and goes to talk to the two men.

"This is bad, isn't it?" I ask Ben.

He crawls a few inches forward in the back. "It's stupid. Maybe we'll get by without it turning out too bad. Hey!" His body twitches against the bales. "Do you see that?" Ben points to an alley up the block. It's a thin passage between houses, too narrow for cars.

"What?" I say.

"Nothing, I guess." He continues to stare. "I thought I saw somebody over there. Probably just paranoid."

The Jeep's back door swings open. Ben climbs out. The two Salvadoran strangers scoot the first bale outward.

Pelo comes to my window. "Hold this, Chinita." He drops a paper wad into my hands. "We'll split it up back at the ranch."

The bills are wrapped up in newsprint and rubber bands. I rip the bundle open on one side. The bills are all American hundreds. I lift my hips and shove the wad down the front pocket of my baggy work jeans.

The men from the house carry the first bale inside. Pelo stands between the car and the front door and supervises.

Ben comes around to my window. "Does the money look okay?"

"Looks green," I say.

The men come back for the second bale. Looking in the rearview mirror, I study their faces. They look bored by this, perhaps annoyed that I keep the motor running. Whatever quality possessed them to start a rival business to this town's true crack house isn't showing in their eyes. They don't look ambitious, reckless, or cold-blooded. Perhaps they're like Pelo: a bit of greed and a bit of stupidity mixed together in dangerous proportions.

Ben turns back to the tiny alley up the block. He takes a few steps down it, then comes back.

"See anybody?" I ask.

"No." He shakes his head, then turns and gives it one more glance. "I must be losing my mind."

The men come back for the third bale.

"*Vamos*," Ben tells them. "We're not getting paid by the hour."

"Ben," I say. "Would you mind driving home?" My hands are sweating so hard that they hurt. Plus, I'm not quite sure what corner of La Libertad we've ended up in, or how to get back to the hotel.

"Not a problem," he says.

I pull up the emergency brake and climb out. The two Salvadorans step toward the front door of the house. Pelo paces on the pavement, holding his elbows with his hands. Ben takes a step toward the car and grabs the door handle. He stops and says, "What's that sound?"

All five of us pause to listen. The piercing whine of a police siren cuts through the night air. One of the Salvadorans mutters "*¡Hijo de puta!*" Both of them dash back inside the house and slam the door.

"What the fuck?" Pelo says.

"Get that bale out of the car!" Ben yells at him.

Pelo nods and goes for the trunk.

"Malia." Ben turns and grabs me by the elbows. "Run. Use the alleys. Get back to La Posada and wait."

I can barely hear him now as the sirens approach. By the twine, Pelo tosses the last bale at the blue house. Thousands of dollars' worth of cocaine bounce off their front door.

"Go!" Ben shouts to me again, and hops into the driver's seat. Pelo climbs in on the other side.

I take off sprinting. The Jeep's tires squeal on the concrete. Red and blue lights briefly illuminate the walls on either side of me. My flip-flops pull hard at the spaces between my toes.

Moonlight drips down into the alley and spreads a thick glow, like frosting, to the tops of all the windows and doorways. A dog barks, and I pray it won't bite me. My torso slams into somebody. I mutter a string of apologies, then feel for that wad of dollars along my hip bone.

I cross a carless street and continue into another segment of alley. This one is more crowded. Lights are on inside a few of the buildings. Others have cook fires outside. Smoke from burning wood and plastic bags rises and winds through the walls and over rooftops. Several sets of eyes turn toward me as I pass. Voices call out to me: *"Muchachita," "Mamasita," "Ven aca, mi amor."* I keep on running, more lost now than when I started. I run faster, my rubber soles slapping the rutted cobblestones, wanting out of this concrete ravine.

The next section of alley is even darker. Two bodies sit crumpled in corners. I make out their hands and faces in the moonlight. A plastic lighter sparks up and burns at the end of a short glass stem. A sound like a bubbling hiss. I jump over their feet and run on.

The alley ends and a burst of salt air fills my sinuses. My eyes take a second to adjust to the open spaces. I'm staring at the sea.

The lights from the pier tell me that La Posada is to the east. Along the shorefront street, I walk slowly, trying not to attract attention. Some fishermen sit on the seawall, already preparing their nets for the next morning. Closer to the pier, a group of drunks blasts *cumbia* music and clangs bottles together.

La Posada is locked. I wonder if anyone bothered to tell Kristy what we were up to tonight. Without hesitation, I climb the tree alongside the wall, half-expecting to cross paths with some petty thieves. Once inside, I put the money underneath our mattress and lock the room. In the hammock outside our door, I wait for Ben to return. As the hours tick by with no sign of Ben, Pelo, or the Jeep, I come to realize that I'm doing more hoping than waiting.

25

During last year's Holy Week, Ben convinced me to take a few days off from the water project. La Lib tends to fill up with drunken merrymakers from the capital at Easter time. All the forecasts called for surf. The timing was good for me, as Cara Sucia's workers also expected a break.

We rode a slow bus to Usulután, in the east of the country, then hitchhiked to a remote part of the coast meant to have great waves. Ben had been there once before, with a traveling surfer from Australia.

At this time of year, all of the stones were still painted with the colors and initials of political campaigns. Most bore the red, white, and blue of ARENA—the U.S. client party that's held the presidency for years. The reds and yellows of the former guerilla party were well represented. Third parties gained some ground, including one that deftly usurped a green-and-gold look from the Brazilian soccer team.

Our final ride came from a pickup truck selling melons. The vendor let us ride in the back, along with our surfboards, backpacks, and tent. Melons rolled from side to side with each hill and bump. The driver often stopped to bargain with local merchants.

Ben tapped on the cab once we reached the tiny coastal town of El Cuco. It was smaller and less conspicuous than I'd expected, no sign of hotels or other tourist infrastructure. It looked to be little more than a sandy street shaded by tall palms. Humble restaurants and stores lined either side.

"This way," Ben said.

We walked down to the coast. In the shore break, unrideable tubes—hollow and sandy—stood up tall and then collapsed upon the steep beach. There was swell.

"It's a bit of a walk," Ben said.

We made our way west, packs on our backs and boards under our arms. The town gave way to tall bluffs above the black sand. They said this area was littered with uncrowded breaks, but where would we sleep?

Soon, I saw a point in the distance. Not made up of round boulders like Punta Roca or K 99, this was a jagged outcropping of land. One small whitewashed building stood atop its far end.

"That's the spot." Ben pointed. "It's not quite as long or hollow as La Lib, but we'll have it to ourselves. Mostly sand bottom."

For the rest of the walk, I stared at the distant foam taking shape until I could make out the takeoff spot and some work-able sections.

"Don Goyo!" Ben hollered.

"What says the man?" a big-bellied Salvadoran called back.

We'd come upon a family's home and compound at the base of the point. A small adobe house stood against the bluffs, along with a separate kitchen and composting latrine. A woman washed dishes at a cistern. Two shirtless boys turned to stare. Dwarf coconut trees sheltered the packed sand of their patio. The man with the belly came to greet us.

Ben shook his hand. "Do you remember me?"

"Of course." Don Goyo's face was dark and deeply lined by the sun. His grin was wide, his teeth white and straight.

"This is Malia." Ben put a hand on my back.

"*Mucho gusto.*" I shook Don Goyo's hand.

"Chinese?" he asked.

"No," I said. "Hawaiian." It seemed the simplest explana-tion.

"Hawaiian!" He was impressed. "Pleased to meet you."

"Do you have space for us?" Ben asked. "We brought a tent."

"Of course," Don Goyo said. "Over there, in the shade." He pointed to a spot under the tree at the edge of his compound's perimeter.

"Perfect." Ben nodded.

"Meals?" Goyo asked.

"Please."

"Beer? Bottled water? I'll send the boys to town."

"Yes and yes." Ben took some bills from his pocket and passed them to Don Goyo. "Keep the change."

"Very good." Don Goyo crumpled the money inside his fist. "This is your home now. Relax." He smiled again.

We thanked him and went off to the spot he'd indicated underneath the tree. Don Goyo walked toward his house, calling out for his two sons.

"He seems nice," I said.

"He's great. Here's the deal: He enjoys the occasional beer and cigarette, but the wife won't let him waste money on vice. Long as we offer him booze or smokes, we'll stay on his good side."

"Got it," I said.

"She's a good cook, too. Little heavy on the salt. Let's get camp set up and paddle out."

We raised Ben's tent and stowed our backpacks inside. I changed while he waxed up the boards. As I went to leave the tent, I stopped at the flap and took in the view. A set hit the point break and threw a small barrel at the takeoff section, then formed a fun wall the rest of the way in. The wave was perfectly framed by the rainfly, the water a stone's throw away. In my native city, this kind of view would have been worth several million dollars.

"Did you see that?" Ben said. "Let's get out there."

For the next three days, we traded fun waves at our own personal point break. We rose at sunrise and surfed the morning glass until we were starving for breakfast. In the shade, with the tent fully unzipped, it was possible to nap briefly before breaking out in a sweat. We often walked to town for lunch or Popsicles or simply to kill time. Once the wind died down in the evenings, we'd paddle out for our sunset session and surf until dark. Don Goyo's wife stacked our dinner plates with beans and fried fish. His sons were thrilled to carry boxes of beer and ice back and forth from the store for a few extra coins. In the middle of the night, Ben and I made love, with the sound of the sea so strong inside our ears, I half-expected our tent to wash away.

One afternoon, Don Goyo lowered a cluster of dwarf coconuts from one of his palm trees. He gave lessons on opening them with a machete. I was lucky not to lose any fingers. The six of us spent the afternoon drinking the milk and eating the nutty flesh.

Each night after dinner, Don Goyo joined us at our tent. Ben would roll him a cigarette and offer him a beer. He asked questions about our country, confirming rumors and truths that he'd heard from returned Salvadorans. Did one really need a license to catch fish? Was it truly legal to carry a gun down the street but not an open beer bottle? Were there hospitals for dogs? We all agreed that he was lucky to live where he did. That was perhaps my favorite thing about Don Goyo: the contentment and peace he felt toward his home, his half acre of paradise.

On our final morning, I woke and saw Ben seated just outside the tent. The rising sun had not yet broken over the bluffs opposite the ocean. On the sand in front of us, a herd of cattle walked in the direction of town. A dozen bony beige cows, driven by two teenagers with short sticks, ambled along the tide line, their steps muffled by the sand, their long shadows stretching out toward the sea. They studied our tent and the ocean in turn, unimpressed by either. Behind them, the waves at the point waned in size, but they were still clean and perfectly shaped.

"Morning." I sat down beside Ben and put my arm around

his back, felt that manta ray–shaped muscle below his shoulder.

"You sure you want to go back?" he asked.

I grinned. "The water project needs me."

He sighed. "I'm ready for this. I'm ready to do this full-time for a while."

"How do you mean?" I asked. "Uncrowded waves? Sleeping on the beach?"

He turned to face me. "That and being with you."

Blood rushed to my cheeks.

Ben looked back to the ocean, the cows now gone. "We should travel once we're done," he said. "Buy some wheels, hit the road for a while before real life catches up."

"You mean, like, Mexico?" I asked.

"That'd be fun." He furrowed his brow. "Fuck it. We could go all the way to South America."

I laughed at the audacity of the idea, then saw that he wasn't joking. "You're serious?"

"Why not? Our combined readjustment money. Both our airfare payouts. I brought a little savings with me. It'll be a nice chunk of change."

"How do we get back home once we're done?"

Ben shrugged. "Sell the car. Teach some English in Chile or Argentina. Get a credit card. People do it all the time."

Don Goyo's rooster crowed and startled us both. I put a hand up over my heart.

"Could be the trip of a lifetime," Ben said.

I nodded. Suddenly, I was being persuaded. A minute of silence passed. I laid my head down upon his shoulder. Both of us stared out at the point. The waves looked worth one last paddle out before we made the journey home.

"Ben." I lifted my head again. "I want to finish up this aqueduct. It's important to me."

He smiled and put a hand around my back. "I get that. This would be after. You'll deserve a vacation."

"Yes," I agreed, the very notion rising up without warning and forming itself into a convincing peak. "I'll deserve it."

26

In the morning, a hysterical Kristy shakes me awake. I'm still in the hammock. No sign of Ben or the Jeep. "Chinita? Where is everybody?"

By which she means, *Where is Pelo?*

"I'm not sure," I say. "Probably the police station."

"The police?"

"They chased us last night. It's all a big misunderstanding." In fact, it was more a case of too much understanding too fast.

"What will you do about it?" she asks.

I don't quite know how to answer that question. But now, in the daylight, it seems plausible that I could head down to the station and talk this all out. "I guess I'll go over there, see if somebody will listen to me."

Outside, a man pedals a creaking three-wheeled cart full of produce. He has a loudspeaker and microphone attached. In a robotic monotone, he mutters the prices of plantains, potatoes, onions, and mangoes. Kristy turns to him, then stares back at me and sighs. Frustrated, she walks off to buy vegetables.

I shower, then do my best to dress up like somebody who could cause consequences for a local cop. From out of the mattress bundle, I take a hundred-dollar bill and tuck it into my bra.

On the way out, I tell Kristy to be sure to watch our bedroom. She seems hurt by this remark, but I don't much care.

The police station isn't far. I've walked past it hundreds of times but never had any business there—not even when we'd captured burglars in our hotel room. The interior reminds me of the public schools I've seen in this country: the furniture too small for those who sit at it, the blue-and-white two-tone walls painted the colors of the Salvadoran flag, the stiff uniforms likely sewn by the mothers of those who wear them.

An officer with a crew cut waits behind the counter. He holds a phone to his ear and listens to somebody on the other end, uttering the occasional "Yes" or "I understand." He doesn't seem to notice that I've entered.

I put both hands on the counter. He looks up at me, then goes back to muttering and agreeing. Finally, he says good-bye and hangs up.

"Can I help you?"

"Did you bring a gringo in here last night? With red hair?

A beard?" I use my hands to draw an air beard over my own face. "I need to see him."

The officer wrinkles his eyes as if deep in thought. In the ensuing minute, I nearly come undone. Only now do I allow myself to consider the much more terrible possibilities of where Ben might've wound up last night—that he might've been dealt with by the criminals, and not just the crooked cops.

"It was two gringos, was it not?"

I exhale so hard, it ripples the fabric of my shirt. "Yes." I nod. "But I don't give a shit about the other one." If there were some way I could lay the whole blame on Pelo, a button I could press to force him to take the fall, believe me, I'd do it in an instant.

The officer shakes his head. "Sorry, I can't help you."

"That's too bad." From out of my bra, I draw the hundred-dollar bill and lay it flat on the counter with both my hands. "You must get thirsty doing this job. I'd like to offer you a little something, for a soda."

He looks down at the bill, then back up at me. "Let's go." One meaty hand gestures for me to follow, the other grabs the hundred from off the counter. On his wrist is the expensive watch that Pelo wore yesterday.

He leads me out a back door. We cross a courtyard and enter another bare and boxy concrete room. This one holds a card table and two small plastic chairs.

"Wait here," he says.

I nod.

He starts to leave, then turns back to me. "The beard, right?"

"Yes," I say.

He shuts the door and I wait. For a few minutes, I wonder if he's taken off with my money. What could I do about it if he had?

The iron latch jangles and the door swings open. I see Ben's face, backlit by the morning sun. One of his ears is swollen and crusted in dried blood. His wrists are bound with tarnished cuffs. The same officer's hand rests on his shoulder.

I run over to hug him, but Ben says, "Don't!"

We stare at each other, our faces only inches apart. I take a confused step back.

"It might be better if he doesn't see too much . . . affection." Ben gestures with his head toward the policeman.

I nod. The two of us sit in the plastic chairs. The officer leans against the back wall.

"Did they do that to you?" I can't look away from his ear.

"It happened last night," Ben says. "It's not so bad."

It looks bad to me. "What do we do now?"

"Not sure." Ben shrugs. "Doesn't seem to be much actual law enforcement going on here. We haven't been charged or anything legal like that."

"What happened to the last bale?" I look over at the officer leaning on the wall. He shows no signs of understanding English.

Ben laughs. "The cops got all confused. They finally put it in the squad car and dropped it off at the real crack house."

I don't find this funny.

"We were there for a while, waiting in the car."

"So it's true," I say. "The cops are in the pocket of those guys?"

Ben nods. "They're definitely pulling the strings with us."

"Is that a bad thing or a good thing?"

Ben squints and jukes his head back and forth. "Best case,

they'll decide we've learned our lesson and let us go. Worst case, they'll think we've seen too much. I'm not sure there's anything we can do about it either way."

"I have to do something." The words hiss their way out of my mouth.

"Malia." Ben cringes as though about to remove a splinter. "It might be better if you get out of this town. If these guys decide to do anything drastic, they won't want any loose ends."

"What?" I'm taken aback. "There's no way!" I want to tell him I'd never leave him here. Instead, I say, "I don't even have a passport."

"Get to San Salvador, then. Someplace safer. Even Cara Sucia." Ben turns toward the guard for a second, then back to me. "I'm worried about you."

"I'm worried about *you*!"

He nods and stares down at the table. "All I wanted was a fucking surf trip."

The guard looks at his new wristwatch and says, "*Ya*."

"What should I do?" My eyes water.

"Be careful," Ben says. "Whatever else happens, this situation is not going to leave La Libertad. I'm sure of that."

The guard puts a hand on Ben's shoulder. "*Vamos*."

"I love you," I say.

"I love you, too, Malia."

I follow as far as the door while Ben is taken away.

For the next hour or so, I pace the courtyard of La Posada. By the looks she gives me from the kitchen, it's obvious that Kristy expects me to find a solution to this mess. I have a seat in the dining room and ask her for a beer.

She slams the bottle down on the table and gives me an angry glare.

"Kristy?" I stop her before she walks back into the kitchen. "Did you lose anybody, in the earthquake?"

"No one close to me, thanks to God," she says. "My mother was on a bus from San Vicente. They were among the last ones to pass by before the tragedy there."

One of the more gruesome episodes brought on by the quake was a landslide on the Pan-American Highway. Several buses full of people were buried alive in dirt and mud. It's a busy route, one that most Salvadorans must travel at one time or another. While not the deadliest aspect of the quake, it is perhaps the one that has most captured the imaginations of us, the survivors.

"We were both lucky," I say.

"Yes. You heard about Don Adán's family?"

"No." I realize that I've not seen the owner of La Posada in several weeks. "What about them?"

"His in-laws lost their home, outside Santa Tecla. That's been the biggest change for me. I've hardly seen the owners since."

"I didn't realize," I mumble.

"They may try to sell this place. The señora never liked the business. I hope my job is stable for a while longer." She walks back into the kitchen.

I carry my beer up to the roof and stare out at the rectangle of visible ocean. Not long ago, Ben and I were twenty-four hours away from leaving this place, from the trip of a lifetime. That kind of freedom—the very idea of it—feels unthinkable to me now.

The sun creeps into the last quarter of the sky. I have to figure something out.

In the bedroom, I find my baggy jeans and hiking boots—the clothes I once wore to work on the aqueduct. I tie my hair back in a tight ponytail. Thankfully, that wad of bills still waits under the mattress. I pass them through my fingers a few times. It's plenty. The ceiling fan sticks at the far end of its turn, lets out several clicks, and then goes the other way. I put a hundred dollars under the pillow. I break the rest of it up into four rubber-banded packets and put those into the four pockets of my jeans. I tuck one tightly folded Salvadoran bill into the palm of my hand.

Outside, the sun has begun to set. I leave La Posada and head for the crack house. My only plan is to get Ben out of that jail, or die trying.

I don't allow myself to hesitate crossing the street or at the stoop. My fist knocks against the red wood of the door. I let a long breath out through my nose.

The door opens a few inches and a bearded face sticks out. "What do you want?" He blinks hard. "¿*Mota?*"

"No," I say. "I want to enter."

"Sorry." He pushes the door toward me.

"Here." I hold up a fifty-colón bill. The rumor is that one must pay to go in, but I've never heard why or how much.

He tenses his nostrils and takes the money from my hand. Then he pulls the door open and gestures for me to come inside.

With one long stride, I cross the threshold into this, the last forbidden place in La Libertad. My eyes dilate in the dark. The doorman goes back to his post as soon as I'm inside—with no mention of any change from my bill.

The only light comes from several small red bulbs burning at low angles along the walls. It reminds me of old pizza parlors. I see a few bony bodies seated on the floor, the spark of a lighter from the corner of my eye. This first room is connected to a narrow hallway. A gas stove sits upon a table in the corner by the door, a round tank of fuel at its side, blackened pots stacked atop its grill. The place smells of body odor and pool chemicals. Along the walls are posters and centerfolds of naked women. Gang signs and initials are scribbled onto the white rounds of their breasts and buttocks.

As my vision improves, I make out the face of Peseta. He sits on an overturned milk crate against the wall, next to others. Our eyes meet. He wags his index finger back and forth, warning me not to speak to him.

"What do you want, *mi niña*?" A tall man materializes from the hallway. He is shirtless, in American-style oversize jeans, his chest covered in gang tattoos: MS, 13, long-nailed demon hands making a series of signs. He wears a leather belt that has EL SALVADOR written in blocky stencils, alongside pictures of cowboy boots and cacti. He smiles and shows a golden front tooth. Along his forehead runs the phrase *Pardon Me Mother,* in a bluish cursive script. He looks me up and down, grins.

"I need to speak to whoever's in charge around here," I say.

He laughs hard, throws back his head. "What do you think this is? The customer service department?"

"I have information," I say, "about what happened last night."

That gets his attention. He nods for a long moment, then motions for me to follow him. Peseta and I exchange one last glance before I head down the hall. He shakes his head back and forth like a disappointed parent.

Pardon Me Mother pounds on the last door at the end of the hallway. "*Macizo,*" he says to the wood. "Got something out here that might be of interest to you."

Pardon Me cracks open the door. He puts a hand on my shoulder and roughly ushers me in.

Inside, it's like a room from a totally different building. A ceiling fan rotates slowly above; its lamps keep the room well lit. A man in a white guayabera sits at a large desk. His pockmarked face has no tattoos. His hair is oily and black, well along into male-pattern baldness. He wears wire-frame glasses that look a few years out of style. A ledger notebook sits before him. The place reminds me of the doctor's office where we took Pelo. In a chair beside the desk sits the same police officer who took me to see Ben this morning. He cocks his head at the sight of me. In one corner, there's a large iron door that looks like it leads outside to the alley.

"What in the devil is this little Chinese girl doing in my office?" asks the man at the desk.

Pardon Me Mother clears his throat. "She says that she was there last night, *Macizo,* that she has information."

The cop leans over and speaks into the boss's ear.

The boss removes his glasses and rubs at the space between his eyes. "All right," he says. "Let's hear what you have to say."

"Yes, sir." I swallow. "This is all a big misunderstanding. You see, we believed we were doing this errand for you, for your ... organization. That big-haired gringo, the one with the eye patch, he's an idiot. He made arrangements with those other ..." I struggle to come up with a word that they won't find offensive. "Other salesmen. Ben—the bearded one—and I, we didn't know. We thought it was a service to you. Instantly, we saw the error."

The boss stares on at me, impatient and unmoved. "You were there last night?"

"Yes."

"To whom did you deliver those goods?" he asks.

I pause. "It was a blue house, a few blocks from here. There were two men. I didn't recognize them."

"And the original delivery?"

"By sea." I suddenly feel useful, like I have something to offer. "There were two of them as well, their faces covered with handkerchiefs. At the cove we call Kilometer Ninety-nine."

The boss turns to the policeman, who offers him a nod. They seem to know all this already.

The boss turns back to me. "Is that all?"

I decide to lay all of my cards on the table. "I have the money. I assume you have the product or know how you can get it. I need the bearded one back. That's all I ask."

The boss crosses his arms in front of his chest. "Where are you from?" he asks me in perfect English.

"The States." I switch to English as well. "Hawai'i, actually."

"Do you know much about the Conflict?"

"The Conflict?"

"Yes. The civil war that took place in this country not so long ago."

It's the last question I expect him to ask. "A little," I say. "I've lived in El Salvador for nearly two years, most of the time in a small village north of here. Some of the families there fought with the Frente, most with the army." I shrug. "It's hard not to hear things, under those circumstances.

"Have you heard of El Mozote?" His English is excellent.

I nod. "I visited. Almost two years ago."

"You've been there?" He raises his eyebrows. "Seen the little memorial with the silhouettes?"

"Yes," I say. "It's very moving."

The policeman's chair creaks as he leans back and crosses his legs. As I thought this morning, he doesn't appear to understand English.

"I was there, you know," the boss man continues, "on that day twenty years ago. I come from a village nearby. I lost my family then. You understand what happened, yes?"

"Rape," I say. "Murder. Women and children all killed for no good reason. Some pretense about finding the guerilla."

"Little girls." He holds up the palm of his hand to indicate a short stature. "Ten or twelve years old. Can you imagine? They cut off heads until their arms were tired and their machetes were dull. Then they used the machine guns."

Tears well up behind my eyes. The room goes silent but for the slow rotation of the fan above, like the blades on an old helicopter.

"The journalists always mention that those soldiers were the ones trained by the gringos."

I manage to whisper, "I'm not really a gringo."

"But I tend to think it's impossible to train anyone to commit that kind of brutality."

I nod.

"These young men today"—he points with his lips at Pardon Me Mother—"they will never suffer the way that my generation suffered." He shakes his head. "And still they walk around as if they have some chip on their shoulder."

I turn toward Pardon Me Mother. He doesn't understand a word. I wonder if the two of them are related.

"Let me ask you something," the boss says. "What do you believe you were doing there last night?"

"Last night?" With the El Mozote story, I've nearly forgotten my reason for coming here. "I thought we would make some fast money. Cash was stolen from us recently. This . . . this errand—it seemed a good way to settle things. That's all."

The boss man nods. "Some fast money. A way to even accounts." He turns to the cop momentarily, then back to me. "It's interesting. I hid in a tree and watched twenty years ago as those so-called soldiers committed all those horrible acts— killing children as if they were breaking open anthills. I asked myself, How can one do such things? Now I understand that they couldn't see it for what it was. If I had asked one of those young men, all he would have said was, 'I was pulling a trigger, following orders.' And the superiors—who are even more irredeemable—they'd have simply said they were winning a war, saving their country from godless communism. Do you understand what I mean?"

"I think so," I say. "It all depends on the frame of reference. If your focus is too narrow or too wide, you can obscure the act itself. Not see it for what it is."

From the main room down the hall, a ranchero song suddenly blares. Pardon Me Mother turns his head toward the sound, unsure if he should go and silence it.

"So when you say that you were only interested in some fast money, a small measure of economic justice, I have to ask myself, Does she not understand the kinds of consequences associated with this thing that she did last night? Or is she just stupid?"

"Consequences?" After following his meandering line of thought for so many minutes, I'm now confused. "You mean for the users?" Is this man about to lecture me on the dangers of drug abuse?

"What I mean," he pounds one meaty fist upon the table, "are the consequences of starting a rivalry in my business. Have you any idea the sort of bloodshed that occurs whenever there's a power vacuum in this industry? Young Salvadoran men—my friends and family, in some cases—will have to die by the dozens if anyone presents a real challenge to me in this city." He shouts now, both hands clasped upon the desk's edge, flecks of his spittle dotting the top. "So tell me: Why should those two moronic gringos be spared?"

I fear that my legs might collapse beneath me. The scariest thing of all, I find, is that he's absolutely right. "I swear to you, I didn't know there was any rivalry. All I did was drive. It was that other gringo who made the arrangements with the men from the blue house."

"Of course." He shakes his head and snickers. "Only driving—turning the wheel and pushing the pedals. Only earning a little fast money."

Pardon Me Mother and the policeman tentatively laugh along with him; neither knows why.

"I thought we were working for you," I say.

"Oh yes! I forgot," he says sarcastically. "You were performing a service for me. You were on my side, right? Tell me: Do you know what they called that operation in El Mozote?"

"Operation Rescue." Why do I remember that?

"That's correct," he says. "Operation Rescue." He smiles, nearly laughing at the absurdity of it.

We pass a tense few seconds in which the only sound is the music from down the hall.

"I have your money." I take the four wads of dollars out of

my pockets and drop them all upon his desk. "I need Ben released; then we'll be no more trouble to you."

The boss man quickly puts all the cash into one of his desk drawers, as if the sight of it is somehow unseemly.

"I'm sorry," I say. "Please."

He lets out a big sigh, looking bored by the whole exchange. He turns to the policeman and says in Spanish, "Let those two idiots go already." He shakes his head, still staring at the cop. "If there's any thing that's more trouble than one dead American, it's two dead Americans."

"Or three." The cop points an index finger in my direction, like a pistol.

Everyone but me laughs.

The cop rises from his chair and lets himself out through the iron door at the side.

"Thank you," I say to the boss man. I fight a sudden urge to prostrate myself at his feet, to kiss his ring or touch the edge of his garment—some timeless and Catholic show of respect.

He stands up from his chair and shrugs. "It's only logical, really." He pulls the drawer open, removes all the money I gave him, and stuffs it into a paper bag. He rolls the top down and makes a handle, like it's a big sandwich.

"Well done," he says to Pardon Me Mother. "She's all yours. Nothing too rough, eh?"

"*Simón*." Pardon Me smiles and nods.

"How's that?" I stop myself before asking what he means by "She's all yours."

The boss goes to the iron door. Pardon Me Mother reaches out and runs the back side of his first two fingers down my cheek.

"*¡Tranquila!*" he hisses, as if I were a horse about to be broken. The gold tooth flashes from between his lips.

"What the hell?" I say to the boss in English.

He opens the door, turns back to me, and shrugs. "It's how things are done. Your friends have suffered for their offense. Isn't it fitting that you suffer a little as well?"

"You can't just offer me to him!" I swat away Pardon Me's hand.

"You'll survive," the boss man says. "In this country, we've been doing it for decades. Who knows? Perhaps you'll even grow stronger."

The iron door shuts with a clang.

Pardon Me Mother steps toward me. "*Vaya.*" He undoes the buckle of his belt and slips it out through the loops of his pants. "You can relax, or we can do this the hard way. Your decision."

The sight of him physically sickens me. The door is only a few meters away, on the room's far side. With both hands, I push him in the sternum and let out a groan. He's more solid than I expected. My shove doesn't move him an inch. I step high and try to run around him instead.

Then the blow. The belt is wrapped around his hand. I hear the sound before I feel anything. It's a crack like an old tree falling—the sound of something strong giving way. The taste of sweaty leather fills the inside of my mouth, followed by the mineral warmth of blood.

Finally, there's the pain. It's like a foreign thing along my lips and teeth, under my gums, my skin. My vision goes grainy, then fades to black. In my former life, this would be the part where they'd blow the whistle, when everybody would take a step back and the grown-ups would come onto the court. But that life is thousands of miles from here. My limp body bends and twists through the blackness as through a big wave after a wipeout.

With my tongue, I try to count my own teeth but can't keep the numbers straight. When I open my eyes again, my face is down against the plastic top of the desk. My arms are bound behind me somehow—both bent so far, they feel broken. I move my hands a little and brush the low-grade leather of that same EL SALVADOR belt.

There's an audible grunt, then a sudden gust of air against my hips. With one violent motion, my jeans are pulled down to my ankles. Pardon Me Mother steps back into my field of vision. The tattoo on his forehead still asks forgiveness, but his eyes offer no penance.

"You see." He reaches one hand up to the tight bundle of my arms. "This would all be so much easier if you would just relax!"

He torques an end of the belt. One arm feels as if it's about to come away at the shoulder; the other is numb from fingers to elbow. I try to resist, but that grinds my aching mouth farther into the desk. Pardon Me Mother slaps my ass with his open hand, and that feels like the only part of me that's not about to shatter.

He lets go of my arms. I shut my eyes and open them. Now Pardon Me has his own dick in his hand. It's crooked and uncircumcised, like a length of knotty wood or one of those blind subterranean moles. He spits into his palm twice and then rubs the saliva into the skin of his cock. I squirm with every remaining muscle but get nowhere. Even my feet are bound by the wad of denim around my ankles.

Now I can't see him, but I feel him pull at my arms from behind.

"Get away!" I scream through a broken mouth. "Help!" I can't tell if it's English or Spanish or just some soup of syllables.

Pardon Me's whole body presses me against the desk. His kneecap pushes my legs apart. I feel that crooked dick against the inside of my thigh. He puts one of his hands over my mouth. He hardly has to cover it, only to pinch and prod at the wound enough to shut me up.

Then that same hand—now wet with my own blood and spittle—is below my navel and moving lower. The tears come hard, wetting my cheek and pooling up on the plastic top of the desk. They make a puddle right in the spot where I laid that money down—which I believed would be the last sacrifice I'd have to make in this room.

"Stop! Stop!" I squirm and kick, but he has my lower body pinned against his. His palm presses into my pubic hair. Two moist fingers pry me open and make way for the ragged fingernail of a third.

"Relax," he hisses into my ear again.

Finally, I wonder if he's right. I cannot stop him, no matter how hard I try. Is this my punishment after all? I've been trying to undo fate for weeks now. I couldn't simply accept the earthquake or the loss of my project. Even the stolen passport wouldn't convince me to give up on the trip. Will it take being raped by a gangster to teach me that this nation and this world are indifferent to my plans? The fight drains from my limbs. I blow a hot breath out through my bloody lips. Relax. Stop fighting. Surrender.

In that very instant, the pressure on both sides of my pelvis abates.

"That's enough, Cheecho. ¡Basta!" A different voice is in

the room with us, speaking a gravelly Spanish. "Take a step back."

Those two heavy hands come away from me. No sweaty, stinking male flesh touches mine. The sensation is so liberating, it's as if I've learned to fly.

"Remove the belt," says the same small voice.

I close my eyes as my arms roughly come unbound. To my surprise, they're both still attached to my shoulders. Pins and needles fill the numb one.

"Pull your pants up, Chinita. I'm very bashful."

I'm finally able to turn and see who's come to help me. Though he hardly reaches Pardon Me's chest, he has a death grip on his ponytail, and a small silver blade—it looks like a butter knife that's been sharpened on both sides—held tip-first against my attacker's windpipe. It's Peseta.

I pull up my pants and fasten them. Pardon Me twitches and snorts, but Peseta keeps a steely grip on the hair and the knife.

"Thank you," I manage to say.

"There's the door, Chinita," Peseta says. "I'd go if I were you."

"You're a fucking dead man, Peseta!" Pardon Me shouts. "You hear me? That's a promise."

I can't help but stare at Peseta. "What will you do?" My eyes scan the room for something heavy, an object big and blunt enough to bash Pardon Me's face in.

"Don't worry, Chinita." Peseta grins from behind the bigger man. "I'm just going to have a little talk with my old friend here. We have history, him and me. You run along."

"But what . . . what will they do to you?"

"We'll fucking kill him, that's what!" Pardon Me shouts.

Peseta tightens his grip. A red dot of blood appears on Pardon Me's neck. "These assholes have been trying to kill me with their crack rocks for ten years. Maybe they'll have more luck with their guns and knives."

Someone bangs on the wooden interior door to the room. Peseta has locked it from this side. "Don't speak!" he hisses at Pardon Me.

My feet feel planted to the ground.

"Go on, Chinita!" Peseta scolds now. "There's the door. Do this one favor for me." He pulls hard on the other man's pony-tail. "Go!"

I nod. He's put himself in grave danger to save me. The least I can do is allow myself to be saved.

"Thank you," I say again, then open the iron door.

For the second night in a row, I make a desperate late-night run through the streets of La Libertad. This time, it's much shorter, and I know exactly where I'm going.

The gate is open at La Posada. I'm shocked to see the Jeep parked inside again, in front of Pelo's stupid stack of cement. In all the commotion of the last twenty-four hours, I'd forgotten that we owned the thing.

"Ben!" I scream. He comes running from over by the room. We meet halfway through the courtyard and he wraps me up inside his arms. I sob against his chest, staining his T-shirt with tears and the blood from my mouth.

"What happened to you?" he asks.

"I was at the crack house," I say. "I got them to let you out."

"Are you all right?"

"Barely. It got ugly."

Ben's face goes pale, like he's unsure whether or not he wants to know more. His ear is swollen and still crusty with dried blood. "Let me see your mouth," Ben says. He tugs open my mouth and grimaces. "Your lip's split. And your gums are swollen up, but the teeth look okay."

I'm shocked that none are missing.

Pelo walks over to join us, eating pork rinds from a bag. For a moment, the three of us stand there in relative silence, broken only by Pelo's crunching. Our three wounds have us looking like the "See no evil, hear no evil, speak no evil" monkeys. Or some stupider version of them that never quite learned their lessons.

"Hey, Chinita!" His mouth full, Pelo overenunciates the words, as if speaking to the locals in his poor Spanish. "What about the money?" He rubs a thumb and forefinger together. "You still have it?"

"The money?" I take a step toward him, fresh anger coursing through my veins. "*The money?*" I take another step, but this time I slap him across the face.

"Oww! What the fuck?" He touches his own cheek. Reddish pork-rind dust dots his chin. "It was only a question."

"All you care about is your fucking money." I pound my balled-up fists against his chest, my vision all blurred by rage and tears. "Do you have any clue what happened to me tonight? I nearly died because of you." And Peseta may still die, I think, but I can't quite bring myself to say it. "All because of you and your dumb-ass plan."

I land one square blow to his rib cage before Ben grabs me from behind and pins my arms to my sides. Pelo shakes his head and slinks off toward Kristy's room.

"I fucking hate you!" I follow the words with a hasty wad of spit, but it falls short of him and lands on the dirt of the court-yard.

Ben pulls me several paces away. "Easy, Malia. Easy," he whispers into my ear. "You're okay now. We're all right."

"I want to leave. I need to get out of here. Now. I don't give a shit about our trip anymore. I just want to go."

Ben's restraining hold morphs into something more like a hug.

"And I want to talk to my dad. I need to see him. I want to go home."

"Okay," Ben says. "We can do all that. Fuck South America. We'll go to Hawai'i. Together. I don't care where it is, as long as we go together."

The moment he says that, I hug him back—as hard as I ever have. Kristy closes and locks the gate to the courtyard. Back inside the hotel, back inside Ben's arms, I finally feel like we might indeed be all right.

"But Malia, we have to wait until morning. It's not safe right now. You get that, don't you?"

The idea of not running from this place, of settling in—even for just one night—is like a strong medicine that takes a second to swallow. "Yes," I admit. "You're right."

"Let's go to bed," Ben says. "We can bail first thing."

I nod. We start toward the bedroom.

"How'd you get the car back?" I point to the Jeep.

Ben shrugs. "The cop handed me the keys when they let us out. It was behind the station the whole time."

Ben stops right in front of our room, takes me by each hand. "Malia, what happened to you tonight?"

I shake my head. "Could we talk about it later?"

He nods, then gives me another hug.

Before we climb into bed, I double-check the door lock and find the jar of Valium that Peseta brought to me yesterday. I place two of them on my tongue, like I'm receiving Communion and the little yellow pills might become the flesh of my ragged Savior.

27

Toward the end of our Peace Corps training, Jim, the country director, interviewed each of us one by one. Our impression was that he'd use this information to decide where to send us. There was a rumor that the Peace Corps always gave you the opposite of what you asked for—say the beach and you get the mountains. That idea seems silly to me now, as if our bosses had nothing better to do than play games with us and build character.

Alex, Courtney, and I waited our turns. We wondered aloud whether we might end up close together.

I was the first to be called in. Jim had a pad of paper and a stack of files. We introduced ourselves and exchanged a firm handshake.

"I've looked over your materials," Jim said. "Very impressive."

"Thanks." I wasn't sure what about those documents might have impressed him, but I didn't bother to ask.

"So, Malia." He closed a manila folder that lay on the table between us. "Why do you want to be a Peace Corps volunteer?"

His question caught me by surprise. I'd been anticipating something about urban versus rural, inland versus coastal. In the end, I settled on the honest answer, mostly because I couldn't come up with anything more compelling. "I want to see the world."

Jim nodded, as if that were an explanation he'd heard before.

"I come from a small island," I said. "A lot of the people there never leave. I got my degree and my student loans, and realized I was about to find a job and work away the rest of my life. I thought I should see some other places first. But I didn't know where to start."

Jim scribbled on his legal pad; it couldn't have been more than a word or two. "Was this a hard decision for you?"

"It wasn't hard for me." I stared down at the yellow paper, unable to make out his writing. "I've never looked back. But it was hard to break the news. My father would rather I'd gone straight to a career or graduate school. I'm not sure he fully understands what the Peace Corps is. He sees it as an indulgence."

"I have to be completely honest," Jim said. "In a case like yours—a trainee with your level of technical skills—the assignment is usually a no-brainer. It's likely to choose you, so to speak. But I suppose I should ask, to be fair: Do you have a preference as to where you live?" He smiled.

"No," I said. "I joined up willing to go anywhere in the world. I still feel that way."

He nodded and wrote another illegible note.

That night, Alex and I sneaked a liter of cheap vodka into Courtney's host family's house. The three of us sat out on the open porch attached to her bedroom. We mixed the vodka with a pink and clumpy powered drink mix inside a plastic bottle. Alex passed out cigarettes. The sun set behind one shoulder of the volcano.

"What did you guys say when Jim asked why you'd joined the Peace Corps?" I was surprised we'd not discussed it already.

"Pshh." Courtney rolled her eyes and blew out a lungful of smoke. "I came up with some crap about wanting to save the world and tried to keep a straight face." She took a slug of the makeshift cocktail, then passed it to me.

Alex was in one of his distant moods, staring out at the San Vicente volcano. We heard Spanish arguments and a crying baby from inside the house.

I took a sip and passed the bottle to Alex.

Somebody banged on the iron of the bedroom door. Courtney rose to deal with it.

"What about you?" I asked Alex. We'd not yet kissed at this point in training, but it was something I'd thought about.

He held the bottle up to his eyes and checked the level of the liquid. "I told him I joined because I wanted to be a better person." Alex gulped the drink.

Suddenly more attracted to him, I stared at his face until it became awkward and I had to turn away.

"*Sí, sí*," Courtney shouted into the house. "*Momento*, okay?" She closed the door and came back to join us.

Alex passed her the bottle and she took a long pull from it.

"So," Courtney said, "what were we just talking about?"

"Nothing," Alex replied. "Saving the world and other impossibilities."

28

I wake from a dreamless, sweaty slumber caused by the pills. The paralyzed weight of my own body feels like an anchor pulling me downward and tethering me to the bed.

Ben shakes me before first light. "Chi-ni-ta," he whispers.

With blurry eyes, I see two big pieces of sweet bread in his hands. I rise and sit up on the bed, take one of the sticky rolls and have a bite. My swollen mouth still aches, but I'm able to chew.

"Can we leave now?" I ask.

"Hold up. Let's talk this over for a sec."

"Let's just go, Ben. Let's throw our shit in the Jeep and go. Get out of here."

"Not quite yet, Malia." Ben puts a hand on my shoulder. "In a couple of hours, maybe."

"Why? What are we waiting for?"

"The surf," Ben says. "It's going off."

"Waves?" But before he can answer, I hear the roar of the ocean coming from outside.

"The point's firing," Ben says.

I nod, finish the sweet bread, and grab the bikini hanging from the doorknob. "Let's go surf, then."

Ben smiles, and scratches a comb across the wax on my board.

Kristy has not yet awakened or opened the gate, so we head up to the roof. I wait while Ben lowers himself down the tree. Once he's on the ground, I hand him the boards and climb down myself.

In bare feet, we walk out along the path toward the point. I've not traveled this route in over a week, and already it feels unfamiliar. We pick our way across the boulders in front of the cemetery—the bandits still sleeping in—and past the few big houses at the far end of the point. Once we come to the rusty pipes, Ben lays his board down and does a windmill with his arms. I start to put in, but he says, "Wait."

I turn to face him, surfboard under my arm.

"Look." Ben extends one finger toward the ocean.

At the point, the first wave of the first real set of this surreal swell breaks. A perfectly shaped double-overhead bomb, it pitches at the takeoff and stays top to bottom all the way through to the inside. Ben and I watch four more break after it—riding them with our minds—then we paddle out.

There is no wind. Inexplicably, no other surfers join us. Salt water stings my hurt mouth a little, but not as badly as I feared. Once in position, we don't wait long for another set. Ben takes the first wave. I watch him hit the lip once—in that compact, functional stance of his—and then disappear down the line.

Wanting to take off deeper, I paddle over the second wave and go for the third. It breaks so far outside that the Mother Rock isn't a problem. Straight away, I can tell it's as good a wave as I've ever ridden. If given the power, I'd not move one single drop of water in any direction. The face is fully workable, but I've got barrels on the brain.

I surf conservatively through the first section, pumping up a little speed, staying in the trim. In a fatter section, I do a big cutback and steal a view of the curl.

Farther inside, the wave jacks up along the point. I plant a hand in the face—up to the fingertips, up to the wrist, then up to the elbow. Like some amateur, I first try to lean backward into the tube. The nose of my board rises and the hull pushes water. I crouch lower and shuffle a step forward on the deck—my front foot dangerously close to the waxless region.

Low as I can get without lying down on the board, I turn my eyes up toward the lip and watch the arc of dark water circle all the way across. It's bigger than the barrel I was in six months ago. I can stand straight up. Worried about going too deep, I take my arm out from the face and gain speed inside the tube. I reach up with one hand and touch the watery ceiling above me. Still shedding the effects of the Valium, I wonder if this isn't all some sublime dream.

Over the echoing rush of the barrel, a hooting human sound reaches my ears. I look out the almond-shaped door to this green-glowing room and see Ben there in the distance. He sits on his board, both fists held up in the air, howling like a jackal at the shack I'm in. That vision—of my lover happy and proud of me, surrounded on all sides by water and speed—is the most beautiful thing I can remember seeing. The tube is more like a centrifuge than a pedestal: a place where impurities are cast off by motion, and only the purest and most basic stuff remains.

The memory of my last tube—and the close-out that ended it—looms high in my mind. I pump my way out on the next section, and lose sight of Ben. On the messier inside bowls, I do a couple of big carves. The wave finally closes down. I turn and paddle back out.

The sets are so long and consistent that Ben and I see each other only in passing. Even when we're both on the outside, we find little to say.

Ben was right all along: Surfing is a way of life. The forsaken sport of my forsaken ancestors, it isn't something I could outgrow or get over. It's worth years of waiting to get a morning like this at a spot like the point. And that's the thing about surfing: You could lose your job, your money, your family, your home, all of your best-laid plans. Your world could crumble right before your eyes. But at the end of the day, a perfect wave is still perfect.

Every accomplishment in my life—my education, my hard work, my altruism—they're all like a currency that could supposedly be cashed in for pleasure, comfort, or security sometime in the future. Surfing isn't that way. In a world of paper and promises, surfing has real value. It's like gold.

We stay out for over three hours, until my arms hang limp at my sides. The sun rises and reflects off the water. The day's first onshore winds start to turn the surf messy. Ben holds up a single finger to indicate one more wave and we'd go in. I nod. We'll quit while we're ahead. Still, I cannot understand why none of the locals have paddled out by now, especially after such a long flat spell.

While we ride white water in on our bellies, it becomes clear that something is wrong. Clouds of dust and smoke rise from town. The Hotel Sandra along the waterfront is now renamed the Hot Sand. The other letters lie scattered upon the beach. The seaside restaurants, where the mariachi bands played during our sunset sessions, are in ruins. We leave the water and climb the stone stairs in front of the beach.

All of La Libertad—what's left of it—takes to the streets. Old women cry and pray. Young men argue over shovels and water. Bodies lie about, already dragged from the buildings. Some people are dead, others dying. Dust is everywhere. The people and their clothes are all shades of gray. Ben and I look ridiculous: baggy bright-colored shorts, neon triangles of spandex, wet hair, surfboards under our arms. The only things in the city not covered in that gray dust, we are like two cartoon characters walking down a real-life street.

"What happened?" I ask stupidly.

"C'mon," Ben says.

La Posada is only half there. The more expensive strip of rooms, on the ocean side, still stands. The cheaper rooms, where we stay, are rubble. Our bedroom is nothing more than a mound of bricks and dust. Had it not been for our dawn patrol, Ben and I would be underneath it. This morning, surfing the point literally saved our lives.

The kitchen and dining room are rattled but not collapsed.

Kristy's bedroom looks intact. The too-high stack of concrete bags fell straight into our Jeep. The windshield is shattered, the hood bent inward, the grille cracked and dangling. A high-pitched hissing sounds from the radiator. Inside, the cab is full of smashed glass, broken chrome, and cement dust.

From the kitchen, Kristy limps toward us, letting out violent screams. Mascara lines streak their way down her face. At what hour did she rise to apply her makeup? Something must've fallen on her foot. I can't make out what she says, but I figure it's more of the hurried and desperate prayers that I heard on the heels of the first earthquake.

"Where?" Ben shouts back at her. Kristy points toward the pile of rubble in the corner. Finally, her words arrange themselves into sense: Pelochucho. Ben and I look over at the ruins of Pelo's room. The sun rises a notch higher, clearing the hills in the distance and hitting us right in the eyes.

Ben moves chunks of roof and wall with his hands. I follow. Kristy collapses against one of the Jeep's wheels. We pick through the mud and concrete. Rebar and chicken wire hold together some of the bigger pieces. I notice that the walls on this part of the hotel weren't made out of bricks or concrete blocks at all. It's adobe, just covered over with a cosmetic layer of cement *repello*—like so many of the recently fallen structures in this country. The ceiling, on the other hand, is poured concrete. The building behind it, which butts up against our fallen wing, is three stories, and casts a shadow over the ruins as we excavate them. I wonder if another tremor isn't on its way, and if those brick walls might cover up Ben and me, in another layer above Pelochucho.

Kristy sets her injured ankle in her lap and prods it with her hands. I find an electrical cord and pull. Once it goes taut,

I tug a bit harder. A ceiling fan with lighting fixtures breaks free of the pile. I lift it by the busted-up blades and toss it to one side.

"There," Ben says. "There he is."

On first glance, I don't notice, not with all the dust discoloring everything. But it's the small of Pelo's back, the gray seam of the board shorts he slept in. There is no chance of survival. A piece of the ceiling—concrete and rebar, half a foot thick and a yard wide—covers his upper body. Pelochucho is dead several times over.

I stand and stare at the ash-colored section of flesh that we've unearthed. Kristy whispers curses at the cheapskate builder of La Posada—I think she means Don Adán, or maybe his father—and the manner in which this part was constructed. She's right. Ben picks the pieces from Pelochucho's legs. I see his small feet. His limbs are crooked and limp, in unnatural postures—so many broken bones.

"A little help," Ben says. He wants to move the section of ceiling off the head and torso. Still in bare feet, we struggle to stand amid the shards and chunks of glass and mud. Ben counts to three and we both lift. Once we have it up at waist level, we switch our grip and flip the whole piece over.

There lies Pelochucho's head. It is a cone of flesh containing the ingredients that might've made up a face: some teeth, an ear, the hair that earned him his nickname, the eye that we all worried over. I take a few steps back and turn away. Ben kicks off the smaller pieces from around the torso. I fold my arms on one side of the Jeep's dark rear window and rest my head there. This is too much. Somebody needs to pull out the power cord and reboot my life.

Ben stumbles forward through the rubble. He gets sick along

the brick wall of the adjacent three-story building. With one forearm, he wipes his face, then turns straight back to the body. With the sheets from Pelochucho's bed, Ben wraps up the dusty corpse. He lifts the bottom sheet by its corners and ties them into a knot above the ankles. He does the same under the neck. Ben finds a wool blanket—which wouldn't have been used on a night so hot—and wraps it around Pelochucho's head.

Still limping, Kristy brings a ball of twine from the kitchen. With his teeth, Ben rips the twine into pieces and ties up the bundle that he's made of Pelochucho's remains. It's as if Ben has done this before.

My body slumps down along the side of the Jeep. Before I know it, my elbows rest on my knees and my ass is on the dirt of the courtyard.

Once Ben has the shroud tied to his satisfaction, he comes over to the Jeep. He finds his hiking boots in the back and laces them up.

With a closed-eyed groan, he tries to hoist the blanketed bundle up onto one shoulder. Pelochucho's body looks shorter than normal, his small feet sticking out one side of the wrap like a sick joke.

"Ben." I point to one corner of the ruins of Pelo's room, indicating the wheeled hard-shell surfboard case we failed to notice. "The coffin."

Ben nods and then pulls it free from the rubble. He lays the case open beside the body. I lift the feet. It's a perfect fit. Ben closes Pelo inside, then lifts one end of the case and rolls it along. The coffin's wheels bump and wobble upon the uneven dirt of the courtyard, but Ben doesn't mind. As he disappears out the gate, I wonder where he's going, why I'm not going with him, and when he'll be back.

I reach around the wreck of the passenger-side window and manage to turn on the Jeep's radio. A newsman says what we could've guessed: An earthquake even stronger than the first has hit, with an epicenter located somewhere inland from La Libertad. Landslides have closed all incoming roads. It's one month, to the day, since the first earthquake. The exact date of the Monkey-Faced Baby's prophecy.

Kristy resumes her sobbing. She wobbles over to me and lays her head in my lap. I wonder if she quarreled with Pelochucho last night. Did she sleep in his room? How many hours had she been up and out of the bed before the chunks of concrete rained down? I imagine the swirling hurricane of second guesses that must now wreak havoc through her mind—the list of things she might've done or not done last night and this morning to bring him out of that bedroom.

I stroke her hair and whisper in English, "I'm sorry." The Spanish version of this phrase translates literally to "I feel it," and that seems disingenuous; I can't comprehend what she is feeling.

The voice on the radio goes on to say that relief boats are at the ready but that "large and violent seas" are preventing them from being launched. After an hour or two, the battery runs out of juice and the radio goes dead.

Ben is gone for hours. I set up a couple of chairs for Kristy—one for her to sit in, another to elevate her ankle. From the freezer, I salvage ice. It melts quickly in the hot sun. Once that's gone, I use orange Popsicles. This causes a sticky puddle of syrup and artificial coloring, which is instantly teemed by hundreds of small black ants.

Fingers spread wide, I place my hand in the center of the sweet orange-and-black puddle. My handprint exists there for a few seconds after I pull the hand away, outlined by the little black bodies. Then it fades once the ants resume their feeding.

After a while, I get the feeling that Kristy is humoring me. It's only an insignificant sprained ankle within a swarming scene of death and destruction, but that's all I can handle.

The sun sets and Ben still has not returned. I take out the tent from our Jeep and set it up there in the courtyard of La Posada, out of the range of any falling walls. Amid the ruins of our hotel room, I find most of the contents from our bedside table—my Valium, a gallon of drinking water, the faded surf magazine we'd all read too many times, the pages of Pelo's hotel contract, which now might be useful only as kindling.

I wipe the dust from off the top of the water bottle, then use it to wash down two of the Valium. That's the only way I'll get any sleep tonight.

29

How could it be that only one year ago my life was so different? I rose before dawn and put on jeans and boots. I stuffed a water bottle, my pager, and the altimeter lent to me by one of the NGO facilitators into my day pack.

Cocks crowed as I made my way up the darkened center of Cara Sucia. Niña Tere made me coffee as she did each morning. Nora and I sat sipping together at the table. She was wearing her starched school uniform. I had on my filthy work clothes.

Niña Tere prepared plastic bags full of food for both of us. The first northbound bus of the day rumbled uphill, audible for miles at that hour. A few dogs howled as it came. Rambo rose and wagged his tail. Nora kissed her mother, said good-bye to me, and went off to school.

Niña Tere poured me another cup of sugary coffee and brought out a couple of rolls stuffed with refried beans. We sat eating.

"Going to be hot today," Niña Tere said.

"Yes." From outside, I heard a few men milling about at our meeting spot along the road. "I should get going."

Niña Tere nodded.

Out on the street, I put on a more serious face.

"Don Mauricio." I reached out my hand.

"*Ingeniera.*" He smiled and shook it. Mauricio was a young member of the village council, and he'd taken the lead with organization. On a computer at the Peace Corps office, I'd made a spreadsheet of names and dates for him. Each morning he checked off the workers as they earned the right to their household water.

The men themselves were a mix of older patriarchs, wearing collared shirts and straw hats, and teenagers in T-shirts and baseball caps. Young Felix was there every day, yawning and complaining about the early hour, his grandmother's screams still sounding from their little house.

Once the sun had risen higher, we started on our long commute, Mauricio and I in the lead. Many of the men carried picks and shovels over their backs. Others carried only the iron implements and a machete, hoping to hew wooden handles from tree branches once the tools were needed.

Though much of the village complained about the long walk to reach the spring, I'd come to enjoy it. These hours of the morning were the most pleasant in El Salvador: the air still cool from the previous night, no diesel exhaust yet belched out by the buses, a low-angle sun casting dramatic shadows off all the trees and houses. Even the village drunks had found their beds and not yet started on another bender.

We stopped for a rest and a snack at the bodega. The owner of the house brought out our Stillson wrenches from his bedroom.

Mauricio finally spoke. "Okay, boys, let's get to work."

Chago and Chente, two strong teenagers, were the first to load up. They laid pieces of grain sacks over their shoulders, then lifted each end of one six-meter-long galvanized pipe.

I put one of the Stillson wrenches over my own shoulder, which was about all I could bear. Early on, I'd fantasized about helping to carry one of the big pipes, but watching the men struggle along the steep sides of the river valley had cured me of that.

We set off down the narrow trails, grabbing at the thin stalks of coffee trees as we went. At last, we reached the pipeline's stopping point. I asked Felix to help hold the Stillson while I clamped it onto the pipe fitting. He blushed a little as I leaned across him to tighten the wrench.

Chago and Chente groaned under the burden, which seemed to grow heavier the second they stopped walking. Several other men rushed over to shoulder it for them.

I crouched along the existing pipe as if it were the barrel of a gun. The men raised the rear of the new pipe to align the threads.

"Up in the back," I called. "To the river. Good. Toward me a little more. All right, now!"

They held the pipe still while Mauricio turned the big wrench. Once the threads caught for a rotation or two, we attached the other wrench to the new pipe and set about screwing it in. I liked this part. Felix often hung his whole bodyweight from one end of the wrench, feet kicking in midair, giggling and hooting. Sometimes two or three guys hung on at a time.

Once that pipe was tightened, we moved on to the next pipe. And so it went: Our aqueduct advanced in six-meter baby steps. By lunchtime, we'd laid three pipes, which meant it was a productive day. We took our break by the banks of the river, alongside a tall waterfall. Mauricio made a quick fire and we all toasted our day-old tortillas in the coals. Chago and Chente stripped down to their underwear and went for a swim. They climbed to the top of a high rock by the falls and traded flips into the deep pool. It might've been a scene from an old Hawaiian postcard.

A swim sounded nice, but I knew better. Already, it was a semiscandal that I spent my days working in the woods with all these men. If the gossip mill heard that I bathed with them as well, I'd become a walking confirmation of everything Salvadoran women suspected of American girls.

Instead, I ate my lunch, crunching through the blistered outer layers of the retoasted tortillas. As I returned the trash and dishes to my backpack, I saw that Ben had sent me a page: "SWELL COMING IN. HERE NOW. SEE YOU TOMORROW."

I'd almost forgotten it was Friday. I put the pager away and signaled to Mauricio that we should get back to work.

He stood, whistled, and gestured to the boys.

I smiled as we walked back to the aqueduct. I had good waves nearby, meaningful work, and a wonderful boyfriend. Now, I'd do anything to get back that version of normal. It's laughable that I ever thought of that part as hard.

30

The next morning, I step out of the tent, still groggy. Ben sits in a hammock strung between two of the remaining columns. He rubs his eyes with his fists. Hiking boots are on his feet—still, or already. Tied around his forehead is a white cloth that reads RESCATE, the Spanish word for "rescue," in Magic Marker. I nod in his direction, but don't say anything.

"Morning," Ben says.

"What did you do with Pelochucho?"

"I found some guys. They buried his body with others. It wasn't pretty, but he's underground."

"That took all day?"

"No. Afterward, I helped more people out. There's lots to be done around here."

I find my surfboard under the wrecked Jeep, run my hand over the wax on the deck. It still has plenty of traction. I roll my neck a few times, then gather up the leash.

"What are you doing?" Ben asks.

"There're still waves." I hear them crashing against shore even now. "Sure as hell won't be any crowd. I'm going surfing."

"You can't do that, Malia. We've got to help." He is matter-of-fact.

"Fuck that. I quit being a hero. Remember? It was all your idea."

"This is different. People are alive under there. We quit the Peace Corps, but we're still human beings."

"What's the point?" I ask him. "I spent two years trying to help that one little village. And then"—I snap my fingers—"boom. Like that. A waste of time."

"You'll regret this," Ben says. "Trust me."

"Do you know what happened to me the other night, Ben?"

"What, while I was in jail?" His head cocks to one side.

"This close." I hold up my thumb and forefinger and pinch a centimeter of air. "I came this close to being raped by some fucking Salvatrucha drug dealer. Trying to get you back." I feel the tears along my cheekbones. The burning in my gums doubles.

"I didn't know." Ben shakes his head hard. "You didn't want to tell me. Who was it? Tell me who it was. I'll go find Peseta and—"

"Peseta's the one who saved me. He's probably dead now because of me. Because of that ridiculous plan that you and Pelo came up with." There's still more anger in me than I realized. "And don't you dare think up some kind of half-baked revenge scheme. This isn't the high school parking lot; these guys are real."

Ben looks down, ashamed.

I lower my voice. "All I wanted was to leave, to get out of here."

"Sweetheart, I'm sorry." He reaches out a hand and tries to touch me.

I move my shoulder away from his fingers. "You want me to help this town? Forget it. I'm going surfing." I walk away, my board under my arm.

Outside of La Posada, things grow worse. People carry machetes and clubs. Abandoned stores and businesses are rummaged through for anything of value. Teenage boys fight over firewood and ripe coconuts. The final semblances of civility threaten to erode fast.

The point is firing. Sets of four and five waves, double-overhead, barreling, dead wind. It's one flawless thing, an oasis of perfection, within a vast desert of both natural and man-made disaster.

I realize then, or remember perhaps, that a surfer's idea of perfection is different from everyone else's. It isn't abstract or inscrutable, some shadow on the wall of a cave. We know what it feels like—perfection—how it looks and the sound it makes.

And here it is right before my eyes: world-class waves all to myself. But somehow, the point suddenly has strings attached. It tempts me like one of those fast-talking salesmen in the Faustian stories, asking only for my soul in return. Were the surf mediocre, I'd put in without a second thought. But right now, the heaven that's in the water shows the hell that's on land in greater relief. I still think most of these development and relief efforts are pointless, on a long-enough time line. But in this place and at this moment, it suddenly isn't about the results anymore. It's simply what I ought to do, an end in itself.

Weeks ago, I came across a rare kernel of wisdom in an article from that same faded surf magazine; it feels appropriate now: "Surfers are not free to live in the moment; surfers are *forced* to live in the moment."

I turn around and walk back to La Posada.

Ben is still there. Water boils on his camp stove. He squats beside it, brushing glass and ants from a piece of salvaged sweet bread.

"You're back," he says.

"I want to help you."

He smiles. "Get your boots on, and find something you can drink coffee out of."

I put on my boots and baggy jeans, along with the tank top I'd borrowed and then stolen from some new volunteer in San Salvador last week. Ben pours my coffee into a tin cup from the cab of our ruined car.

"I'm sorry, Malia." He puts his hand around mine. "I'm sorry for what happened to you, for getting us into that mess in the first place." His eyes are moist and twitchy. "It was my fault."

I nod and look away from him, not wanting to talk about it anymore.

After breakfast, Ben pulls two shovels and a pick out from

under the Jeep. With a marker and the remains of a torn T-shirt, he makes me my own RESCATE bandanna. We leave La Posada. We walk within sight of the crack house, but it's a pile of rubble. By one of its fallen corners, a crude tent has been built from a black tarp. I make out the bearded doorman from the other night, but don't see Pardon Me Mother or the boss man.

Soon enough, I understand that Ben didn't work alone yesterday. We're joined by two older crack addicts—men I can remember seeing around town. They are keen to help out, and introduce themselves as Flaco and Alacrán.

As the four of us walk together, I suddenly think of Crackito— the young human punching bag with whom we ate breakfast a few mornings before.

"¿Y Crackito?" I ask Flaco.

"No" is all he says. "No, Chinita." Flaco shakes his head and looks at the ground.

My next inexplicable thought: I hope that boy was high as Mount Everest when the earthquake happened. I hope he still had a little of my money, or that he'd stolen something in the night that was worth a big hit from a borrowed stem, when whatever doorway or makeshift shelter he'd found to sleep under had come crashing down upon his head. This is the best fate I'm capable of imagining for little Crackito.

First thing, we find an old man and a young woman trying to lift chunks of concrete where a two-story house has fallen. The four of us put down our tools and help with the heavy columns. The work is difficult. It takes everybody at once to hoist the bigger debris. Soon we see a blackish foot from which dangles a rubber flip-flop.

"Look," Ben says.

The old man and the woman come over. They call out a name a couple of times: Jacinto. The woman cries. The old man has already resigned himself to the worst. The two of them clear the rest of the rubble from the body. We all turn away, as if it's a sort of rite that we owe to them.

Through tears, the woman uncovers the dead man's face. Her husband? Brother? The old man shakes Ben's hand and thanks him. They speak softly. Ben motions toward our two Salvadoran comrades. The crackheads stand there leaning on their tools, with gaunt frames and vapid expressions, like a postapocalyptic rock band posing for a photo. The old man walks over to them, reaches into his pocket, and gives them each a bill and a few coins. He says, "God bless you."

They nod and mutter, "*Gracias*," then drop Ben's tools and wander off.

"Where are they going?" I say to Ben.

"To buy crack."

Ask a stupid question, I think to myself.

"Once they get back, we need to move inland. Here it's just fallen houses. There it's worse. Landslides and homes tumbling down the bluffs."

The corpse is nearly clear now. I try not to look, but I can tell that he's wearing blue jeans cut off below the knees. Whoever it is, he must've been somewhat successful; it's a nice home.

The old man approaches us with a nearly full pack of menthol cigarettes. "Would you like?" he says. "I don't smoke."

Acting on a mix of politeness and indifference, we take them. It isn't until after Ben has lit us both up and I've taken a couple of drags that I realize the cigarettes must've come from the dead man's pocket.

While we smoke, the woman wraps a blanket around the corpse.

"Can you two handle things from here?" Ben asks the old man.

He nods.

"Where will they take the body?" I ask Ben in between drags.

"To that mass grave those guys started." He points with his hand. "Where I took Pelochucho. I don't like going there too much." Ben blows minty smoke. The crackheads reappear around the corner. Their eyes now cloudy like unfresh fish, they are no less somber. Two more walk with them. Now six, we start up the hill to Las Lomas, Ben in the lead.

"We saved three people who were pinned down yesterday," Ben says as we walk. "But it was easier. They were screaming and stuff."

As if on cue, a woman's cry is followed by a clatter of metal. We turn in the sound's direction. The frenzied shouts finally take the form of words.

"*¡Auxilio!*" It's a fat woman with wavy hair and pale skin. She stands over two young boys, both of them digging furiously with bare hands at a pile of dirt littered with scraps of corrugated metal.

"He's alive!" she shouts.

We run over. Sure enough, somebody is beating from below on a piece of the metal roofing, one corner of which has been unearthed. Muffled shouts come through the dirt. It looks as though this was an adobe house, which has fallen down and also been partly covered by the collapsing bluffs.

"Careful, careful," Ben shouts as our crackheads dig through the earth with their hands and hoist the heavy chunks of adobe.

"*¡Niños!*" Ben shouts at the two boys. "Go and find some water. Fast!"

They run off. The fat woman stands behind us, muttering "Help" and "He's alive" alternately. She dances from one thick leg to another. Finally, Ben and I are able to lift the corrugated-metal square.

I expect something beautiful, the happy ending of a sappy movie where the buried man hugs his wife as the score reaches its crescendo. Instead, I am terrified.

The first thing that hits me is the smell of shit and piss that rises out of that hole. The trapped man sits up from the waist and gasps for air. The space that the section of metal made for him resembles a coffin. Now upright, he looks like a shabby vampire. In the more than twenty-four hours that he's been under there, his body has evolved into something meant to live that way—his skin pale and moist, his legs crammed together and looking as boneless as two earthworms. He throws a hand up to cover his eyes against the sun.

In some ways, for me, this is more difficult than finding the dead body. I wonder if all of us, walking around La Lib now, are truly survivors. Or are we trapped in a kind of limbo state somewhere between life and death? A state that might even be worse than death. Nobody else shares my reaction.

His eyes still closed, the undead man mutters "Claudia" between shallow breaths. Ben helps him out of his hole. When the reunited pair finally embrace, it's more a matter of her holding him up. His long-numb limbs struggle to move, and soon enough she sets him down onto the ground. The children return with a shallow bucket of water, and the man takes several trembling sips. "Papá!" the boys shout. Too weak to embrace them, the father reaches out to brush his fingers against their cheeks and shoulders.

Ben and I sit down. I worry about the crackhead situation. We helped for only ten minutes or so, and now there are several of us. This family doesn't look like they have any spare cash to contribute to our cause. While nobody forces the issue, the crackheads stand around awkwardly; one of the new guys—the smallest among them—looks particularly restless.

The woman wipes dirt and debris from the man's face and hair while he continues to force down water and blink furiously. She shouts an order to the kids and they disappear into a hut of plastic and cardboard on the far side of their fallen home.

The children return with a cold pot of boiled potatoes. "*Toma*," the older one says, and sets them down in front of us. Ben and I aren't bashful. The smaller boy runs back inside and produces a dish of salt. The crackheads are slightly more hesitant, but they tuck in soon enough. I am hungry, and with all the awful smells around, this meal has the right degree of blandness for me to stomach. A new guy, the small one who's been looking restless, takes a couple of bites, then chucks his potato to the ground. He grumbles something I can't understand. Flaco shushes him.

After two or three of the cold potatoes, Ben brushes his hands together and stands. "*Vamos*," he instructs the rest of us.

The family thanks us all and asks for God to bless us. They are still in a state of overwhelmed shock. I get the feeling they don't quite understand who we are or what exactly we're doing.

"*¡Qué mierda!*" shouts the smallest crackhead once we're out of earshot. The others reprimand him in a Spanish so hushed and slang-ridden that I can't follow, though I assume he expected cash for helping the man. To me, it's fairly obvious that the family would've dug the body out within the hour, whether or not we'd shown up.

At first, Ben doesn't appear to pay attention, but then suddenly he stops walking and turns to the complainer. "Weefer, why don't you fuck off, then? Nobody promised you anything. There's no minimum wage here. That family didn't have shit to give you. Walk away, *pues*." Standing there with the headband on, bare-chested, lean from skipped meals, glaring down at a rival, Ben looks exactly like the real Chuck Norris in his prime.

Weefer—I gather that's his name—spits on the ground, then walks off muttering curses.

Ben walks onward. We follow.

There are no more dramatic screams or critical rescues. Everyone around us resigns themselves to the slow grind of excavating bodies. I feel self-conscious about the silly RESCATE bandanna upon my head.

Soon enough, we fall in, helping unearth a house that is badly buried. An old woman and a small boy dig through the rubble with sticks. Few words are exchanged; we take our shovels and move earth. The boy communicates by pointing and making a sort of bleating noise through his sinuses. As the minutes and shovelfuls go by, and I watch the old woman gesture and signal to him, I understand he is deaf as well as mute. We carry the dirt away in buckets and grain sacks. This family also looks too poor to pay us anything. It's a good thing that Weefer left.

The minutes spent digging turn into hours, and I wonder if there truly is a house underneath all this dirt and dust. The moment that thought enters my head, my shovel hits a piece of corrugated metal. We hoist out the heavy chunks of old junk—tire rims and broken cinder blocks—used to weigh the sheets of roof down. All of us put aside our shovels and pick

through the pieces with caution. Now that the sounds of digging diminish, I can hear the perfect waves breaking in the
distance.

This time, we find a hand first. I'm the one to spot it. We
make short work of clearing away the rest of the dirt. It's an old
man's body. Like Pelochucho, he was caught sleeping in. Large
adobe bricks fell all around, though his body isn't crushed like
others we've excavated. Nobody speaks, but it's obvious that
his cause of death was not falling debris, but live burial. The
old woman and the little boy cross themselves and cry. The boy
makes honking sounds in between his sobs. We back away.
Ben passes out menthol cigarettes.

The woman and the boy wrap the body with sheets and
blankets, just as Ben did with Pelochucho. She takes pieces of
twine that were strung along the bottom of the bed frame and
uses them to tie up the bundle.

Once we've finished our smokes, the old woman approaches
Ben and me. She shakes Ben's hand, then hands him a folded
stack of American dollars.

Ben is incredulous. "Where did she get this?" he asks me as
the woman walks back to the body. "Look at this place."

I stare into the hole that was their home. The boy honks away
over the bundled-up man—his grandfather, most likely.

"They must be getting *remesas* from the States." I think of
Niña Tere and her husband, Guillermo. "The boy's parents, or
one of them at least, probably send back cash. Maybe she doesn't
realize what it's worth. He"—I point to the twine-tied blankets—
"probably took care of the finances."

The crackheads approach and steal glances over Ben's shoulder. I hear one whisper, "Dollars."

Ben wraps his fist tighter around the money, then shoves it

into the Velcro side pocket of his board shorts. He is flustered—feeling guilty about taking this woman's money, but knowing that the crackheads will never abide his giving it back.

"Wait," he shouts down to the woman and the boy. I didn't notice, but they are making fruitless attempts to lift the body.

"We'll help you," Ben says. He turns to the crackheads and gestures with his arm. Two of our helpers hoist either end of the body to their shoulder level; once they have it up, the third one supports the sagging middle.

Ben assures the woman that it's better this way. She asks God to bless us all—making our team of three possibly the most blessed crackheads in the world. The boy bleats a few more times.

Our crew doesn't look happy about the extra work, but they are placated by the possibility of serious payment.

"Wait a second," Ben instructs once we're out of sight of the dead man's house. He goes around behind me, and counts the money against the small of my back. The three pallbearers turn and try to look.

"Keep going," Ben calls out. The edges of the bills tickle the bare skin below my shirt.

"How much?" I ask.

"Almost three hundred," he says. "It's mostly twenties. I'll give them three each and keep the more mismatched bills for us." He stuffs the wad of money into the back pocket of my jeans. Ben smacks my ass lightly, as if sealing the bills there.

Immediately, I wish she'd never given us that cash. It feels heavy as an adobe block in my pants, as bad an omen as the wads that Pelochucho flashed around a few short days ago, the big ones I had to hand over to the drug boss. Worthless to us under the circumstances, it's nothing more than a burden, a source of trouble. Once Ben pays these guys their cut, there is no chance they'll be back to help for days.

I don't mean to be judgmental. They are good men, in their hearts. Their left hands don't know what their rights are doing. In many ways, their acts of altruism are no more selfish than my reasons for joining the Peace Corps—or Alex's reasons for working with the Red Cross. But their addiction is too strong. The source of their short-term pleasure is too easy, too close, too available.

Soon enough, we arrive at the makeshift mass grave, and it's easy to see why Ben dislikes it. Mounds of dirt are piled up at one end, all sprinkled with a layer of lime, like confectioner's sugar over pound cake. Closer to the entrance, on the town side, bodies are covered in thin layers of earth. A couple of burning tires dribble out columns of black smoke around the perimeter. Above, buzzards fly in patient circles, kept at bay, it seems, by the toxic smoke. The flies are not so easily dissuaded. Most of the corpses are wrapped in blankets and twine like the one that we brought, but some are just bodies, dead in their clothes.

It's obvious that the architects of this place never expected it to grow so large, even in the first two days of its existence. They've already begun moving the dirt around near the entrance, expanding it in the direction of town. I wonder how long it will take before this mass grave swallows up the whole port, until it connects with the graveyard on the point, and La Libertad is nothing but dead bodies and killer waves.

The most unsettling part of the mass grave is the men working there. They all have on long-sleeve shirts with collars pulled up against the flies and sun. Handkerchiefs or pieces of cloth cover their faces from the stink—not unlike the Colombians who gave us those accursed cocaine bales. They work—digging

and dragging corpses, sprinkling lime, and fanning the fires—
with a slow, persistent cadence, like real-life grim reapers.

"Who are these guys?" I ask Ben. "The . . . attendants?"

"Who knows?" he says. "The rumor is that they're guys who
lost everybody. Guys who have no idea what happened to their
families or loved ones—where they were at the time of the
quake. They're *esperando* to come across the bodies." To describe what these men are doing, Ben chooses the Spanish verb,
which means both to hope and to wait—another word that
cannot be satisfied. "But my theory," he goes on, "is that they're
guys who somehow did wrong by the ones they lost. The way
they seem obliged to do this shit . . . it's like they believe they
can make up for something by serving the dead."

Our three crackhead helpers hand off their burden to one
such man. He doesn't speak to them, just drags the body off to
a pile, where a cloud of flies scatter. It's like watching the dead
bury the dead.

We walk away from the grave and back toward town. The
crackheads ask Ben about the money. He takes the bills from
my pocket and hands them each three twenties.

"There it is," he says. "*Gracias.*" But we're invisible by then.
They are off toward the crack house, not like men celebrating,
but like men on a most urgent errand. I think of myself this
morning, standing at the water's edge with my surfboard.
These men are not free to indulge; they are forced.

"We can forget about seeing them for a while," Ben says.

The crack house—or its temporary shelter—will probably
be the last place in La Lib to take currency. Everywhere else
will soon accept only barter: food, water, fuel. I wonder, in the

event that we're stuck here much longer, if the dealers won't find a way to get more raw cocaine into the port before the rescuers arrive.

The sun is low along the horizon. We walk back to La Posada with shovels over our arms. I keep thinking of the self-appointed undertakers at the mass grave, for whom even hope is death. Isn't that the logical end of our efforts? Isn't that what we will be reduced to tomorrow, once that many more hours have passed? Won't all relief work become, at some point, merely a process of burying the dead?

We find the gate locked back at La Posada. One of the columns holding it up has been bent by the earthquake; it closes cockeyed, but keeps us out regardless. Still wobbling a bit on her bad leg, Kristy comes over with a key ring and lets us in. She's cleaned the place since we've been gone—cleared the rubble and broken glass around the kitchen, made little caches of food and supplies.

"At last," she says. "You're back. I've been worried; I had no idea where you'd gone. The people here, they're getting desperate."

I'm not sure if she's afraid for us or for herself. For the first time, I understand how lucky we are: caught in an empty hotel, with plenty of food, and only the three of us. But if things go on like this much longer, our luck could be our undoing. La Posada will be a prime target for looters and thieves, once it comes to that.

Niña Tere once told me a story about how, when the farmers burn the sugarcane fields, a mass of snakes comes writhing out in a tangled, swirling mess—a rolling wave of refugee serpents—a few feet in front of the fire. Is this what has become of us here in this city? A homeless bunch of earthbound creatures, slithering our way toward the next temporary hole, choking and strangling one another as we go?

I wonder briefly why my grandfather never told similar stories about the cane plantations in Hawai'i, then remember that we have no snakes on the islands.

Kristy takes a key from off her big ring and extends it toward the two of us. "Here," she says.

I reach out and take it.

"We've got to keep this place locked up at all times. I see how the people are looking at it."

I put the key in my pocket. Ben walks over to the side of the Jeep. He opens the rear hatch, sits on the bumper, and unlaces his boots. I take off the RESCATE bandanna.

"We won't be gone so long tomorrow," I tell Kristy.

"*Ojalá*," she says.

I walk over to our corner of the courtyard, sit in Ben's hammock, and unlace my own boots. One then the other, they fall to the ground with dull thuds.

Ben rummages through the back of our car, taking a rough inventory of its contents. Finally, he appears from the side with a half-full bottle of Nicaraguan rum.

"What do you think?" he asks me. "Cocktail hour?'

Barefoot, we walk up the stairs to the roof over the undamaged part of La Posada. My heart flutters at the top of the stairs, but I figure that this building has weathered two bad quakes already. It can hold us for another hour. Our patio chairs still stand undisturbed from a couple of nights ago. The sun is now in its final stages of setting. Down the coast, fires in the cane fields burn away, past the landslides, where the road is impassable.

"Swell's dropping," Ben says.

I look out at the point. If this is a set wave that we're seeing, then he's right.

"What's the tide doing?" I ask.

"Filling back in. I think high tide was around ten today. And it's real high, with the full moon and all." Resting on a cinder block by our chairs is an empty jelly jar that we used as a beer glass days ago. Ben blows the dust out of it and pours in a couple fingers of rum.

"Do you think it's a good idea to leave Kristy here by herself? She seems to think things are going to get ugly—looting and whatnot."

"The boats should get here soon, now that the surf's coming down." He slurps the big shot of rum.

"And if they don't?"

Ben grimaces. "If people come in here to steal from us—food and gas and stuff—then maybe they need it more than we do."

"From now on," I say, "we won't find anything but bodies under the dirt, will we?"

Ben shrugs and shakes the jelly jar upside down. "You know, if we dawn patrol"—he pours more rum into the glass—"we might get a nice tidal push, maybe some punchy waves."

"That's true." For a second, I wonder if this isn't a joke, the old bait and switch.

Ben passes the glass of rum to me. "Maybe the looting won't start until after breakfast."

I roll the rum around in my mouth for a second before swallowing. "Maybe we should go surfing tomorrow."

"Tomorrow," Ben says the word in that occasional Southern drawl of his. "Tomorrow we can do whatever we want." He doesn't mean this as permission, but as a basic—and in some ways, a difficult—fact of life.

We trade shots of rum for a while longer but don't speak. Surfing, I realize, is so much simpler than living. If you're too far inside, don't go. If you're too far down the shoulder, you can't make it. And if you're right in the pocket, then any semblance of a decision fades away. All mistakes or misjudgments— you pay for them within a half second. I thought there should be some similarity in this earthquake thing—both are a matter of responding to nature. But it isn't the same at all. Each new happening holds no clear response, and every misstep inspires days of second-guessing.

When the bottle is empty, Ben hands me the last glassful and says, "We'll get on it first thing." He squeezes my shoulder and makes his way down the stairs. I finish the last shot in two sips, then head down myself. He is already asleep in his hammock. I crawl inside the tent. This time, I need no Valium to get me through the night. And I wonder if that—the ability to fall asleep without trouble and without pills—is reason enough to go on with the exhaustive work of burying the dead.

31

I think I'm dreaming. Short, soft breaths puff along my face. A child with small lungs moves over me. Something shuffles beside my head. The breath smells bad, like rotten fruit but also chemicals. This is not a dream. Somebody is in my tent with me, and it's not Ben. He goes for my Che wallet.

Without thinking, I push him hard with both hands and curse in English. "Fucking sneak thief motherfucker!"

The tent cloth whooshes with motion. He tries to scurry his way outside the door on knees and elbows, but I grab him by his wrists. The two of us wrestle our way through the still-open flap.

Out in the courtyard, I scream, "Ben! He was in the tent!"

Ben snaps upright in his hammock. He sees the two of us struggling in the dark. I hold tight to each wrist. The thief thrashes and convulses like a snake in my hands, tries to kick me in the knees. To Ben, it must look like some bizarre dance of violence.

"Weefer!" Ben screams. It's the guy who briefly helped us. "*¡Mañoso culero!*" Unlike me, Ben remembers how to speak Spanish. He runs over and puts Weefer into the same kind of headlock he used on my first night here. Also like that night, I notice how comically small the crackhead in Ben's arms actually is. I wonder if it could be the same person.

"Let me go!" Weefer screams.

From her own room near the kitchen, Kristy emerges, shouting. She screams for the police, which is almost laughable, under the circumstances.

While Weefer thrashes around in Ben's arms, I go for one of his pockets—dodging his flying knees and elbows, airborne spittle everywhere. I manage to pull out my Che wallet. In the process, a small pink piece of glass falls to the dry earth of the courtyard. I pick it up. One end is charred and black. The other end is broken off.

"Fucking crackheads."

To help me access the other pocket, Ben switches his grip, pulling upward. Somehow, Weefer gets one of his arms free. It swings toward me in a windmill motion. I take a step back.

In a blur of spinning limbs, Weefer reaches up and then appears to pat Ben on the back. The two of them freeze, their arms around each other: Weefer on his tiptoes and extending his head up at Ben's, Ben leaning forward, toward the smaller man. It's like Weefer wants to whisper something into Ben's ear, or kiss him on the cheek.

Then Weefer is gone. The speed with which he climbs up the stairs to the roof and then scurries down the tree is almost comical—like the old sped-up footage from silent movies. Ben goes to his hands and knees, wheezing as though he's just surfaced from a two-wave hold-down. Blood pours from his back. I look. A little metal stalk blossoms to one side of his spine.

"Take it out!" He coughs the words.

I'm frozen: waiting for the punch line, not getting the joke.

"Take it out," Ben pleads this time.

I nod, then wrap my fingers around the silver stick and pull straight up. It's that butter knife sharpened on both edges— the same one Peseta used to save me, or one that's identical. Ben turns over on his back, arms out at his sides. This isn't right, I want to say. Ben told me himself that they never carry weapons when they come in to steal. No, I shake my head, incredulous. Go back! It's an illegal move. Over the line! From underneath Ben's back, puffs of dust blow out with each of his belabored breaths.

"Kristy!" I shout. "*¡Llame a un médico!*" I finally remember how to speak Spanish.

"You'll be okay," I say to Ben. At that point, I still believe it.

"I can't breathe."

"Kristy's calling a doctor."

He smiles at this, as if trying to laugh, seeing the absurdity that I've missed in the very notion of calling anyone, let alone a doctor.

"We should've left here," he says with great difficulty. "We should have left here a while ago, sweetheart."

"No!" I say it out loud now. "No. We survived!" The equation simply doesn't add up: Ben's will to live was greater than two major earthquakes, but less than a fucking butter knife? It can't be so. I put my hand on each of Ben's round shoulders. "Listen to me: We're the survivors!" I shake him as I shout, but he doesn't stir. "We're the survivors!" I say it again and again.

Sweetheart is the last word Ben says. I turn him onto his front, thinking I can plug the hole in his back somehow, with my fingers or with the same towels we used to hold together Pelochucho's face. But by the time I have my hand over the wound, it is too late. That manta ray of muscle across his back now feels as limp and lifeless as a supermarket steak. No air comes in or out, only blood. Ben has drowned to death on dry land.

Beside him, on the dirt of the courtyard, I curl myself into a fetal position, spooning his body one final time, blood soaking into my shirt. I cry until my face hurts, muttering words like *fuck*, *goddamn*, and *love* every so often.

An hour passes before Kristy finally comes and pulls me off the ground. She helps me over to the hammock where Ben had slept before I woke him. She covers me up with a sheet, then covers Ben's corpse with a thick wool blanket. I can smell him still in the thin nylon strings of the hammock. Drained of tears, I tremble and hyperventilate away the rest of the night.

A random bit of wind blows in with an odd, metallic smell to it. A few drops of rain fall—raising small puffs of dust about the courtyard—and then grow into a heavy downpour. I wonder, if this rain had started an hour earlier, would it have kept Weefer at home?

For the first and perhaps the only time, I feel a suicidal urge. The unknown suddenly looks more appealing than this world. I think of what Alex had told me about pretending and not pretending. For me to go on living, another year or another seventy years, I'll have to pretend every second not to be haunted by this night.

32

In the morning, buzzards circle overhead. Kristy asks for my help. We take the already-flat spare tire from the Jeep and carry it over by Ben's body. I watch as she empties some kind of fuel from a glass bottle, then strikes a match and sets the tire on fire. From the kitchen, she brings a small bag of white powder—lime for making corn tortillas. She lifts the blanket and dumps the powder over Ben. We both know it isn't enough, and that there's no way to get more.

"We can't leave him here," she says. "The buzzards."

I look up at the black birds rotating above. Impossibly, the worst is not over yet.

I know a little about death in this climate from the people in Cara Sucia. If somebody had a bad fall or accident in the countryside, and died out of earshot, buzzards were the most reliable way to find the corpse. There's a method of measuring how long the person has been dead by what's been eaten away. They call it the "law of the vultures." The eyes are the first to go, then everything around the mouth and nose. Only once the dead flesh is tender enough do the buzzards begin to pick the body apart.

I can't handle this. I walk out of La Posada. Thin ribbons of smoke spiral upward from elsewhere—cook fires, perhaps, or other burning tires. Every car parked along the street has been broken into. Auto glass litters the ground. Many of the still-standing walls have crude signs written in charcoal or white-wash across their sides: HELP! SMALL CHILDREN, ONE BURIED ALIVE! But it's obvious that all these words are days old by now; their messages no longer carry much weight.

At the remains of one such house, the word HELP is written, with an arrow pointing at a doorway. A small dark-haired girl pokes a soot-streaked face out the door. The arrow on the wall points straight to her head. She chews one of her fingers and stares at me with big eyes. We lock gazes momentarily. I keep on walking.

Along the road that leads to the Pan-American Highway, I take long strides, my hands on my head. I pull out fistfuls of hair, looking around for someone who might help me now, in the absence of Ben.

In post-earthquake La Libertad, there are neither embalmers nor refrigeration of any kind. I have no way of communicating with anybody from Ben's family, short of swimming twenty miles down the coast, or hiking over dirt loosened by landslides. And what could the family members do if I did get word to them? There'll be nothing but picked-over bones and buzzard shit left to repatriate. I have to handle this on my own, and handle it here. And this, the greatest tragedy I can imagine, means nothing to anybody else around. My problem is the dead body of someone I love—a problem more common than a headache in this place.

I turn and walk back toward La Posada. What are my options? I can't stand the thought of burying Ben in that mass grave. He hated it there. In some ways, that was the one aspect of this earthquake that he couldn't handle. It would be impossible to bury him anywhere else. All the ground left in La Lib has been claimed by the newly homeless.

Kristy still tends the tire fire when I return, studying the buzzards overhead.

"Kristy," I say, "do you have any tools?"

She produces a drawer from her own room, a hammer and some screws inside. Last night's rain caused the cement bags that fell on the Jeep to break and then harden. Now the whole thing is a big sculpture of steel and masonry that will have to be jackhammered away. I manage to free Ben's collapsible multitool from the glove compartment, along with the roll of tie wire he used to fix my flip-flop. I go to work setting a series of screws into the decks of our two surfboards. With one broomstick and a set of notched two-by-fours, I make crosspieces so that the boards will float side by side, like a raft.

I think of my education then, as I sort through pieces of old crates and broken furniture, scraps of wood that will soon be precious for burning. Years ago, I must've learned calculations and equations for testing the strength of such things. Now, I bounce them in my hands or push against the grain with my thumbs. If I judge a board sturdy enough, I attach it length-wise over the crosspieces with a mess of nails and wire. Eventually, I have a raft that won't come apart when I shake it.

Ben's sleeping bag is in the Jeep. It's a technical model from an American gear store, with a hood for the head. I unroll the bag and undo the zipper all the way. With a deep breath, I get his feet in. Kristy helps me turn his body over. I zip him all the way up, facedown, wrap the insulated hood over his head, and cinch up the string. Kristy brings out the same ball of twine that we used with Pelochucho. We tie off the bundle at the neck, waist, and feet.

Now I need a way to move him. The only thing with wheels inside La Posada is the Jeep, and that's not going anywhere. I sit on the packed dirt of the courtyard for several minutes, my head resting upon my kneecaps. This is ridiculous: my pride in making a stupid raft, without any way even to get it to the waterline.

A rhythmic squeaking sounds from the street. I stand and run over to the front gate. An old man rolls a cart toward me. It's the modified bicycle from the other day. The produce it carried and the loudspeaker are both missing. The vendor stands upon the pedals to make the dry wheels turn; they ache for grease with each rotation. I shout for him to stop. He parks in front of the gate.

I ask to borrow his cart, but he wisely refuses. After some haggling, he trades it for Ben's hiking boots and all the American money that the woman gave us yesterday—the money that led to Ben's death. The old man studies the bills for a while, not certain that they'll again have value. I'm more than happy to be rid of them.

On the roof of La Posada, I find the empty rum bottle from

the night before. Kristy lends me a section of plastic tubing, and I siphon gasoline from the Jeep's tank into the glass bottle. I pile the body, the raft, and the bottle of gas onto my new cart, along with more of the twine from Kristy's roll. In the kitchen, I find a tin of cooking lard and use it to lubricate the chain and gears.

The back half of the bicycle cart has one wheel and a seat. The front has two larger wheels and the cargo area. At first, I'm able to pedal my load. I head around behind the restaurants of the point, past the graveyard, and come to the end of the road. A dirt path runs alongside the last few structures. There, I dismount and push it from the side. Once the path runs out, I struggle to move the cart over the big round rocks that give Punta Roca its name. The swell has dropped considerably. We would've been bored had we surfed today. It's just past noon. The sun is high and strong in the sky. I sweat through my clothes.

Finally, I make it out to the very tip of the point. Ben was right about the tide. It recently turned, and now it sucks out hard. The black stones along the waterline grind together with each surge like a giant mouthful of teeth.

I place my matches and the bottle of gas on a dry stone above the waterline. With our two surfboard leashes, I lash Ben's bundled body down to the raft's crosspieces. After minutes of pushing and dragging, I manage to move the cart far enough into the sea that the raft floats when the surf comes in. My boots fill with water and sand. My jeans cling to me, soaked.

I fetch my bottle and dump the gas over the whole works. With three matches all struck at once, I set fire to the bundle.

Wading out into the water and avoiding the rising flames, I give the raft a final push.

The retreating tide carries it quickly to sea. I climb out and watch from the shore. I watch as the wobbling flotilla grows smaller and the flames fade farther on out toward the horizon, my lover's body burning away just above the surface of the salt water. Soon, the fiberglass decks of the surfboards blister and become engulfed in the blaze. Toxic flames of blue and green sizzle alongside Ben and the smoke around him grows blacker still. A rogue gust of wind pushes him westward, toward Kilometer 99: the closest thing to the Elysian fields that Ben will ever know.

But it's not until he's even farther out to sea, farther out than even the biggest of channel boomers that ever broke upon his beloved point, that the crosspieces burn through beneath him, and Ben's body slips into the Pacific Ocean at last.

I watch a while longer as the rest of the raft burns out and then sinks. I stand there staring for a few more moments at the water's edge, amid the ruins of a city called freedom.

I pick up a single stone and throw it out into the sea after him. My cart still parked at the tide line, I turn and walk back to La Posada.

Kristy moves the tire fire over near the gate. She prepares a meal of rice and catsup for the two of us. We eat in silence. Once we're done, I go to my tent and find the rest of the Valium. Though the sun has not even set, I take three of them and drift toward a deep drug-induced sleep inside Ben's hammock. I think I'm halfway hoping—or perhaps only waiting—for somebody to come in and stab me then, or for the walls of the stubborn air-conditioned wing to crumble, and get it all over with already.

As the effects of the pills take hold, I wonder with closed eyes if I've been wrong about Alex and my father all along. Maybe it isn't so much that they see life as a long-suffering contest. Perhaps, rather than seeking out the greatest possible pleasures— the way surfers do—they spend their lives guarding against the worst of all pains. At this moment, I would trade all the waves in the world to somehow get Ben back. The times I spent with him are the silver and shining memories scattered along the banks of my life. Someday, I hope to have the strength to pick them up and make something useful from them.

I wake up late. Kristy boils water on Ben's camp stove.

"Good morning," I say.

"There are rumors." She looks up. "They say the roads have been opened. Everybody's heading down there to meet the relief trucks."

"That's good," I say. "Let's hope it's true."

I open the gate and walk toward the waterfront, as if to check the surf. Whether or not the roads have opened, people believe they have. In the street, everyone hurries about. Many carry bags. The people I pass are all on their way to the east end of town, where the trucks from San Salvador are meant to arrive.

On the beach, just beyond the stairs, two dogs have gotten stuck together while fucking. They stand ass-to-ass, stumbling in clumsy circles and trying to see each other's eyes. Down the leg of one, a spray of blood is matted into the fur. The looks on their faces are confused more than anything—as if wondering whether it's their own appetites or only nature that led to this predicament.

The swell is way down, barely rideable, even if I did still have a board. Farther out, to this side of the horizon, an iron ship heads right toward me. I watch as it rounds the pier and makes its way into the cove, closer than I've ever seen any vessel come to the point. Its hull is black and full of rust. A red-and-white flag flies from its bow, with the word *Rescate* written there under a cross.

A couple of Zodiacs embark from it, weighted down with about a dozen people, heading to the beach. Once they get to the shore, they all shout and point and then split up into three groups. One runs in the direction of the pier, another straight inland, and the last group comes toward my spot on the steps. I light one of the dead man's last menthol cigarettes. The first two people to approach me are Salvadorans. Wearing orange life vests with the Red Cross logo, they ask in Spanish if I need medical attention. I tell them no.

The last person from their group, panting from the walk through the sand and pulling wet khakis away from his legs, is Alex.

"Malia! Oh my God!"

We embrace, our forearms pressing hard into each other's backs. Then it suddenly becomes awkward and we let go.

He wears a baseball cap that reads EL SALVADOR, EARTH-QUAKES, 2001.

"I was hoping to find you. I'm so glad that you're all right."

He's the last person I expect to see today. "I'm glad that you're all right, too." It doesn't sound stupid until the moment I say it.

"Listen. I've talked to my director. There's a lot of money coming in for La Libertad right now. It's become our number-one priority. I told him about your Peace Corps experience, your engineering background, your knowledge of the area. Anyways, he's keen on hiring you. We'll be working together!"

"I'm not interested, Alex." I let out a mouthful of flavored smoke.

"What?"

"I think it's time for me to leave this place. It's well past time for me to go."

"Malia, think about this. Think about your life for a second."

"Chuck Norris is dead," I tell him.

"The movie star?"

"No." I have a hard time saying it out loud. "Ben. He was stabbed the night before last. And you know what? My life is, unfortunately, all I ever think about." I take the hat off Alex and put it on my own head.

He doesn't know what to say.

I kiss him on the lips, tell him good-bye, and return to La Posada.

As I'm about to enter the hotel, the sandal that Ben repaired finally breaks; its rubber sole dangles limp from the severed strap about my toes. I step out of both flip-flops, leave them there before the gate, and cross the courtyard in bare feet. I set about gathering spare clothes and other necessities from the back of the Jeep and the ruins of our room.

"Chinita?" The voice that calls my nickname is so sheepish and hesitant, I don't recognize it as Kristy's. "I have to speak to you." She limps over from the kitchen area.

"Speak to me?" I'm so focused on getting out of here—finding a way to the embassy and persuading them to get me out of this country—that I don't have the patience for a sentimental good-bye, even from her.

"Chinita, listen." For some reason, she's not wearing the heavy eye makeup that I've never seen her without. "I have something to tell you—something to give you, I suppose." She looks down at the dirt of the courtyard.

My first thought is to try to say politely that I'm too busy. But when Kristy takes from behind her back a clear plastic bag with that tiny blue booklet inside, she has my full attention.

"My passport," I say.

"I'm very sorry." Her gaze goes back to the ground. "I thought you'd be able to get another one straight away. It wasn't supposed to create a big problem." She meets my eyes for a moment. Tears start down her cheeks. "I thought that we looked enough alike, I might not need a smuggler. I'm so sorry."

I open up the bag. Along with my passport, there's the woven wallet, the card for the bank account I'd assumed was emptied, and that Red Cross business card that Alex handed me at the Peace Corps office less than two weeks prior, when things were so different.

"What about the envelope of money? Do you have that as well?"

"No." She shakes her head. "The real *mañoso* took that. I heard him leave, chased him away, really. But I saw your passport left inside the wallet. I thought it was an opportunity, especially with Pelochucho back in my life."

I open up the cover and have a look at my smiling image from a few years back. It was a decent plan Kristy had. We do look alike, especially without the eye makeup. She probably would've passed through immigration.

A part of me wants to scream, to tell her that she should've come clean days ago. It might've saved me a world of trouble. But instead, I say, "I forgive you."

She doesn't look satisfied, expects more anger, perhaps. "But I must also apologize about all of this, about Chuck Norris as well."

"How do you mean?"

"Had I not taken the passport"—she uses her lips to point at it—"you two might have been gone before the earthquake."

A dozen thoughts tumble through my mind. Where might I be if my passport had never gone missing? Ben and I could've made it to Nicaragua or Panama by the time the quake hit. Maybe to the South American continent by now. Ben might still be alive. But what am I supposed to do? Blame her?

"It's okay," I say. "You had no way of guessing what might happen. I forgive you for all that as well."

"Thank you." She nods, then walks away.

"Kristy!" I say. "Wait a second."

She turns and steps back toward me.

"Do you want it?" I hold the passport out toward her. "I can get an emergency version from the embassy; it would allow me to travel home. You might make it to the north, without a smuggler."

"No." She shakes her head. "That's generous of you. But I'm not interested. This is my home. I've never truly wanted to live in your country. It was only for him." She gestures in the direction of Pelochucho's former room. "I didn't care about where so much. I simply wanted the two of us to be together."

"I see." I nod, then look down at the passport inside my hand. It suddenly seems a silly offer. Why would anyone pretend to be me?

I lace up my boots and dust off my backpack. I dig out Ben's passport from the Jeep's glove compartment. I fix Alex's Red Cross cap atop my hair. With an old rag, I force the sharp blade of Ben's multitool to stay partly open—for quick access in case of trouble—and put it into the front pocket of my baggy jeans.

"Kristy," I say, handing her the key that she insisted I hold on to the other day, "I don't need this anymore. I'm leaving El Salvador."

"Of course," she says. "Your family must be worried about you."

"Will you be all right, by yourself?"

"Things should improve now that the aid workers are here. I'll go stay with relatives in San Salvador once I get a chance."

"Thanks for everything," I tell her.

"Thanks to you," she says. "Take care of yourself." Though I know it's only an expression, it sounds more like a good piece of advice that I'll have a hard time following.

Once, only a few days ago, it was still possible to tell the crackheads from the rest of La Libertad's population. Now, all the young males wear the crackheads' look: gaunt and dirty, dressed in rags, desperate for and yet disinterested in things like food and sleep. As I walk around the streets for the last time, we all scramble like ants from a busted-open colony. I come across an empty lot where the Red Cross has set up a station. The workers offer rehydration fluid and medicine. There is no rhyme or reason to how they distribute. Soon, fights break out over unidentified bottles of pills. A glass jar full of *suero* shatters upon the ground.

The young relief workers look a little terrified, and I can't help but hold their hubris against them—their self-righteous notion that they're somehow capable of answering to or undoing the very motions of the earth.

I make my way to La Libertad's one ATM, double-checking for my newly returned bank card through the fabric of my jeans. For the first time in several days, I'll need money, and I'm curious to check the balance. I have the card, all right, but when I come to the cash machine, it's in pieces. The screen is charred and black, as if somebody tried to burn it or blow it up. It lets off a piercing beep. There's no way I'm putting my card inside.

As I walk away, a young man squats down on the step in front of the unopened bank. I do a double take. He puts his face in his hands, then turns it up again, his eyelids half-open.

"Weefer?" I'm staring at Ben's killer.

He looks over. He doesn't recognize me, but he seems to understand that I'm not from here. "Hello, my friend!" he mutters in broken English. "Give me a small gift, won't you, please?" He holds up his empty palm, expecting a coin.

It would be so easy for me to kill him. Even without the knife that my fingers now squeeze, I could choke him to death with a strap from my backpack, crush his head with a rock. I could do it in front of a crowd of people and nobody would look twice or cause me any consequences at all. The strange thing is, I don't feel anger toward him. I still want Ben back, but I can't be bothered with any sort of revenge. I feel a little sorry for Weefer, but mostly, I feel like I understand him, understand what it means to need your fix—a fix that makes no sense to most of the world. In the end, I leave him there with his glassy eyes and his open hand.

A little farther down the road, workers at another relief station give out blankets and mattresses, with as much disorder. I wonder how soon they'll start cutting the mattresses in half, how many blankets will simply be used to wrap up the dead.

Near the end of town, I spot a Salvadoran man in uniform starting an empty pickup truck with a Red Cross insignia, preparing to leave. I whistle and beg a ride. Thanks to my stolen cap, the driver allows me to hop in the back.

"Chinita!" I hear the shout as I turn for my final look at Puerto La Libertad. I turn to see who called to me. The sight of him almost makes me fall down there in the pickup; it's Peseta. His T-shirt is held out in front of him, its little cloth hammock filled with jars of free medication. Somehow, he's managed to stay one step ahead of the gangsters, the drug dealers, the falling walls. Perhaps it shouldn't be a surprise. I hold up a hand—finger and pinkie extended—and give Peseta a *shaka*. Of all the labels that have been slapped on him over the years—surfer, addict, runner, hustler, urchin—none of them quite does him justice. What Peseta is most thoroughly is a survivor. He smiles and holds up two fingers on his free hand, making a peace sign with supreme confidence, as if he is mayor of this chaos, the president of this small apocalypse.

The pickup clears the excavated landslides. I ask to be let out before it turns inland toward San Salvador to resupply. From there, I cross the *desvío* and flag down one of the big sugarcane trucks. The cab is full, but they let me ride atop the rolling two-story pile of charred stalks with the rest of the laborers. I feel a kinship with them. If not for all the noise, I'd explain that I, too, am descended from sugar-plantation workers, a part of their clan. We gnaw the syrupy juice from out of the blackened lengths of cane as the driver passes carelessly on the Litoral's blind curves. Trees, fields, and the textile sweatshops whiz by at ninety miles an hour, until all of El Salvador is nothing more than a sweet and blinding blur of nature and injustice.

At the turnoff for the airport, I tap on the cab and the truck stops. I give the Red Cross baseball cap to one of the workers. After thanking the driver, I cross the parking lot to the terminal. My clothes and backpack are now black from the soot of the cane stalks, but at least that covers up the stubborn bloodstains on my jeans.

The smell of fried chicken inside the airport is overwhelming; everyone carries on boxes of Pollo Campero for their relatives in the States. I find an ATM and a TACA counter, and within minutes I have a one-way ticket for Los Angeles.

On the other side of the security barrier, I buy some chicken and a Coke and sit watching the planes take off. I think briefly of the families in that hamlet on the hill above Kilometer 99. I hope they get to keep both their land and the money Pelo paid them for it. Perhaps that can be one small crumb of justice to fall from this tragedy. Maybe they understood the deal better than I did, knew something about the nature of fortune that I never quite grasped.

The boarding call begins for my flight, and I can almost feel Honolulu's trade winds, smell the old wood of my father's house. Suddenly, I wonder: What will El Salvador look like from the air? Will it be a mess of collapsed buildings and muddy landslides? Will I see Cara Sucia from up there? Could my mark on this country—a few lines of useless silver among the endless greens and browns—be seen from such heights?

The other L.A.-bound passengers stand and line up at the gate, chicken boxes in their hands. The voice crackling across the loudspeaker is incomprehensible, but I know that it's my section being called. Something comes over me. I rise up and turn away from the Jetway. Before I know it, I'm running out of the terminal, past security and the baggage claim and out to the street. I have to hold up a hand to shield my eyes from the afternoon sun as it beats down so hard upon this, a world that never asked me to save it.

34

It's hard to say what went through my mind. For a moment, the time line of my life unraveled before me like a vast stretch of ocean seen from a high ridge. I could tell which regrets would stick, and which mistakes I could still fix.

I found a taxi right outside the terminal. Once again, the road to Cara Sucia seemed so much shorter when not traveling by bus, as if the whole nation were shrinking beneath my feet. In less than one hour, I stood in the doorway to Niña Tere's house.

"Malia?" she said, a bit shocked.

"Can I stay with you for a while?"

"You can stay here as long as you like. It's our pleasure."

The second quake hadn't been nearly as strong in Cara Sucia or its environs. The people there were less traumatized than anybody I'd seen for days.

By the next morning, I'd met with the village council and convinced them to repair the aqueduct. It was less regimented than the previous phase of construction. Everyone—even women and children—formed a disorganized mob and dug ditches for the distribution lines, the pipes that would run from the tanks into their homes. Every pick and shovel in Cara Sucia swung for weeks on end. It became a sort of social event, like an Amish barn raising. The work was slowed by constant mischief and coffee breaks, but it got done.

For my part, I took a handful of the best workers—the ones who had real construction experience, or at least a good work ethic—and led them up to the spring. Like before, we used red clay to move the river and dry out the area around the spring box. With an unsightly mess of stone and concrete, we sealed up the sides, where our box had come apart during the first quake.

From there, we worked our way down. I spent all of the money in my recovered bank account on cement and pipes. In some cases, we were able to replace the galvanized sections. In others, we laid PVC and covered it over with a stone and concrete sleeve. All the while, I told the workers—and myself—that our goal shouldn't be to build an indestructible water system, but to make one that could be repaired in the event of floods or earthquakes or other acts of God. Flexibility, I reminded them, is more important than strength.

I spoke to my father about what was happening. He was confused but patient, glad that I sounded so safe and stable over the phone. I never told the Peace Corps or anybody else what I was up to. It took weeks to summon the strength, but I managed to write a letter to Ben's family. I didn't say much about who I was, but instead emphasized Ben's last days in La Lib, the hero that he had become late in his final act. Hopefully, his father and brothers would find something to admire in that.

At night, in my little bed inside Niña Tere's house, I often kept myself awake wondering where Ben and I might be if things had turned out differently, if we hadn't met Pelo, if we'd never quit in the first place. I guessed which country we'd be in by now, my mind making the southbound journey that my body never could.

Might we be surfing that long Peruvian left, riding backside for the first time in years? Might we be in Patagonia, staying in one of those cabins in Torres del Paine that Ben sometimes talked about, standing on the banks of a blue-green glacial lake, staring up at snowcapped peaks reflecting the pink light of dusk, alpacas grazing at their base? How long would it have taken us to reach the Tierra del Fuego—that place that even my imagination lacks the vocabulary to describe? Ben might've tossed that southbound stone he so often spoke of into the sea.

That seemed the cruelest part to me: that he couldn't have lived at least one more year. Had he gotten to the bottom of that continent, spent twelve months doing exactly what he wanted, his life would've felt a hundred times more complete.

Without any sort of institutional bureaucracy, with only a personal bank account for a budget, with no lip service about sustainability or empowerment or whatever, the job went incredibly fast. I worked from dawn till dusk every day, and got home in time for a giant dinner and a bucket bath at Niña Tere's.

Was I happy during this time? I was unconflicted, which seemed like enough. Had my *kuleana* been in Cara Sucia all along? Even that seems like an oversimplification. I'm still as cynical as ever about development and relief. This was more about finishing what I'd started, getting a baby-faced monkey off my back.

On the big day, my work crew finished up at the tank and walked back to the village. I went to Niña Tere's house and told her to open the valve on the faucet, the one that had stood there useless above her cistern for so many months. A series of oddly human sounds came from the tap—gurgles, coughs, throaty breaths. She grimaced at me and started to close it again, but I told her to wait. After a minute or two, a slow dribble finally came from the pipes. Soon, the gravity-fed pressure built up, forcing the water out in a straight, strong arc. Nora clapped her hands and ran in circles. Rambo barked. Whoops and hollers erupted from the surrounding houses. Old ladies thanked the same saints they'd blamed for the earthquake. A couple of guns were shot in the air.

Niña Tere wiped away the beginnings of tears in her eyes, and we went out to the street. People splashed their dry courtyards. Spouses dumped bucketfuls of water atop one another. Somehow, a pair of mischievous teenagers made water balloons—as if that was some instinctual adolescent skill, born into even those children who'd never had running water in their homes. I wondered if I should warn everyone not to be wasteful, but I decided it was a good idea to bleed the air and pressurize the lines.

All the people from the village came up to offer congratulations, even some timid hugs. *"Ingeniera,"* they said, "the water has finally fallen."

Niña Tere held on to my hand as we watched the celebration. "What will you do now?" she asked me.

"Now," I said, "I have to go home."

I left there the day after the water arrived. I didn't mean to be cold about it, but it wasn't fair to my father to stay even one minute longer than necessary. The members of the village council wanted to throw a party for me, but I assured them that it was better this way, that the Cara Sucians congratulate themselves for the project, rather than some short-term visitor.

I found myself at the airport again, not even four full months later. This time, I boarded my flight.

Back here in Honolulu, it didn't take long to find the job that I've had for years now. It's an engineering and architectural firm that specializes in green homes for rich people—mostly on Maui and the Big Island. The ironic part is that much of my work these days involves designing exactly the sorts of features that Pelochucho wanted for his ill-advised resort: retaining walls, erosion-proof drainage, seismic foundations.

It's a good living. After a year or so in my father's house, I moved into my own apartment in one of the tall glass towers near Ala Moana. It's on a high floor, far above the street noise, and has an ocean view.

But at the hotel restaurant where I agreed to meet Alex, I find it hard to summarize my life these days.

"Do you keep in touch with anybody from El Salvador?" Alex asks me as the food arrives.

"Not much." I shrug. "It isn't something I'm proud of; I thought I'd always write, to Niña Tere at least. But nobody has Internet access in Cara Sucia, so . . . it just tapered off eventually."

"I know what you mean." He finds the steak knife and cuts into his meat. "And who has the time?"

In the booth beside him, Alex's elder son quietly accepts the small morsels of food that his mother makes for him. As Courtney predicted, Alex has been touring the world with the Red Cross for years now. He went straight to New York City after El Salvador, from there to sites around the Indian Ocean, then to New Orleans, Haiti, Central Asia, and so on. He married a beautiful Indonesian girl he met doing tsunami relief. They have two young boys. The four of them stopped to spend some vacation days in Waikiki on their way back from visiting her parents in Jakarta.

I was shocked when he called my office and asked if I'd join them for dinner. Apart from a few odd e-mails, it was the first time we'd spoken since that day by the beach in La Lib. He looks happy—quite bald now, and softer around the middle. The scars along his forearms have almost completely faded away. I enjoyed chatting with him about his life but find that I do not envy it. The very idea of all that destruction all the time, it unsettles me. Important or not, it seems an unbalanced way to live, always focused on the globe's most desperate scenes. Even the constant plane travel sounds unbearable.

His kids are cute, and well behaved, but they don't make me want any of my own. Alex's wife seems nice enough, but she is quiet and hard to have any sort of conversation with. She mostly minds the boys while Alex and I talk.

Alex refills my wine, and asks the waiter for a second bottle. "You still surf?"

"I've got a couple of boards," I say. "I go if the waves are good, and if I have the time." I take a sip from my glass. "Where are you headed to next?"

"D.C. for the rest of the year, then on to Afghanistan." He rolls his eyes. "Two of my least favorite places."

As the plates are cleared, Alex's second bottle arrives. It's totally unnecessary, as he and I are the only ones drinking, and we barely finished the first. Nobody wants dessert. Their mother takes the boys upstairs to bed. Alex asks me to stick around and help him with the wine.

"Think you'll ever go back there, to El Salvador?" he asks.

"I doubt it. By the end, it was so much effort to close that chapter of my life, I've never wanted to open it back up."

He nods and fills both our wineglasses up to the brim. "I'll tell you one thing: I sure wish you'd stayed on in La Libertad, worked that site with me. What a shitstorm that town was." He looks up at me with a cocked eyebrow. "Who knows how things might've worked out?"

I shrug. "Who knows?"

"I'm really sorry about what happened to Ben down there."

I look at the sea and the night beyond him. The sun has set, but lights from the waterfront restaurants still light up the incoming waves. "It was a bad thing, a tragedy."

"You think of him often?"

"Sometimes." I still can't bring my eyes back to Alex's.

"Being married now . . ." He struggles for words. "I guess it's clear how easy it is to end up with somebody for the rest of your life, you know. It's almost like you have to kick and scream to keep that from happening, after a certain age."

"I guess."

"Did you love him? Really love him?"

I reel my gaze in, and nod. "We were in love; I know that. We were in love like only twenty-three-year-olds can be. Naïvely, recklessly. Would we have stayed together had he lived? I can't say. Would it have worked—the two of us—under any other circumstances, at any other place and time? I'm not so sure about that, either." I turn the glass around on the table. "In a way, it doesn't seem fair to hang all those hypotheticals on it, you know?"

"Still smoke?"

"No."

"Me, neither. If I bought some, would you have one with me, for old times' sake?"

"I'd rather not."

He gulps down more wine. "Should we go somewhere else? I'd love to check out your place."

"Alex." I move the wineglass out of the way and lower my head closer to the table. "This was a nice evening. It's good to see you. Why don't you go upstairs to your family now."

I stand up, and at that very moment a band breaks into song in the bar adjacent to this restaurant—guitar and ukulele, a falsetto singer. They play an old Hawaiian standard. And though I don't understand much of my mother's family's language, I'm sure it's a song of farewell. I want to ask Alex if he's still depressed, if witnessing all those disasters helps anymore, if he pretends to be happy in front of his kids, if he ever became a better person. But I don't know where to start, and the music is so loud, so I simply say good-bye.

He stares at me and lets out a dark smile. Some of that old intensity is still in his face, in spite of the baldness and the wine-purpled teeth. That swollen vein still squiggles down the side of his forehead. "It's nice to see you, too. Good-bye."

It's a short trip home through an oddly beautiful night. Gusts of cool conditioned air blow out from all the storefronts along Kalakaua Avenue. I'm asked for money by cardboard signs, by steel drummers, by human statues painted silver. I pass Japanese tourists with shopping bags, mainlanders with sunburns, a local couple arguing too loudly, a pack of wet teenagers carrying surfboards. Waikiki is, in a sense, the opposite of La Libertad—a beach that everyone has heard of, perhaps the most famous in the world, the origin of surfing, rather than its frontier. But like La Lib, Waikiki's reputation is just as incapable of containing its reality.

I cross the Ala Wai, and the street turns darker and quieter. My building is only a short walk away.

Inside the elevator, two twentysomething local girls are on their way up to a party on another floor. They carry a six-pack of beer and a bakery box. The taller one gives the younger one relationship advice. Her truisms run together into a blur: All guys think x; all girls have to learn y. "I've seen it a million times," she says.

Once the elevator stops at their floor, the shorter one and I lock eyes for a second. She breaks the gaze and hurries down the hall, as if I were staring at her in judgment. The truth is, my look held more envy in it than anything else. I hope she doesn't learn too much too fast. I hope there's a little more time for her to be reckless and innocent, in love and whatever else. The elevator stops on my floor. I get out and enter my apartment.

Feeling dizzy from the wine, I pour myself a tall glass of water and walk over to the window. In the moonlight, small waves form on the reefs just past the shore. The surf fills in and recedes along the tide line: that place where one enormous, constantly moving thing meets another enormous, constantly moving thing—and the two of them take from each other and give to each other and change each other all the time.

I wonder if the taller girl from the elevator could distill my relationship with Ben down to a single bite-size lesson. And if so, what would it be?

I'd like to say that—when it comes to remembering Ben— I think of all the good times: the sunset surfs, the long, lazy meals, making love in a sandy rented bed. Unfortunately, my mind's eye most often zeros in on his burial at sea. I can't help but see it every time I look out at the Pacific Ocean: the chemical flames that rose up around him like a ghost, the tide that ripped him finally away from dry land and all its misery.

Perhaps it was that image that taught me the lesson I'd needed so badly to learn, the point that I'd missed all along: In a fallen world, you're not always free to choose. Our way of life, it turns out, wasn't entirely up to us. All my doubts, all my second-guesses, they were like little affronts to fate—fistfuls of sand hurled toward an indifferent ocean. The truth is that—in a fallen world—all one can do is stand up often, and with grace.

Nowadays, I find I'm grateful to live in a city like this, with good waves and my family nearby. It's funny: All the plans that were kicked around back then, and pretty much all I ever saw of the world was La Libertad—that place called freedom, which, like freedom, could be both beautiful and terrible all at once.

AUTHOR'S NOTE

Kilometer 99 does not exist. It's an imaginary surf spot drawn from aspects of several different breaks in El Salvador, Peru, and Mexico. Most of the larger locations in this novel—La Libertad, San Salvador, Santa Ana, Los Planes de Renderos, Sunzal, etc.—are depicted realistically. Though there are places called Cara Sucia in El Salvador, the one in this novel is fictional (which is also the case with El Vado and El Cedro).

Most of the details regarding the earthquakes that hit El Salvador on January 13th and February 13th of 2001 have been rendered more or less as I recall them or as they were recounted to me by friends and associates. The greatest fictional embellishment in this story is the severe damage to La Libertad caused by the February quake. (La Libertad survived both earthquakes with relatively minor damage.)

It's also worth mentioning that El Salvador's beaches now draw a large number of traveling surfers. It was much less of a destination in 2001. Many of the beaches described as empty and desolate in this novel are now booming with hotels, restaurants, and tourist shops.

Technically, El Salvador had switched their official currency to dollars just before the time in which this novel is set. However, I preferred to use colones, the former currency, for issues of both clarity and aesthetics. It's also come to my attention that there probably was no ferry service around the Darien Gap during the time Ben and Malia considered driving to South America. However, I chose to keep that detail in as I recall many travelers suffering from the same misunderstanding.

ACKNOWLEDGMENTS

I could never have written this novel without all the kindness and generosity I received along the way. Thanks to Jennifer de la Fuente for her help, candor, and resourcefulness. Thanks to Hilary Rubin Teeman for her incredible feedback and guidance; I can't imagine the book without her input.

Mahalo to my invaluable early readers: Malia Collins, Stuart Holmes Coleman, Kristiana Kahakauwila, Paul Diamond, and David Fogelson. Thanks especially to J. Reuben Appelman, the brilliant writer and critic, whose honesty, insight, and enthusiasm have been indispensible to my work.

The bulk of this novel was written in a four-hundred-square-foot apartment that's always hot, often loud, and occasionally overrun with ants. There's nobody on earth I could share it with other than Dabney Gough. Thanks for her patience, her support, and her constant inspiration.

Most importantly, I owe a great big *gracias* to all of the wonderful friends with whom I shared my time in El Salvador. My superiors in the country office were the best bosses I've ever had. My fellow volunteers were the greatest colleagues I'll ever know. I'm particularly indebted to the many wonderful Salvadorans who accepted and looked after me—particularly those from the Ayala family of Cantón Palo Grande. The beauty, warmth, and resilience of that country and its people have never stopped affecting me.